I0524129

ROB WILLIAMS

Second Edition

Gathering of Six
Local Crime and Global Conspiracy

Rob Williams

Gathering of Six
Published through Winged Publications
http://wingedpublications.com/

Printed in the United States of America
Second Edition: 2023

ISBN-13: 978-1-0881-4475-6

In dedication to my soul mate and wife,
Gwyn,
my four children, and grandchildren.
Rob Williams
September, 2019

Forward

Power corrupts, society undermined, means to ends justified:

An investigation into the kidnapping of an Atlanta waitress by the local police and the FBI becomes deadly while shadowy forces move with unimaginable arrogance below the radar. Humans yearn to know secrets; it's in our nature. An unlikely duo, a daughter of one of the wealthiest families and a relatively poor construction worker, stumble unto a secret society with the ability to shape world events. Like chess masters moving pieces across a board, members of this group position elements of the world as they implement a radical design planned over several centuries -an ultimate restructuring of the world. Just as the world isn't as it seems to be on the surface, people can be much more interesting if we look much deeper. Though worlds apart in education and privilege, Sam and Megan find that they are similar souls.

Chapter 1
Disappear

MISTY CALLAHAN COULDN'T help herself. She shook uncontrollably; urine flowed into her jeans. Lying on her stomach, her head arched back toward her hogtied legs by a rope fastened to the gag in her mouth. Tape covered the gag. She attempted to remember details of what had happened earlier that night while walking to her apartment from an Atlanta bar that closed at 2:00 AM. Her eyes blindfolded, Misty tried to focus on elements of her surroundings. She understood that she was riding in the trunk of a car, but had no idea how she got there or where she was going. Her intense discomfort was the only thing that distracted her from utter terror.

The car stopped. She listened for sounds, grasping for an indication of what was to come. Misty heard the engine die, and then a muffled curse before a car door opened. The vehicle rocked slightly before the door closed. The trunk was opened, and clean night air entered the space where she lay. Traffic could be heard in the distance.

"What?" a deep male voice mumbled. "You peed in my car? OK, I guess I can see how that could happen."

He was silent for a moment. She then felt a heavy hand on the small of her back.

"I want you to listen very carefully," she heard him whisper.

He's close - must be leaning over me.

Fear gripped her when he took hold of one of her legs, and Misty shuddered as a powerful arm slipped under her waist. With one smooth move she was lifted out of the trunk and placed on asphalt.

God, he is strong!

"This is your lucky night," the voice continued. "If you do exactly what I tell you, you have a good chance of staying alive. I'm going to cut the rope fastened to your legs, but if you make any sound or attempt to struggle – I'll finish things."

Her face fell forward with the cutting of the rope. Every muscle in her body ached intensely. Her hands were still tied behind her back, and her ankles bound. Misty felt his hand on the back of her neck.

"There's a MARTA station just a few blocks away," he clearly stated. "I'm going to set you free, but it's up to you if you want to go on living. Nod your head if you understand."

She nodded, her neck aching.

"Don't go to the police, and make sure you never go back to your apartment – ever. If you do, you will die. I'm leaving your purse here on the pavement. I'm taking your phone, but I'll leave your money and credit cards. A bus line runs a couple of streets over. Take

MARTA to the airport and buy a ticket to somewhere very far away. There are people who want very bad things to happen to you, and if you're found – you'll wish you were dead. Do you understand?"

Misty nodded again.

"If you don't have enough money for a plane fare, take a bus. But get away from Atlanta as fast as you possibly can, and never come back. Don't even tell anyone that you are from this city. Go somewhere - wait tables – anything. You may want to move again after a while. I mean this."

He paused again, reminding himself of her fate if he were to carry out the orders he had been given. He placed his huge right hand on her back.

"I'm going to free your hands, now. Leave your ankles bound and your blindfold on until after I drive away. I'm taking a huge risk leaving you here alive. I'll be watching as I leave, and I can't risk having you identify me. Stay still until I am long gone, or I'll have to finish things. Once I'm out of here, you need to disappear – and fast. Do you understand?"

She nodded.

Placing a knee on her shoulder, his powerful hands worked quickly to free her hands. Misty let out a soft moan as her hands fell to her sides. Confident that she would do exactly as instructed, he removed his knee and stood.

"Remember what I've told you. Don't doubt a word. You have to disappear."

Still blindfolded she listened to his steps and the opening of the car door. Terror flooded her mind. She didn't move. The engine started, blasting hot exhaust fumes over her.

Is he going to back over me? No, he wouldn't have bothered untying me.

The sound of tires rolling over pavement diminished as the car begin to move away. She remained frozen. Misty waited until she imagined he had traveled far enough to not witness her stirring before moving a muscle. She slowly raised her aching arms above her head and rolled onto her back. Misty pushed herself into a seated position. Her hands trembled, as she removed the blindfold.

This is a very dark alley.

Her mouth, still gagged, she began working on her bound ankles. She felt anger towards the hands fumbling at the duct tape.

I have to find a stupid edge on the tape! I have to be gone in case he changes his mind and returns.

At last, her nails found an edge of the tape and she began pulling it away. Her legs felt slightly numb as she staggered to her freed feet. Misty quickly snatched her purse from the pavement. Moving toward a dimly lit street at the end of the alley, she ripped the tape from her mouth and removed the gag. *MARTA. Is there really a MARTA station nearby?*

Glancing up the street to a brightly lighted area, she moved as fast as her legs would move in that direction. Before she knew it, she was at a full sprint. At the corner, her heart felt relief when she spotted a bus stop at the next block.

"I need to be away from here, and fast," she heard herself whisper.

Over one of the rolling hills of the city lumbered a bus. It seemed like an eternity before it came to a stop in front of her.

"Please take me to the first station," she mumbled, fumbling through her purse for her thirty-day pass.

"I'm in no hurry," said the driver. "You're my only rider for now."

She suddenly felt embarrassed when his eyes spotted her urine-soaked jeans. Shoving the pass at him, she hoped he didn't smell her condition. He nodded and turned his attention to the street before them. The bus began to slowly move forward. Misty quickly moved eight seats back.

Maybe he won't catch a smell from here. I'm disgusting, but there's nothing I can do about it right now. The guy warned me not to go home. The airport! Airport shops will open in several hours. I'll find something.

Taking perfume from her purse, she attempted to mask the odor by spraying her jeans. Every few seconds she saw the eyes of the driver glancing back at her in the bus mirror.

I'm alive, and headed toward safety. I'll probably never see this driver again. Pee should be the least of my concerns –still, I'm gross. He said that people want to hurt me, do very bad things to me! Who wants to do this to me, and why?

People and scenarios ran through her mind in flashes. She had waitressed for two years in that Atlanta bar. She had come in contact with thousands.

Any one of them could have been behind this – but why?

Relief flooded her mind when she spotted the MARTA station. Yet, her hands still trembled.

From here I can catch a train to Hartsfield.

———·●·———

"WILL YOU BE CHECKING a bag?" asked the woman at the airline counter.

"No, I'm traveling light," replied Misty.

"Your flight to Colorado Springs will board at 10:15 AM," she stated, handing her the ticket.

The airport contained a few overpriced shops, offering select clothing for women. Misty boarded the flight dressed in an expensive pair of slacks. They were a total mismatch with her shirt. She earlier attempted to wash the soiled jeans in a restroom sink, and then placed them in the shopping bag that once held her new slacks.

Anything is better than what I've been wearing. I don't know anyone in Colorado Springs, and that's what is needed. Hopefully, I never run into anyone I've met here. At least I don't have to worry about family.

———·●·———

TJ TURNER PULLED HIS old Crown Victoria into the garage of his East Point rented house. He hadn't finished the kidnapping job, and that meant he should personally exercise the advice he had given Misty. The huge man popped the trunk open and scanned it for evidence of its earlier occupant. There was a faint smell of urine, so he sprayed it with air freshener that he kept in the glove box. Confident that it was reasonably clean, he quickly made his way inside the house.

From the bottom of the closet in the spare bedroom, he retrieved a large duffle bag. He loaded it with clothes and moved to the nightstand. The drawer contained a nine-millimeter pistol. TJ wrapped the handgun in a faded T-shirt, and strategically placed it in an outer pocket of the bag. He opened the door of the nightstand, revealing a small gun safe. After opening it, he emptied it of ammunition and a spare pistol. Everything was wrapped in a towel and placed inside the bag. His bedroom closet housed a larger gun safe, where he retrieved stacks of cash. He placed two hundred dollars in his wallet and shoved the rest into the duffle bag.

Tossing the heavy bag over his shoulder as if it was a down-filled pillow, he couldn't stop thinking about his abduction of Misty. He had snatched her from behind as she walked past a large tree near a sidewalk in front of a vacant lot. His huge, gloved hand covered her mouth, muffling her short cry. TJ easily lifted her off her feet, and he quickly carried her into the darkness of the empty lot. Holding her down, he injected a tranquilizer through her jeans and into her hip. Within moments she was unconscious. His eyes quickly adjusted to the darkened surroundings. Just before he placed the duct tape over her mouth, he paused. In this still moment, he studied the features of her face in the faint lighting. In her face, he saw a person he once loved. Flashbacks of eyes filled with love and compassion flooded his mind. He suddenly felt the full weight of delivering his victim over to brutal people, where she would suffer horrible abuse. As he prepared her for transport, he couldn't shake an overwhelming sense of guilt. TJ knew what it meant for him if he didn't follow through with his orders. He would have to be on the run to avoid being snuffed out.

He moved to the kitchen. There, he collected a couple of flashlights and packed them as well. TJ paused, considering whether anything else should be packed. With the duffle bag in hand, he opened the door leading into the garage.

His chest was immediately nailed with probes from a Taser, generating 1200 volts delivered in a series of 100 millisecond pulses. Disrupting neuron communications between TJ's powerful skeletal muscles and his brain, his body stiffened before dropping to the kitchen floor. Two large men quickly synched his wrists behind his back with duct tape, and then used more tape to bind his ankles. Duct tape also quieted his mouth, before they dragged him to the Crown Victoria and shoved him into the trunk. One slammed it shut, while the other went after the duffle bag. Tossing the bag in the back seat, he dropped into the driver's seat and started the engine. The car backed from the garage, and slowly moved down the street. The other man followed in a car that had been parked a block away.

TJ was muscle. His job was to physically handle people. He had beaten men to the point that they were left as drooling brain damaged imbeciles. This was supposed to be an easy job. He was to simply overpower a much smaller individual and transport her to a particular location. In the darkness of the large trunk, his present situation was overcome with images of Misty Callahan. Though he was ordered to not rough her up, thoughts of her probable fate had hung in his mind. TJ had seen the condition of a body he had been given orders to dispose of. It was as though something much larger than himself had taken hold of him, moving him to drive Misty to that alley and release her.

I just couldn't do it. I should have gone with her, but I'm sure she would have identified me to the police at some point. Even if she grew to trust me, I'm sure they wouldn't have let me off. They would have hunted us both down relentlessly.

Now, it was TJ in the trunk of that same Crown Victoria. However, his dread exceeded that of Misty's. He knew no one would give him a warning and send him out of town.

Chapter 2
Saturday Morning

A STRANGE COMMOTION in the parking lot behind Sam's inner-city apartment captured his attention Saturday morning. An unusual conversation between two very different neighbors lured him out onto the back porch, stealing him away from breakfast.

Betty Sue Jackson was a responsible Christian woman in her late thirties. She wasn't a Bible-thumping zealot, but rather a clear-thinking regular church goer who was as practical as they came. She always had a tidy appearance. Her clothes weren't expensive, but clean and well matched. Sam liked her.

Mr. Murphy, a functioning drunk, was the other person. He was in his early forties, married and had fathered several children. In a drunken stupor, he sometimes gave his smallest daughter the chore of taking the family kitchen garbage out to the dumpster in the rear parking lot. She was too small to operate the opening on the side of the container, so she would place the bag of trash on the asphalt at the base of the dumpster. Consisting of leftover food items, the garbage was an open invitation to flies and rats. Rats easily tore open the bag and scattered the contents. Sam had witnessed Betty Sue cleaning up the resulting mess on a couple of occasions. She never lodged a complaint. It was a job that needed doing, and she quietly did it.

This day, inebriated Murphy held two wooden boards together at the corner of the aging green dumpster. The simple fact that Betty Sue and he were involved in a loud early morning discussion was unusual. Sam found the subject matter to be even more interesting. While bent over at the waist with her right arm reaching inside the opening of the stench-filled container. Betty Sue shouted instructions to Murphy.

"Come here and take my end! I'll swap with you. Come take hold of my stick."

Murphy obediently laid the stout pieces of wood down on the parking lot pavement and staggered toward the woman. He awkwardly moved his frame into the opening of the dumpster, aligned himself with Betty Sue, and took hold of her long stick. Both their heads were now inside the container, their backsides pointed in Sam's direction.

"Don't let go," the woman ordered. "Press hard and don't let it back out."

It was a beautiful sunny morning. With no concerns of having to be at work, Sam dropped into a seated position on the porch with his feet resting on the third step.

What in the world are these two up to?

From the conversation and what he visually observed, Sam soon understood. A rat had entered the container through a rusted hole in the bottom corner and eaten its fill of garbage. Too fat to fully exit the hole after eating, it was trapped with its head sticking out of the hole.

Sam had seen plenty of rats. When he pulled into the parking lot at night, the headlights often revealed several sets of glowing red eyes. Sometimes when he started his truck in the morning, a few rats would scramble out from under the vehicle.

Convinced that Murphy had a firm grasp of the situation within the dumpster, the woman made her way to his previous position at the exterior corner. Still pressing the rat from behind with the stick, the man's head raised briefly to watch her. She quickly picked up one of the wooden pieces held earlier by him and took careful aim. With one determined swing, she dealt a powerful blow at the bottom corner of the dumpster. The rat's severed head sailed across the parking lot.

"Wow!" Sam whispered.

Seeing the bloody head of the rat on the asphalt, Murphy withdrew from the dumpster and immediately let the contents of his stomach plaster another area of the parking lot. Betty Sue dropped the piece of wood and walked away. The job had been handled to her satisfaction. Mr. Murphy then slowly rambled across the parking lot and entered his apartment. Sam lifted his face toward the cloudless blue sky.

What a Saturday morning. I wonder what the rest of the day will bring.

While some Atlantans were reading a paper on a Saturday morning over coffee, others in poorer sections of the city were waking up to bizarre scenes. It had been over a year since Sam had a working TV. He hadn't really missed it. Unimagined by others in more wealthy parts of town, this neighborhood sometimes offered cheap forms of entertainment. Such was the case this Saturday.

His neighborhood was rarely dull. On several occasions he had witnessed acts of violence. This Saturday morning offered no threat of someone being shot, only an oddity that ended poorly for a fat rat. The disturbance at the dumpster was over. The parking lot was empty of people, and the morning air of the city was quieter than on weekdays. Sensing no cause for alarm, Sam continued to relax on the back porch. He closed his eyes and leaned back. The morning sun graced the scene, warming Sam, the rat's head, and Murphy's vomit.

By the time Sam returned to his breakfast, his attention was redirected. He focused on the thickly painted small drop-leaf table where he sat.

There must be at least six coats of paint on this thing. I just hope I don't have to do a lot of sanding before I can put a finish on the table and two chairs.

His thoughts were interrupted by the ringing of the front doorbell. Sam shoved the last of the bacon in his mouth, and then wiped his hands on a couple of paper napkins before answering the door. A young man and woman stood on the front porch, both neatly dressed.

"Whatever you're selling, I don't need it," Sam immediately announced.

"We aren't selling anything," replied the man. He was tanned and well-manicured. "I'm Michael Wells and this is Megan Adams, and we would like to invite you to our church."

Without saying a word, auburn haired Megan pulled a flyer from a clipboard and handed it to Sam.

Her green eyes locked onto his during the exchange. Stepping out onto the porch, Sam couldn't help but smile.

Michael and Megan, ... M&Ms. She is definitely eye candy.

Sam stepped close to her, and purposely touched her hand as he took the pamphlet. Still looking into her eyes, he found the reaction he hoped for. It was obvious to him that she felt something by the brief contact. He looked down and scanned the flyer.

"Gwinnett County!" exclaimed Sam. "Why in the world would someone from Fulton County drive all the way out there to attend a church service?"

"It's a really good church... with nice people," Megan quietly answered, almost apologetically.

Her eyes had moved down to his tight-fitting tee shirt that covered a muscular chest. Sam used that moment to more thoroughly scan her features, as well. Megan was no more than five feet, two inches tall, but he liked what he saw. Their eyes met again.

The tan 'M&M' can move on. But this red 'M&M' isn't so bad.

"I'm sorry," said Sam. "I shouldn't have blurted that   out."
"Our Sunday school teacher suggested that our class invite people from these apartments," added Michael.

"Why these apartments?" asked Sam.

"I'm not sure," replied Michael. "Maybe you should visit our class and ask him."

"I don't mean to be rude, but we're done here," stated Sam. "You've done your duty. I've been invited."

"Would you at least give us your name?" asked

Megan, as Sam stepped back inside.

"Sam Blaylock," he replied, shutting the door. In the last second before it closed, their eyes met again.

Sam went back to the kitchen. He stared at the rear parking area out of his kitchen window, remembering the rat event, as he began to wash the breakfast dishes. Sam's thoughts shifted back to Megan. Her face was etched in his mind.

That pompous jerk of a Sunday school teacher set those two up. He used naïve rich people in his class to do his "mission outreach" to us poor low life folk - just to make himself feel good. He probably thinks he's earning some kind of brownie points in heaven. People like him make me sick. What a piece of crap! I'm sure it wasn't her idea to come to this neighborhood. She's just a dumb rich kid who doesn't know any better. I hope she wises up to him. She seems nice; I'd hate for her to become a copy of him.

Sam carried the drop-leaf table out to the sidewalk behind the apartment and began the job of stripping the layers of paint away.

"The can says to use in a well-ventilated area," Sam mumbled to himself. "This is about as well-ventilated as it gets."

Sam hadn't seen his father since he was very small. His mother had managed an antique furniture store until she suddenly passed away when Sam was eighteen. After school, he helped carry used furniture from a truck as it was delivered in the back of the store. Sam had the opportunity to watch as pieces were refinished and had acquired knowledge of those skills. Sam felt ecstatic when he loosened the paint with the putty knife, revealing the grain of English walnut.

Just as I hoped! Years of beeswax under the paint has protected the piece. I doubt the two chairs are the same, but I can stain them to be reasonably close.

Sam worked on the table for hours. Over the past few years, he had added pieces of furniture to the one-bedroom apartment. The table and wooden chairs had replaced a cardboard box and two cheap lawn chairs in the kitchen. The box had been turned upside down and sported a tablecloth. He lived alone, so it had sufficed.

Thoughts of the earlier visit by Megan continued to fill his mind, as he placed a frozen pizza in the oven for supper.

I've met others like her at the antique shop. She's a rich girl, and simply doesn't have a clue about how common people live. I doubt she could ever understand someone like me.

Sam's thoughts moved to another Saturday morning. He had been visiting a fellow construction worker who lived in an apartment three doors down. From inside that man's place, the two had heard gunshots from just outside the front of the apartment. They dropped to the floor, crawled to a window, and peered outside. Two men on the street blazed away at each other with handguns, much like a scene out of a Wild West movie.

Neither could shoot. Neither man appeared to be hit. Maybe adrenaline was flowing so hard in them both that it resulted in each firing haphazardly in the general vicinity of the other.

As fast as the incident had started, it stopped with both men running off in different directions. Immediately after the gunfire ended, Sam and his friend raced out onto the sidewalk in an attempt to see where the men had gone. As they stood there, an elderly woman passed them carrying a bag of groceries.

"Crazy boys, playing with guns," Sam heard her say as she walked by.

She didn't appear to be fazed at all. I wonder how long she had lived in in this neighborhood. Gunfire had become so common, that the old woman simply took it as part of her day. This isn't the type of place that attracts people from Gwinnett County. The M&Ms asking me to attend their church were a couple of naïve do-gooders, trying to make themselves feel better by inviting people who are beneath their class. I wonder how they would react if I actually showed up? Would they be embarrassed if I started hanging around, or would they adopt me – sort of like a pet? That Megan is really cute. Maybe I should pay that church a visit. She could be looking for a real man; one who knows how to use his hands.

— • ● • —

MONDAY MORNING, probation officer Russ Blevins reviewed the list of people who had been invited to the church by members of the Sunday school class he taught.

TJ's not on the list. Two officers spotted him in those apartments, but his name doesn't appear. I knew this was a long shot.

CHAPTER 3
RUSS BLEVINS

"**ANY LUCK LOCATING TURNER?**" Vice Detective Frank Reynolds asked probation officer Russ Blevins.

"I'm still working on it," answered Russ. "I hear that you got nothing out of that dealer you turned back out onto the streets."

"That guy is a dead man," replied Frank, putting out his cigarette against the sole of his shoe. "If TJ Turner doesn't kill him, then someone else will. Cutting that garbage with fentanyl has resulted in two deaths already. That kind of thing attracts attention by the press, who in turn, puts cops under the public's spotlight. Distributors who move large quantities of heroin won't tolerate anything that increases pressure on the police to clean things up, including low level dealers cutting heroin with fentanyl. We need to find Turner. I know his type. That big goon will surely screw up, and we'll have him – and he'll sing like a bird to avoid a long prison sentence. A plea deal with him could lead us to someone big. Now that you've lost touch with him, I've had to pull the guy we had on his tail."

"You're right about the fentanyl," said Russ. "As for the 'big goon' comment, TJ's certainly big – but I don't believe he's stupid. The man has issues that makes it difficult for him to remain employed at a normal job, and he's settled for doing muscle jobs for dirty people. For a guy like him, it's easy money to beat someone silly. I hope TJ's 'screw up' doesn't involve beating a man to death."

"It doesn't concern me all that much if he beats a low life dealer to death, said Frank. "That would be homicide's problem."

"No way, man. I can't believe you think it's no big deal if he murders someone."

"So, what, if he kills a scumbag dealer who is essentially killing people with drugs. In one sense, he would be doing the world a favor. I just need him to lead me to who's in charge of distributing this poison."

Frank Reynolds turned and walked away. Russ had politely nodded at the detective's statements, but he didn't fully agree with his assessment of Timothy James Turner – known by most as TJ.

Frank says he knows the type, but TJ doesn't really fit a type. This guy's different. He served years in special forces in Afghanistan, and he left with an honorable discharge. For God's sake, he was awarded a Bronze Star. There's something about him that I can't put my finger on it, but he's not like other muscle heads I've dealt with. Frank doesn't really know this guy.

— • ● • —

THE FOLLOWING SATURDAY morning, Russ decided he would step up the effort to locate TJ Turner. His only lead was given days earlier. Someone reported seeing him in the apartment complex where Sam Blaylock lived. Russ drove to the neighborhood and knocked on the front doors of those inner-city apartments.

Sam was relaxing on his back porch. The apartment had been built in the 1940s, and both the front and rear doors were accompanied with screen doors. There was no central air-conditioning in the aging apartments. During hot summer weekends, it was his habit to leave the front and back apartment doors open – with only the screen doors fastened shut. Sam's apartment was one of the few with functioning front doorbells. Hearing it ring, he slowly rose to his feet.

It's got to be that hot rich chick Megan from that church. I caught her looking me up and down. I knew she couldn't stay away.

Sam's countenance fell as he reached the front door.

"I'm Russ Blevins, a probation officer," said the man on the front porch, displaying his credentials. "I won't take much of your time."

"I make it a point to stay out of trouble with the law," stated Sam.

"Have you seen this man?" Russ asked, holding out a photo of TJ Turner.

Sam glanced at it through the screen door and shrugged his shoulders. "Not sure," he answered.

"He's a big man, hard to miss," replied Russ. "About six-five, with exceptionally wide shoulders. The guy works out a lot and is really bulked up."

"I can't say that I recognize the face, but I've seen a big man wearing a hoody slinking around. There are a lot of big guys in this town. If they don't bother me, I don't bother them."

"This man is TJ Turner, and he's bad. You seem like an honest, hardworking man; and I doubt you would want this fellow to be around. Where did you see the big man in the hoody?"

"About a block down that way. Like I said, he wasn't causing me trouble. He was just walking; both hands in the pockets of the hoody."

"When?"

"About two weeks ago," answered Sam.

"During that heat wave we had a couple of weeks ago?"

"I thought that was unusual. Most people who wear a hoody over their head in hot weather don't want to be recognized. That's why I remembered it. I had my suspicions, but he wasn't bothering me."

"What's your name?" Russ asked.

"Sam Blaylock, but I don't want to be in one of your reports."

"Don't worry, I've asked everyone in this complex for a name."

"I have a job, and I don't want the police pestering me or my employer," explained Sam. "I've seen police come to job sites and create a mess for people. I make a point to do a good job at work and stay out of things that don't concern me."

"I became TJ's probation officer after he was released from jail for assaulting a woman. We believe TJ Turner beat a man down and left him unconscious on a street one night. The guy almost died. Next time, I'm not so sure he'll leave the person alive to talk. Here's my card. Please give me a call if you see him again."

Sam opened the screen door and took the card. He looked it over, then nodded before closing the front door. Sam waited several seconds before slowly reopening the front door just wide enough to catch a glimpse of the probation officer getting into a parked car at the end of the sidewalk. When the vehicle moved out of sight, he closed the door. Sam walked three doors down to visit a fellow construction worker.

"Wayne, did that probation officer come by your place?" he asked.

"Yeah, he came by," answered Wayne Atkins. "Gave me one of his cards, but I tossed it."

"He said that he's looking for a big guy named TJ. He's supposed to be really bad."

"Two key words here – big and bad," stated Wayne. "As long as 'big and bad' stays out my business, I intend to stay out of his. I don't ask for trouble, but I'm ready if it comes my way."

"The probation officer said that he beat a guy almost to death."

"I don't need him beating on me or anyone in my family. But if he does decide to give me trouble, I have the great equalizer."

Wayne reached into a drawer of a lampstand and took out a huge revolver.

"Did you see the movie 'Dirty Harry'?" asked Wayne. "This thing will do the job. Hollow points. They'll leave a hole the size of a quarter when they exit a body. It doesn't matter where you hit the guy; he'll go down."

"You never told me that you had a gun."

"I don't tell many people, but I know you and I trust you. You can protect your place anyway you want, but nobody is bigger or badder than this."

Sam nodded to indicate that he understood. He had once seen a man who had been shot in the face, and it made him sick to his stomach. He didn't own a gun, but he told no one. Sam didn't care to advertise the fact that he was defenseless, should someone attempt to break into his apartment.

If I owned a gun, I don't think I could pull the trigger. All I need is time to get away.

"Do you plan to watch the meteor shower this week?" Sam asked.

"I don't care about that," replied Wayne. "Now, if scientists tell us that a huge asteroid is about to smash the planet… that would be a different thing. If the world was coming to an end, I would raise all kinds of hell before it hit. I'm not staying up to see a couple of streaks flash across the sky. I've seen it before."

"I hear there's going to be a lot of them, so I plan to watch."

"Whatever makes you happy."

That afternoon, Sam bought an amateur telescope for the upcoming meteor show. His sustainable construction wages forced him to save for several weeks to have the disposable income needed to provide himself this pleasure. He also purchased two pepper spray dispensers at a sporting goods store. After arriving back at his apartment, he took one of the canisters onto his back porch.

The guy in the store said that it's good for twenty

shots, accurate up to twelve feet, and contains an orange dye. Time to give it a try.

Sam smiled at the thought of a criminal trying to evade the police while wearing an orange-stained face. He leaned over the back-porch railing. In his right hand, he held the dispenser down and away from him. With a quick pull, a stream of chemicals shot from the end of the contraption. Before he could move away, a slight breeze caught some of the vapors and sent them in his direction. Immediately, Sam found himself in a coughing fit. He retreated back into the kitchen and began washing his face at the sink. Within a few minutes, he was able to breathe normally.

Man, I'm so glad that I didn't get this stuff in my eyes! That was stupid. I should have covered my face.

Sam placed one dispenser in a top drawer just to the right of the kitchen sink, near the rear door of the apartment.

"Well, at least I know it works," Sam mumbled, as he dried his face with a dish towel. "I hope I never have cause to use it.'

He put the second one in a nightstand next to his bed. He rarely had visitors with children, but he considered how he would warn parents with children to keep a close eye on them.

— • ● • —

FOUR NIGHTS LATER, Sam pulled his telescope out of the box and attached it to the tripod that came with it. Because of a streetlight in the rear parking lot, Sam believed his best chance to observe would be from the front sidewalk. Seated in a lawn chair on his front sidewalk, he waited. Within a half hour, Sam witnessed a bright streak across the night sky.

That had to be one! I can't believe how fast it was. No wonder scientists warn people about those things hitting the earth. Moving at that speed, a big one would do real damage to anything it hit.

Sam tried getting a closer look using the telescope, but soon realized the difficulty of focusing on an object moving so quickly. He placed the telescope back inside the apartment and continued watching from the lawn chair.

Buying the telescope was a stupid waste of money.

Sam's eyes grew weary. He had volunteered to work eleven-hour days in the ninety-four-degree summer heat this week. Once his normal sheet metal job of hanging seamless gutters and installing chimney flashing was done at a site, he was to help carry heavy bundles of shingles up ladders to the roofers at other sites. The promise of the additional two hours pay each day over his regular wages caused him to jump at the offer. The owner of the construction company was behind schedule and risked not obtaining his bonus for finishing on time. The crews were pushed to perform at a relentless pace.

If Megan agrees to going out with me for a meal, I'll be ready. Man, she is hot!

Resting in the lawn chair, he had become aware that his body had run its course. His muscles ached and his mind was becoming numb; he was exhausted. Sam placed both palms on his face and began rubbing his eyes. Bringing his hands down, he noticed movement under the streetlight at the end of his block. A man in a hoody stood talking on a cell phone. He froze; not a muscle moved. As though the man had some type of radar, he turned in Sam's direction and began to quickly move toward him. A cold chill ran down the back of Sam's neck, but he purposefully managed to control the panic that was beginning to set in. Deliberately and calmly, he stood and folded the lawn chair. Pretending he hadn't seen the man, he made his way up the front steps and opened the door.

"Hey!" the man shouted in a deep voice. "Hey, I need to talk with you."

As Sam stepped inside, the figure reached the bottom of the steps. Before he could close the door, he heard the man speak in a softer tone.

"Sam, it's me – Russ Blevins – probation officer."

Turning on the front porch light, Sam recognized him.

"What are you doing running at people in the middle of the night?" Sam blurted. "What's wrong with you?"

"The battery in my cell died, and I need to finish a call," explained Russ. "Can I borrow your phone for just a few minutes?"

"You've got to be out of your mind! Wearing that stupid hoody and running at people in the dark like that is a good way to get yourself shot. I thought you were that piece of trash you warned me about – that TJ guy."

"The phone?" Russ politely asked again.

"Come in," Sam said, motioning to the probation officer.

"I really appreciate this," Russ said, stepping into the apartment.

"I'm telling you … somebody else would have shot you," said Sam, nervously pointing his finger at Russ.

"Sit there, while I get the phone."

Sam walked into the kitchen, snatched his cell off the table, and moved back into the living area.

"Don't get me involved with your mess," Sam warned, his eyes fixed on the man seated on the couch. "What if that big guy is out there? What if he watched you enter my apartment? You could be setting me up for something bad."

"I really appreciate this. Not to be pushy, but I need to finish that call."

"You, pushy? You pushed everyone in the apartment complex to answer questions about a guy that you're looking for, and now you've pushed your way into my apartment late at night to use my phone. You're nothing but pushy! Listen, you aren't my probation officer. I had nothing to do with you, until you forced yourself on me!"

Russ held out his right hand, palm up. Sam moved over to the couch and placed the phone in the extended hand.

"Would you mind giving me some privacy?" asked Russ.

"So, is this a private call?" Sam asked. "Do I have to leave my own living room? Maybe I should take a walk outside?"

"You said you didn't want to be involved," Russ calmly replied. "Are you sure you want to listen in on this conversation?"

"You're worse than a sick fart! You're going to run me out of my own apartment in the middle of the night. Please, let me know when I'm allowed to come back inside my own place. Pushy? You're unbelievable!"

Sam slammed the rear door behind him, as he

exited the apartment. Dropping into a seated position on the back porch, he heard his next-door neighbor let out a string of curses about the slamming of his door. The night was warm, the stars were out, and the city was relatively quiet. Under different circumstances, he might have been able to relax there. Suddenly, Sam felt very tired. As he leaned his back against the metal porch railing, his frustrations with Russ reached a peak.

That's enough. I have to face a hard day's work in just a few hours. I don't need this. I have no intention of sitting for an hour on my back porch.

Sam rose and entered the apartment. He approached Russ, with an open hand extended in his direction.

"You need to give my cell back, and you need to leave," Sam calmly demanded. "I've had enough of this."

"That's all I have for you, bye," Russ said into the cell phone, ending the call.

The probation officer stood and handed the phone back to its owner.

"You've been a big help, Sam. A young woman is missing, and I'm guessing that TJ may be involved."

"What?" blurted Sam. "Is her name Megan?"

"Megan?"

"A red head came by the apartment several days ago and invited me to her church. Was it her?"

"No," replied Russ. "A waitress at a bar never showed up for work the next day, and another waitress told the owner that she saw a drunken man harassing her as she left the previous night. She had never missed work. The owner was concerned over her unusual absence and gave the police a call. The police escorted the other waitress to the missing woman's apartment. They found it to be still filled with her things, and dishes still in the kitchen sink. It appears that her departure was unplanned and sudden – possibly not of her own volition. The other waitress said that only her purse was missing. That leads the police to think she may have been taken. They're running a trace on her credit cards now."

"How does that involve you?" questioned Sam. "You're a probation officer, not a regular cop."

"I'm TJ Turner's probation officer. He's missing, and so is this woman. I'm hoping that the timing of both disappearances is simply a coincidence, but I don't put a lot of stock in coincidences."

"Why would this guy take a waitress? I don't get the connection."

"TJ's been known to snatch people and turn them over to really bad people. Because she doesn't own a car, the police can't put out a bulletin tracking her down using a license plate. She's been missing for several days, and they don't have much to go on. You've been a big help, but I need to let you get some sleep."

"Oh, now you're concerned about my sleep? You get me stirred up in the middle of the night with a story about a guy who has been seen in my neighborhood; a huge guy who takes people and beats the crap out of them. A woman is missing, and you think he took her. This is supposed to help me sleep?"

"What made you think the missing person could be Megan Adams?" questioned Russ.

"How do you know her last name? I didn't tell you her last name."

"A little confession; I'm the Sunday school teacher

who organized the visits from the church," answered Russ. "Megan is a member of the class. She must have made an impression on you."

"You don't strike me as a Sunday school teacher."

"What does a Sunday school teacher look like?"

"Not you," answered Sam.

Sam's weary eyes stared down at the floor. Suddenly, as though someone had turned on a switch within him, his eyes flashed at Russ.

"You used those church people to hunt for that TJ guy, didn't you?" accused Sam.

"You're pretty smart."

"You said this guy is really bad," said Sam, his eyes narrowing. "How could you send a naïve girl like Megan out to look for him? What's wrong with you?"

"It was in broad daylight, and I paired women with men from the class," explained Russ. "They were fine."

"Right! Like some Sunday school guy could protect her from a monster like that TJ? You're full of crap!"

"So, I'm a little crappy. We need to find Turner. Plus, I really don't think I placed them in danger. Do you feel like you're in danger around here during the day?"

"I'm not a cute red head from a rich home! I'm a nobody, and bad guys usually leave nobodies alone. I'm not a wimp, and I'm not a badass – I'm more like scenery, like a bush or a light pole. I'm just here. Nobody notices."

"Something tells me that you've learned how to blend in, like a bush," observed Russ. "You're not dumb. Physically, you're in pretty fair shape. You look like you could handle yourself with most guys. I'm guessing that you must have run into somebody who was really bad."

"In this neighborhood, you don't have to look far. In case you don't know, we have crazy people around here. You have no idea what a crazy person will do."

"In my profession, I've run into several disturbed people. You're right. You never know what might set some people off."

"I need to hit the sack," said Sam, pointing toward the front door. "I'm beat."

"Thanks again," Russ replied, stepping out onto the front porch.

SAM AWOKE TO THE sound of his alarm. After turning it off, his bleary eyes stared out the upstairs bedroom window. The rising sun painted the sky with a red glow.

Red sky at morning, sailor take warning. It's an old saying. Oh, please! I just need a normal day of work – no drama - nothing to do with this TJ, and no crap from Russ Blevins. Being around that guy is like Superman being exposed to that green rock. His mess sucks the life out of a person. I feel exhausted already.

Chapter 4
TJ Turner

TJ TURNER WINCED WITH PAIN while riding in the trunk of his own car. Each curve taken caused additional stress on his aching muscles. Until then, he had no understanding of the discomfort he had caused Misty Callahan. Her abduction had been just a job – nothing personal.

I can certainly understand why she pissed in my car.

TJ heard a rumbling sound as the car came to a stop. Fear had been building in him, and survival dominated his thoughts. The car slowly moved forward a short distance. The engine was cut off and the rumbling sound began again. He heard a car door open and close. Suddenly, a loud noise permeated the small space where he was held.

"You doing alright in there?" shouted the man who had just slammed his open palm on the top of the trunk.

The trunk popped open. The two large men took hold of TJ, dragged him from the trunk and dropped him onto a concrete floor like a heavy bag of fertilizer.

He quickly glanced at his surroundings.

They've driven my car into a large warehouse.

Breath left him as the taller of the men delivered three powerful kicks to his side. Recovering, he moaned behind the duct tape that covered his mouth. Hate began to overtake the fear that had been building within him.

If I survive this, I'm going to kill that bastard. Nobody ordered him to kick the crap out of me; he's having a good time with this.

His hands still bound behind his back, the shorter man shoved a pole between TJ's back and his arms. Taking hold of each end of the pole, they lifted him from the floor.

"This load of garbage weights a ton," the taller one stated, as the two began to carry TJ toward an open door, his legs dragging the floor. "Maybe we should cut his legs off. That might lighten the load."

"We'd never get away with just bringing a torso," said the other man. "We'd have to go back and bring a couple of bloody legs. I vote for making one trip."

"What's your vote – one trip, or two?" the taller one teased TJ. "Are you partial to having your legs attached?"

TJs arms were killing him. He ignored his captors and focused on his surroundings. His head facing down, he noticed the pristine condition of the concrete floor.

This warehouse was recently built.

The two dragged him into a room used to store construction items and shut the door behind them. TJ glanced up to spot an empty wooden chair. Brightly colored plastic traffic barrels were stacked along the wall to his left. He had done work for someone who transported drugs in similar barrels. Stacked on flatbeds, no one would have suspected the barrels to contain illegal substances. In broad daylight, large quantities were shipped to various locations for distribution.

I can bet who owns this warehouse.

He was dragged over to an area directly in front of the chair. The two men hoisted his body to a standing position, his feet still bound together.

"Sit in the chair!" commanded the shorter of the two.

TJ lowered his huge frame onto the chair. The two men bound him to this single piece of furniture with ropes. Two sets of construction lights were rolled alongside him and were illuminated. The other lights in the room were turned off.

"Spotlight's on you, big man," said the taller of the two. "I doubt you'll be able to dance on this stage, but I'd put money on you being able to sing. Oh, how rude! I forgot to remove the tape."

The duct tape was ripped from his face in two jerks. TJ grimaced; his skin was left raw. In the darkness before him, he made out the glow of a lit cigarette. He soon heard the footsteps of someone approaching.

"Your solo is about to begin," whispered the man who had removed the tape.

The man then moved into the darkness to meet the person smoking the cigarette. TJ heard indistinguishable murmurs of conversation.

"I want to talk with Tony!" TJ bellowed.

The tall man returned, carrying a small mechanism. He moved behind TJ and fastened the object to his right hand, causing his fingers to be spread out.

Tony Gallucci stepped close enough to the spotlights to be seen. He took a draw from the cigarette, smoke gently rising. Reaching into his jacket, he pulled out what appeared to be two envelopes of cash. The man who had attached the mechanism to TJ's fingers stepped forward to take the envelopes. Without saying a word, he motioned to the shorter man that it was time for them to leave. As the footsteps of the two faded, Gallucci stepped fully into the light.

"Tony…" stammered TJ.

Tony Gallucci moved behind the chair.

"What would you like to talk about?' asked Tony.

Before the bound man could answer, Tony touched the lit cigarette to the tip of TJ's index finger of his right hand. In pain, he let out a string of curses.

"I thought I could count on you," Tony stated.

"I just couldn't do it this time," shouted TJ.

"That's why you're here," replied Tony, touching the cigarette to the tip of the middle finger.

Another assortment of curses followed.

"What's so special about this particular job?" Tony calmly asked.

"Stop, for a minute!" shouted TJ. "Please, just stop!"

"Why?" Tony questioned, moving on to the pinky finger. This time, leaving the cigarette in place for two full seconds. His victim screamed in agony.

"Oh, God" whimpered TJ. "Please stop."

"I guess it would be fair to let you have a say," his tormenter whispered in an ear. "Ok, go on."

"When I got a good look at this girl, it hit me that she looked a lot like my dead baby sister," explained TJ. "It felt like I was about to turn my sister over for someone, to do God knows what to her."

"Family," stated Tony. "Family is important. Haven't I always treated you like family?"

"Yeah… yeah," answered TJ. "But you aren't acting like family right now."

"You were given a job to do," replied Tony. "I trusted you to carry it out. Like a family member, I thought I could count on you. But you burned me TJ That hurts. So, in turn, you have to be burned. It's somewhat poetic, don't you think."

Tony extinguished the cigarette on the tip of the remaining finger of TJ's right hand. After the screams ended, the huge man was crying like a baby. His body shook from a combination of raw emotional and physical trauma.

"So, your sister's dead?" asked Tony.

"Stinking drunk driver," replied TJ, his voice quivering.

"That's a shame, brother," stated his torturer. "It really hurts to lose family. I would hate to lose you. But there has to be consequences when a family member turns on the rest. I'm sure you understand. It just can't happen. You may not appreciate how lucky you are. There's a special place in my heart for you. I'm willing to forgive. What do you say? Would you like that?"

Tony stepped in front of his victim. TJ nodded his head.

"Please," the bound man whispered.

"So, you think you can carry out a few simple orders without failure?" asked Tony. "That would be good for the both of us."

"Yeah, whatever you want," TJ's voice much higher pitched than his normal deep tone.

"See, I knew you could be reasonable," replied Tony. "I just had to explain things, right? I'm sure everything is clear to you now. We just had a misunderstanding, and you simply needed to be taught – like having a personal tutor. Someone who cares enough to take the time to make sure you get it. You won't find anyone else who would give you a second chance. Someone else might just write you off, as unteachable. I would say that another person would leave you in a rather permanent situation. But not me. I like you, TJ. I believe in you. I know you can do better, if just given a chance."

Tony placed his right hand under TJs chin and lifted his victim's head so that their eyes met. He flipped the now extinguished cigarette away with his left hand.

"Are we good now?" Gallucci asked.

"We're good," answered TJ, wearily.

The shaking of his body began to subside. He took a deep breath.

"I'm going to make sure the boys help you back to your place," said Tony. "I believe you warrant personal attention. We're going to keep a close eye on you for a while. You should be mindful of the lessons learned tonight. These two are going to make sure you don't forget. But if tonight's lesson slips your mind, I've given these two men permission to handle things."

Tony stepped toward the darkness, halted and turned back.

"Make sure you put some cream on that hand of yours," Tony whispered. "I need you to be well soon. I have plans for you, and I want you to be feeling good when I next call upon you."

Tony motioned for the two men to come over. Under his instructions, they cut the tape that bound TJ's feet and helped him stand.

"Get that pole out from under his arms," ordered Tony. "It makes him look silly. Take him home."

Turning to TJ, Gallucci pulled another envelope from his jacket and crammed it into the waist portion of the big man's jeans.

"I can't give you what was promised to do the job, because you didn't do it," explained Tony. "But just to let you understand that I really do believe in you, here is a little something to help you along until next time."

"Thanks," said TJ.

"These two thugs don't have that personal trust in you. For their sake, I'll need to leave your hands taped up until they get you back home. I need to make them somewhat comfortable about giving you a lift. Understand?"

"Got it," replied TJ, his voice now returning back to its former state.

The two men escorted him back to his car. TJ was forced into the ample back seat, his duffle bag beside him. His hands were still tightly taped. The taller one operated the mechanism that the raised the warehouse door, while the other dropped into the driver seat. The door rumbled as it opened. The Crown Victoria slowly exited the building and stopped near the car the other man had driven to the scene.

"I'll lead the way," the taller man said, getting into that vehicle.

Soon, both cars were enroute. About halfway back, TJ leaned to the side and used his powerful shoulder to shove the duffle bag onto the rear floorboard. He then lay down on the large rear seat.

"Man, that really took it out of me," he stated.

"What are you doing?" asked the driver.

"My body is killing me," answered TJ. "I just need to just stretch out a little."

"I believe you, but I need for you to sit up where I can see you in the mirror."

TJ quickly slid his taped hands under his butt, and then slipped his legs between his hands so that his arms were now in front of him.

"OK, I'll sit up," he responded.

As quick as a cat, he reached his bound hands over the top of the driver's head and pulled back against the man's neck. With one powerful jerk, TJ crushed the driver's windpipe. The car swerved to the right, and the passenger side front tire bounced onto the curb. The man's right foot came off the accelerator, and the car slowed. A sickening gurgle came from the driver's throat, his hands moved to it after releasing the steering wheel. TJ shoved the man's head to the right, and then rose up and over the back of the seat to take the wheel with his hands. The car straightened. TJ immediately released the wheel and took hold of the key in the ignition, turning off the engine. The car came to a stop.

Still clutching his battered throat, the driver desperately struggled for air. His captive was no longer his first priority. Glancing up through the front windshield, TJ saw the brake lights of the leading car glow brighter. He opened the passenger side rear door and exited the car. Standing outside the car, he opened the front door and pulled the struggling man onto the sidewalk. Leaning in through the open car door, he popped open the glove box and pulled out a .38

revolver.

By now, the leading car was turning around. With the revolver in hand, he quickly moved behind the rear of his car. Headlights of the other car were now illuminating the Crown Victoria. Crouching low behind his car, TJ waited as the car approached. The opened doors of the Crown Vic caused the taller man to assume that TJ had escaped out the rear door, and that the shorter man had chased after him. When the car stopped, TJ rose up from behind his car and fired three shots into the other car. Carefully, he approached the vehicle. Seeing no movement inside the other car, he slipped the gun into the waist of his pants. TJ opened the front door of the car, and immediately his victim fell out onto the street. There was one shot to the chest and another in his shoulder. The man was barely alive, taking in shallow breaths. TJ pulled the gun from his waist and pointed it at the dying man. Suddenly, he knelt and laid his gun down on the pavement near the man's legs. His hands still bound, he opened the pocket of the man's jacket. Taking the cell phone from it, he examined the outgoing calls. He breathed a sigh of relief, finding that no calls had been made over the past fifteen minutes. TJ slipped the phone into a front pocket of his jeans and picked up the gun from the pavement.

"I promised myself that I would kill you, if I had a chance," TJ stated, again pointing the barrel straight at the taller man's head.

Instead, he slipped the gun into the waist of his jeans and took the cell phone from his front pocket. He dialed 911 and told the operator where to find the two severely wounded men. TJ returned to his car and closed the two open doors. His eyes scanned the area for witnesses. Seeing no one, he tossed both the phone and gun onto the front seat. Opening the glove box again, he quickly rummaged through the contents until he found a small pocketknife. Tenderly holding it between the thumb and index finger of his damaged right hand, he worked until he was able to open it using mainly his left hand. Carefully, he cut away at the duct tape binding his hands.

After he merged with the traffic on I75 North, he placed a call with the newly acquired phone.

"This is TJ."

"I can't tell you how good it is to hear from you, TJ," replied Russ Blevins. "When are you going to come see me?"

"I've got troubles – bad troubles - so bad that I can't afford to see you. I want you to know that I meant to do this right."

"Why don't you let me help with those troubles," offered Russ. "You know that you can trust me."

"If I doubted it, I wouldn't be on this call. Listen. A guy named Tony Gallucci owns a couple of large warehouses in the south part of town. They're off Mooreland Avenue and were recently built to store construction equipment. You need to tell the police to pay him a visit. If they search the place, I'm sure they'll find a few interesting items, particularly inside the highway barrels. Make sure that Gallucci never hears my name. If I live through the month, I'll take it as a miracle."

"Can we meet somewhere?" asked Russ,

"I have to put distance between myself and some people, and I have to do it quick," explained TJ. "You've been fair with me. I just wanted to tell you that

I meant to work with you, and that someone needs to check into Tony's business fast."

Placing the phone on the passenger seat, TJ's emotions began to subside. He began to collect his thoughts.

They can't find me using the car. I bought it using cash two weeks ago, and it's a good thing that I've not yet registered it with the state. Talking about timing. Couldn't be better. I might make it to the Canadian border, and cross by foot in a remote area. Maybe, then to Alaska. I just need a little luck.

Once out of Georgia, TJ pulled into the parking lot of a convenience store near a dumpster. He put the gun under the front seat. TJ got out of the car and tossed the phone in the dumpster. He then moved the car near the gasoline pumps to fuel it. Inside the store, he spotted gasoline containers for sale. He paid cash for four large gasoline containers, three Moon Pies, a soft drink, a box of band aids, and a tube of antibiotic cream. He quickly estimated the cost of filling the car and the containers with gas, and also pre-paid with cash.

He first filled the tank, and then the containers. After placing the gas filled containers in the trunk, he applied the ointment to his fingertips. The sun was rising to his right when he entered the interstate highway again. TJ reached for a Moon Pie, consuming it as he drove. His thoughts drifted.

I'm hope the waitress is safe. I hope she stays off the radar, wherever she is.

Chapter 5
Megan

"OUR KEY SCRIPTURE this morning may be found in Luke 12:48," stated the pastor of Valley Springs Church. "For unto whomsoever much is given, of him shall be much required:"

Sam scanned the sanctuary for Megan.

This is a big church, but it shouldn't be too difficult to spot a red head.

"Many of our church members have been blessed financially," continued the pastor. "It's obvious that not everyone is of equal wealth. Some of you were born with very high IQs, enabling much of your success. This was a precious gift from God. Many of you worked hard for what you have. I'm not implying that a person has nothing to do with the level of wealth he obtains. It is absolutely true that choices have a lot to do with a person's success. However, never forget that God granted you the health to do some of the things you do. Never forget that you could have been born in an impoverished and uneducated society. You have been granted particular advantages. Contrary to the view of some, our key scripture points out that God really doesn't treat us all the same. This verse deals with God's expectations of those who have been given much. This scripture indicates that God holds people with wealth as having greater responsibility than those who have little. The wealthy are held responsible to use that abundance in meaningful ways."

Sam wasn't impressed.

I'm sure the pastor views those 'meaningful ways' to mean the rich should fork over money to the church in a variety of ways.

"God could evenly distribute to all, but He doesn't," said the minister. "Do you think you are allowed wealth simply to hoard it for your own pleasure? God is interested in the hearts of individuals, both the needy and those having the capacity to meet those needs. I'm sure that some of you think that your contribution, in the form of heavier taxation to the government, should suffice. Let me share another scripture. Mark 12:14-17 says the following."

'They came to him and said, 'Teacher, we know that you are a man of integrity. You aren't swayed by others, because you pay no attention to who they are; but you teach the way of God in accordance with the truth. Is it right to pay the imperial tax to Caesar or not? Should we pay or shouldn't we?'

But Jesus knew their hypocrisy. 'Why are you trying to trap me?' he asked. 'Bring me a denarius and let me look at it.' They brought the coin, and he asked them, 'Whose image is this? And whose inscription?'

'Caesar's,' they replied.

Then Jesus said to them, "Give back to Caesar

what is Caesar's and to God what is God's.'

The minister paused, allowing the message of the text to sink in. As his eyes scanned the room, Sam's mouth twisted into a slight smirk.

Here it comes. Here comes the part where the preacher sucks money from the congregation. Got to make people feel guilty. He couldn't use this sermon in my neighborhood. We don't have rich people, so he would have to come up with another tactic to reach into the pockets of people.

"Forced taxation doesn't relieve the wealthy from the duty to voluntarily give to others," said the pastor. "Personally, I think that government redistribution of wealth in some ways diminishes realization of personal responsibility towards those less fortunate. Voluntary giving to others is an outwardly expression of what is in a person's heart. God is interested in the hearts of the wealthy in having compassion, such that it actually includes action. In turn, God is interested in the hearts of the less fortunate, such that they refrain from jealousy, envy or anger. Each of us must allow God to shape our heart, as He intends."

Sam's mind drifted to a bleak time in his life, when winter weather prevented him from being able to work. In his construction work, there was no pay when there was no work. Each in his neighborhood had different professions, but were of similar economic levels. Most would be considered to be members of the working poor. The fifty-three-year-old woman in the apartment next door to him was a maid in a local hospital. She gathered used linens and towels, and replaced them with fresh items. Some of the used linens were soiled. Her wages were small. During a tough time of little work, Sam had heard a knock on his back door. Opening the door, he found that neighbor on his rear porch.

"May I come in?" she asked.

"Sure," answered Sam, allowing her entry into his kitchen.

The neighbor marched over to his refrigerator and opened it. After inspecting the contents, she quickly moved to cabinet after cabinet. Her eyes filled with tears, and she quickly departed out of the apartment. Sam was a bit confused.

After a few minutes, he again heard a knock on the rear door. Answering it, he found the neighbor standing on his back porch. This time, she held a large bag filled with groceries.

"Let me in!" she demanded.

The woman emptied the contents of the bag, placing items on the counter beside the sink. It became obvious that she had taken unopened food from her own apartment and given the items to him.

"I've been watching you, young man," she began. "Over the past two weeks, I've not seen you bring groceries into this apartment. Your refrigerator has nothing but a bottle of ketchup, and you've got nothing but crackers and peanut butter in a cabinet."

Sam's eyes fell.

"If you ever run out of food again, you had better tell me," she scolded. "Do you understand me?"

Her eyes still wet with tears, Sam moved in to give her a long and grateful hug. It was one of the most humbling experiences he had ever encountered.

No one here understands this. They think people steal because they're poor. I didn't have much to eat, but I didn't steal. My neighbor was normally as poor as me, but she shared with me out of the little that she had. No one at this wealthy church understands. Sure, we have thieves in my neighborhood; but they would be thieves no matter where they lived or no matter how much they owned. They steal because they're thieves. Good people share, because they are good people.

Earlier in the week, he had read an article in the paper about an executive in a corporation who had embezzled more than one hundred fifty thousand dollars from the business.

It doesn't matter how much or how little people have, thieves are thieves.

Sam's face turned away from the pastor, to find Megan seated on the opposite side of the church. She was alongside two other young women near her age. They were attractive, but Sam wasn't interested.

At the end of the service, Sam moved quickly towards the rear door. He hoped he would catch Megan as she exited the church. A small gray-haired woman took him by the arm.

"Are you new here?" she politely asked.

Sam's eyes dropped.

Good grief! Not today.

He quickly glanced in at the section of the sanctuary where he had seen Megan, but couldn't find her. With a sigh, he turned back to the elderly woman.

"Yes, it's my first visit," Sam answered.

"I'm Dora Hitchcock. I hope you'll come back again."

"I'll consider it," he replied.

"Would you mind telling me your name, young man?"

"Sam. Sam Blaylock,"

"There are a number of Blaylocks in Georgia. Would I know members of your family?"

"I don't think you would know members of my family, but thanks for asking," Sam answered, his eyes periodically darting around the sanctuary. This time, he spotted Megan exiting a side door. He became frustrated.

I should have known this would happen. It's always an old lady. Maybe I'll be able to catch Megan in the parking lot.

"We're having a covered dish luncheon downstairs in the Fellowship Hall," said Dora. "Would you care to join us? We have some awfully good cooks."

"I'm sure you do, but I don't believe so."

"Then, please do an old lady a favor. I sometimes have trouble taking the stairs. Would you take a few minutes to escort me downstairs?"

In silent exasperation, Sam's eyed dropped downward.

"I can't believe this! I give up. This was a wasted trip across town.

He quickly reconciled himself to the fact that his attempt to connect with Megan failed. Calming himself, he looked down at Dora.

"Sure, I can help you."

"I wouldn't ask just anyone, young man. You have kind eyes."

Sam gently took her by the arm.

"Where do we go?" he asked. "I'll need you to point me in the right direction."

One arm locked with his, she used a cane in her other hand to point to another side door. It was then that he more fully took note of her frailty. The shaking of her hand caused the cane to perform a slight aerial dance.

"At your pace, Mrs. Hitchcock. You lead, and I'll come along with you."

"You can stop with the Mrs. Hitchcock," she replied. "Everyone calls me Dora."

"Yes, Dora," he said, with a wink.

"Are you flirting with me?" Dora asked, smiling.

"It's hard not to," he said, returning the smile.

As they slowly made their way down the stairs, Sam heard the constant chatter of church members in the basement Fellowship Hall. Stepping into the room, he saw the raised arms of the pastor.

"Let's ask God's blessings on this wonderful spread before us," the minister called out.

All heads bowed as he prayed. When Sam raised his eyes, he saw Megan standing with those serving food. She turned his way, and their eyes locked. Megan smiled nervously and motioned for him to come over to her line. He nodded.

"Do you know that young lady?" questioned Dora.

"We've met."

"You go on. You've helped me enough already."

"You're not going to get off that easy," teased Sam. "Do you think you're going to bring me down here and just dump me off in this crowd? We'll go through that line together. I'll hold two plates. You load both of them up. I expect you to know who the best cooks are."

"It's a deal," replied Dora.

"How do you know Dora?" Megan asked Sam, as she plopped a large spoonful of mashed potatoes on one of the plates.

"We met in the sanctuary, and she asked that I help her down the stairs," explained Sam.

"Dora!" Megan scolded.

"I simply asked him for a few moments of his time," the elderly woman replied with a grin.

"It was no problem," insisted Sam.

Megan pointed to the elevator.

"She took you," stated Megan. "She's a flirt."

"It was hard not to," replied Dora, using Sam's earlier words. "He is such a handsome man."

———•●•———

AFTERWARDS, DORA DEPARTED by use of the elevator. Sam watched Megan begin to empty the serving tables of pans and platters.

"Need any help?" asked Sam.

"You're a visitor, and visitors aren't allowed to help," replied Megan.

"Since I'm not a member here, I don't have to follow your rules," said Sam, picking up a platter containing two remaining yeast rolls.

"Suit yourself. Bring it in here."

Sam followed Megan into a large kitchen where four women busily cleaned dishes and utensils. He placed the platter alongside her pans.

"I'm surprised you came," said Megan.

"So, you remember me," Sam said, bearing a cocky smile.

"Going to your neighborhood was a first for me," she replied. "What made you decide to visit?"

"I thought you were cute."

"That's not a reason to go to church," she said, rolling her eyes.

"You asked me, and I thought it best not to lie in God's house," Sam replied, making quote signs with his fingers as he said the words "God's house."

Megan turned and headed towards the elevator.

"Where are you going?" asked Sam.

"Upstairs. You coming?"

Without a word, Sam stepped into the elevator beside Megan.

"How did you know that I'm not a pervert, intending to attack you in the elevator?" Sam asked, when the elevator door opened on the main floor.

"Are you?"

"What, a pervert?"

"Yes."

"No, but you didn't know that."

"Well, if you didn't attack Dora, you must not be a pervert," she explained. "Dora is pretty hot, you know."

"I think I might be afraid to be on that elevator with Dora."

Megan chuckled and turned to walk away.

"Where are you going?" Sam asked.

"I don't live here. I'm going home."

"You're being rude.

"No, I'm not," Megan said, walking out the main church exit.

"Why do you want to go home?"

"Lunch is over, and there's nothing else to do."

"How about a movie?"

"Not interested," Megan answered.

"I suppose there aren't any movies currently in theaters that you find interesting. Some might take what you said as a sign that you're not interested in me, but I know that's not the case."

"Why do think that I might be interested in you?"

"You came to my side of town just to find me," Sam said, puffing his chest out. "Any girl who goes to that much trouble must have it bad for me.

"I came to your side of town to invite you to church."

As they stepped into the church parking lot, Sam pressed her.

"Seriously, why did you come to my neighborhood?"

"It was a suggestion of my Sunday school teacher. He said that we should sometimes go out of our way to invite someone to church. Your neighborhood was certainly out of the way."

"Well, you know where I live. Why don't you show me your place?"

"I don't know you," she firmly answered. "I don't know why you think I would invite you to my place."

"Sure you do," replied Sam, with a wink. "You like me."

"I think it's time for me to go home," said Megan.

"Are you going to invite me back to church?"

"Of course," Megan said, smiling. "I don't want to disappoint my Sunday school teacher."

"You got a pen in that purse of yours?"

Megan reached into her purse and handed him a pen. Sam quickly jotted a note on the church bulletin he had earlier shoved in his back pocket and handed it to her.

"What's this?" asked Megan, taking the bulletin from his hand.

"It's my cell number," Sam explained. "I don't want you to have to drive across town again just to invite me to church."

"You set this up with your question about inviting you to church," observed Megan.

"Dora taught me everything I know," he replied, grinning. "If I don't get a call, I'll know that you weren't sincere about wanting me to come to your church. What would Jesus think about that?"

Megan wore a slight smile as she turned in the direction of her car. Sam's eyes followed her, as she walked.

That worked out pretty well. Umm-umm! And I like the way she walks. I'm sure she's been with a number of rich boys, but maybe it's time for her to see what it's like to be with a real man. I wonder how long it'll be before she gives me a call.

Before opening her car door, Megan glanced back at him. She couldn't hide a smile, as she gave him a slight wave. Sam watched her drive away.

Nice car. Either she has a rich daddy, or she earns a hefty salary. I wonder what she does for a living.

The parking lot was almost empty when Sam dropped into the driver's side of his worn 2001 Chevrolet Silverado pickup. He kept the interior clean and neat, but it was clearly a work truck.

I'm kidding myself, she would never get in this truck. It was fun meeting her. I'm sure she has a lawyer or a banker for her guy. But she might think about me. Stranger things have happened.

Across the parking lot, a man in a silver sedan watched. Undetected, he had intently observed the interaction between Megan and this man. As Sam drove out of the parking lot, the silver sedan followed from a distance.

Chapter 6
Misty

***

DETECTIVE FRANK REYNOLDS looked over Misty Callahan's financial report. Recent credit and debit card activity showed she had paid for clothing at a shop at the Atlanta airport and had purchased a one-way ticket to Colorado Springs. There was a withdrawal of a thousand dollars from her Atlanta bank account, by use of an ATM. Other smaller amounts were withdrawn on other dates.

Both she and Turner disappeared at roughly the same time. I don't view this as a coincidence. He could have killed her and is now using the cards. Then again, there's the chance they could be in on something together. I need to find out whether she is alive in Colorado. She could be my ticket for locating him.

He rose from his desk and quickly made his way to his supervisor's office.

"I need to book a trip to Colorado Springs," he announced to his boss.

———•●•———

IT WAS AFTER MIDNIGHT when Frank walked into the bar. He motioned to a dark-haired attractive waitress before taking a seat at a table.

"What will you have?" she questioned.

"I'll have you sit down with me for a few minutes," answered Frank.

Misty had received thousands of similar invitations while waitressing, especially after midnight. The most obnoxious ones came after patrons had downed several drinks.

"I don't think that's going to happen tonight – the boss doesn't like it," she replied, forcing a smile. Her eyes revealed that she was far too tired to entertain a demanding customer.

Frank opened his coat to reveal his badge and shoulder holster. Her empty smile vanished, replaced with a slightly dropped jaw and a bewildered stare.

"Misty, I'm from Atlanta, and you and I need to talk," Frank explained. "I've not yet involved the Colorado Springs police, so this will just be our little talk."

Misty's face went pale; her hands began to tremble. Her eyes darted around the room, and then at the door of the establishment.

"It's best that you not run," advised Frank. "You and I both know that I'm not the one you need to be afraid of."

"I don't want to lose my job," she stammered. "I've not been working here long… you know how it is."

"Like I said, I'm not your problem. I'm willing to let your boss in on this conversation, if you wish. Have a seat. This won't take long."

Glancing over at another waitress, she placed a finger to her lips to indicate that she should not inform the boss. Misty dropped into the seat in front of Frank, her eyes fixed on his.

"How did you find me?" she questioned.

"I'm sure you're wondering whether someone else might be able to find you," stated Frank. "The police have resources that most people don't. I'm interested in who or what caused you to be so frightened."

"Who said that I'm afraid of anybody?"

"You did," answered Frank. "Your entire body is telling me. I need for you to be completely honest with me. Just try to relax. Let's begin with what made you leave Atlanta so abruptly."

RETURNING TO HIS HOTEL room, Frank placed a call to Russ Blevins.

"I've found Misty Callahan in Colorado."

"That's interesting," said Russ. "Do you think the two are working together?

"At first, but I no longer believe they are."

"How did you find her?"

"I found two bars within close proximity of an ATM that she's frequently used. Since arriving in Colorado Springs, she's been making large cash withdrawals. I suspect that she's trying to use cash for most things. At one point, I considered the possibility that TJ had robbed her and was using the card.

However, I found her working at one of the establishments. We had a chat."

"What did she say?" questioned Russ. "Is there a connection with TJ?"

"She said that a large man kidnapped her and caused her to lose consciousness. Misty found herself in the trunk of a car, hogtied. When the guy released her, he warned her of people who planned to do bad things to her. She was genuinely scared of going back to Atlanta."

"Did she get a look at him?"

"She never saw the guy who grabbed her, but she said that he was exceptional large and strong. I believe that he could have been your boy Turner. Her kidnapper warned her to never go back to her apartment, and to immediately leave the city of Atlanta. She told me where he dumped her, and she swore that he'd not contacted her since that event. If it was Turner, I find it interesting that he set her free."

"TJ doesn't make a habit of turning people loose before roughing them up."

"His record indicates that he's not above beating a woman."

"I think there's more to the story of his arrest than we know. That's not my take on him."

"Ms. Callahan willingly gave me her new address while we talked at the bar. After the place closed, I gave her a ride home. We talked there for about another hour. Misty said that her kidnapper told her that he was ordered to take her by someone who would do terrible things to her. She was visibly shaken and begged me to keep quiet about her being in Colorado. I left her my cell number. I thought about going to the local police, but decided to hold off for now. She said she has no idea as to why she was taken or released."

"What do you think?" asked Russ.

"Our investigation determined that she disappeared in a real hurry. She left everything - her clothes, furniture, and even jewelry. Her story fits. Something caused her to not value her belongings, and the evidence itself indicates that her move was completely unplanned. I believe Misty's truly terrified of being found by someone. I honestly don't doubt the kidnapping story, but I'm baffled as to why the guy would let her go."

"Would you mind giving me her Colorado address?" asked Russ.

"Thinking about paying her a visit?"

"My interest is finding TJ. You're right about it being too much of a coincidence for them both to disappear at the same time. Her description of his size matches him. I'm hoping she can give me more information regarding her abductor. Regardless, we need to find him, and this may be the best lead I have."

"I agree," replied Frank.

"Does Misty Callahan have a record?"

"She has a couple of DUIs, and her driver license was pulled."

"So, she's on probation for drinking and driving?"

"Was," answered Frank. "She came off probation last year, but she still doesn't own a car."

"That would indicate that she's more responsible than most. Many DUI repeaters cheat, and drive without a license. It's possible she doesn't trust herself to stay sober. Do you plan to contact the police in Colorado Springs?"

"There's no law against people moving to a different city. I guess you could make a case against her skipping out of her apartment lease, but that's what a deposit is for. Until somebody complains about her breaking a law, there's no real reason to pull in other people. Now that I know she's safe, she's no longer my concern. I believe the kidnapping story, but I have no proof that it happened. Still, I'm going to keep my eye out for another occurrence in the Atlanta area. Maybe she can provide you more luck in locating Turner. You know him better than I do."

———•●•———

ONE LATE EVENING after her encounter with Reynolds, Misty left the bar still petrified of being found by the person who ordered her abduction. Returning to her furnished apartment, she reached for one of the empty large wine bottles placed on top of the chest in her bedroom. The glass was exceptionally dark, and a large label completely wrapped around it. She tossed it onto the bed. Misty snatched a wire coat hanger from the bedroom closet and fashioned it so that it formed a hook. Dropping onto the bed, she ran the wire inside the bottle to retrieve the contents. The bottle held what she considered to be "safety money", to be used if she had to quickly flee to another city. Misty counted the bills fished from the bottle. Consisting of fifties and twenties, it totaled to a little over three hundred dollars.

Still not enough. Soon, I might need to move to another city. That detective found me, and that means others could find me. Why is this happening to me? My old boyfriends can't be behind this. None of them would waste money to hire someone to put me in the trunk of a car – just to scare me. It doesn't make sense. Somebody with big money paid that guy to take me.

She racked her mind, trying to think of contacts with wealthy men. She was attractive, but not the type that would cause a rich man to cheat on his wife. She had dated a number of lower income guys that were up to no good. A thought flashed through her mind.

I remember Ricky talking to a rich guy on a sidewalk one evening. After I walked up and took him by the arm, he introduced me and told me he had done yardwork for the guy. What was his name? Adams. Some rich dude named Adams. I remember his eyes running up and down my body – and right in front of Ricky. At first, I felt a little thrilled that a wealthy dude would be checking me out – but I remember afterwards feeling a little nervous. I can tell that a lot of men undress me in their heads – especially after several rounds of drinks. Ricky told him all about me – that I waitressed at a bar. That was months ago, just before I broke it off with Ricky. Could it be that guy? It could be one of hundreds of those guys who left me big tips. But the guy who grabbed me used the word "people" – more than one. Why would "people" be after me?

Suddenly, she heard a knock on the apartment door. A cold chill ran up her spine. Quickly, she crammed the bills back inside the bottle and then sat motionless. The knocking continued. Misty's fingers fumbled, dropping the large bottle onto the wooden floor, causing a loud thud.

What an idiot! Whoever is knocking knows that someone is home now.

She carefully reached down for the bottle and slowly picked it up. Holding it in a death grip, she closed her eyes. She wished for everything to just go away. Seated on the bed, Misty's body began to tremble. She then heard a voice at the door.

"Misty, my name is Russ Blevins. Detective Frank Reynolds spoke to you earlier. I have just a few questions."

Misty quietly rose from the bed, and gingerly placed the bottle back on the chest. Through the open bedroom door, she had a clear view of her apartment door. She saw a business card slide under the door from the hall outside.

"I know you're in there," she heard the man outside the door say. "Just look at the card. I'm a probation officer from Atlanta, and I'm hoping you can help me find someone."

Misty had worked a trying shift and was in no mood for this.

Why can't these people leave me alone? I may have to get out of here, just to have some peace!

"Leave me alone!" burst from Misty's quivering mouth before she could stop herself.

I'm out of my mind! I can't believe I've started a conversation with this guy. I'm stupid – just stupid.

"I promise that I won't take long," stated the man behind the door. "Did you look at my card?"

Misty nervously walked over to the door and picked up the card. She scanned the words.

"Just look at the card…" the voice said.

"Stop," Misty begged, from her side.

"This situation may be of importance to you, as well. I think you may want to hear what I have to say."

She reluctantly opened the door just slightly, leaving the safety chain in place. She saw a man dressed in a suit.

"Do you realize what time it is?" she asked. "It's late, and I'm really tired."

"I hoped I could catch you at the bar, but I was too late," Russ explained. "I was about a couple of buildings away when I saw you enter your apartment. I promise, I won't take long."

"Will you promise to leave me alone, if I talk to you?"

"I promise. You have my card. If we ever speak again, it will be only if you call me. I promise, cross my heart."

"You left out 'hope to die'. You know, 'cross my heart, hope to die'."

"I got it," Russ said with a smile. "Although, I'm not hoping to die anytime soon."

Misty opened the door fully, allowing Russ to enter.

"Mind if we sit?" he asked.

"I thought you said it wouldn't take long."

"I don't intend to stay long, but you said that you were really tired. We can stand, if you wish."

"No, take a seat on the couch," she said, pointing to the furniture.

Misty took a seat in the accompanying chair, folding her legs under her.

"What do you want?"

"I think it's possible that the man who grabbed you was TJ Turner. I'm his probation officer, and I haven't seen him since you disappeared from Atlanta. You might be interested to know that he called me to tell me that he was on the run. If TJ is afraid, whoever is after him must be really bad. He doesn't scare easily. The guy is huge."

"Did he say that he took me?"

"No, but I believe he did. It's important that I find him. I want to ask you a few questions about the man who took you."

"I don't know anything about the guy, except that something made him change his mind and he let me go. I've never even laid eyes on him."

"You didn't see him?"

"No. After loosening my hands, he left me blindfolded. He warned me not to peek until he was gone. I was scared to death to take it off."

"How about his voice?" asked Russ. "Can you describe his voice?"

"A big voice – I mean, it was a deep voice."

"Anything more distinctive?"

"Actually, he spoke really well. He had a good speaking voice – spoke clearly. For example, he distinctly put the 'g' on the end of words ending in 'ing'."

"The 'g'?"

"Yeah. Like, when he said 'you have a chance of staying alive', he clearly put the 'g' on the end of the word 'staying'. He didn't say 'stayin', he clearly pronounced it as 'staying'. All of his words were clearly spoken."

"Would you say that he sounded well educated?"

"I don't know about his education, he just didn't sound like a red-neck," answered Misty.

"Did he mention anything that would tell you more about him?"

"It's what he did… or didn't do. The guy didn't hurt me when he easily could have. That's all I know. He told me that he was taking a big risk in letting me go. He seemed sorry for taking me. Maybe he's not really a bad guy, at heart."

"The voice could be consistent with TJ Turner's. There are others who would disagree with you about him not being a bad guy. He's been known to hurt people. Like I said, I'm his probation officer. Did he give you any indication of his plans?"

"No; why did those people want him to take me?" questioned Misty. "I don't understand any of this."

"I, too, would be interested in understanding that. Like I said, I believe he's involved with really bad individuals. I need to find him."

"If he's on the run, these people must be after him now."

"I believe so," replied Russ.

"Are they still after me too?" asked Misty, her voice quivering.

"I can't say."

"You're not very comforting, you know that? Good Lord! This seems to just never end. I hoped this whole thing would be behind me once I moved away, but it just keeps on going."

Russ sensed that she was genuinely frightened and seemed almost exhausted.

"I've taken up too much of your night, and I'm sure you're really tired," Russ said. "I'll be leaving now. I sincerely appreciate you allowing me in."

"You're scaring the crap out of me. I'm really tired, but I doubt I'll be able to sleep."

Russ rose from the couch and started for the door.

"Do you have a room?" Misty asked.

"Yes, I have a room."

"Do you have a gun?"

"Not with me. I have one locked in a safe back in Atlanta."

"What good is it doing there?"

"The airlines frown on handguns being brought aboard planes. Besides, I don't really need it with me here. I came here to obtain information about the man who abducted you."

"I did what you asked. I answered your questions. Would you do something for me?"

"What do you need?

"I'm really tired, but my mind is spinning. I'm afraid that I'll lie awake for hours."

"I'm sorry," Russ replied.

"I don't normally do this, but I have to get some rest. Would you mind sleeping here on the couch?"

"What?"

"I need some sleep, and just knowing that someone would be between me and that door would help put my mind to ease. I know it sounds weird?"

"A bit weird. Before tonight, you never met me. How do you know I'm not pretending? How can you be sure that I'm not one of the bad guys?"

"You knew about that cop that came to see me. Besides, I meet a lot of people as a waitress. I usually can size someone up. I think you're real."

"I…"

"OK, I can tell by that dumb look on your face that you don't want to do this. A cop might do it. For a minute I forgot that you're just a probation officer. I shouldn't have asked."

"What about if I check in on you in the morning?" asked Russ. "Breakfast is on me. What about that? I'll come by at 8:00. You've got my cell number on my card. If something were to happen during the night, you can just give me a call."

"Make it 9:00. I've got to get some sleep."

"See you at 9:00 AM," said Russ.

After sliding between the hotel sheets that evening, Russ couldn't shake his conversation with Misty.

That girl's a little crazy. She didn't want to answer the door at first, and later she wanted me to stay the night in the apartment. In some ways, she may be as scary as TJ.

Chapter 7
Adams Family

PARKING IN THE CIRCULAR drive late Friday afternoon, Megan Adams felt assured glancing at the Italian marble fountain that filled most of the space within the circle. She easily recognized the other car parked in front of hers. Gray stones, forming the façade of the massive two-story mansion, projected a sense of strength and wealth to those on the outside. The interior was just as imposing. Stepping through the hand-carved solid oak front door of her family's estate, she made her way to the parlor. Her father, Allen, sat across a walnut table from his banker and financial advisor Charles Worthington. Spotting his daughter, Allen rose to his feet.

"Let me know when you've shifted those investments," her father told the banker. He turned his attention to his daughter.

"Megan, we've just finished. Supper will be ready within the hour."

"Hello, Megan," Worthington eloquently spoke.

The banker was tall and thin, sporting a receding

hairline trimmed with graying temples. His appearance was unlike the stocky Adams, adorned with thick blonde hair. Worthington's visits were less regular than Megan's, but she had seen him at the house many times over the past fifteen years.

"Mr. Worthington," Megan replied, with a nod.

Since her childhood, Allen and Michelle Adams periodically entertained the Worthingtons and another couple in a private adult only weekend party at the house. When young, Megan would always be taken across town to her grandmother's home prior to those events. She was sent to a prestigious boarding school for girls during her high school years. There, she confided in another student about the curious practice of her parents.

"You're lucky that you're sent to stay with your grandmother," replied the other girl. "My parents forced me to attend parties at the house, and I was always bored out of my mind. My mother usually drank too much, and openly flirted with most of the men. She embarrassed me to no end. I wish they had sent me away. It was sickening."

Of the boarding school students, Megan found no other family practicing similar adult only weekends. Megan attributed the unusual event to the fact that very few others in the Atlanta area were as wealthy as her parents.

After moving out on her own, her parents established regular dates for the event as the second weekend of every other month. She had hoped that she would be invited after becoming an adult, but this wasn't the case. It was understood that she was not to visit during those times.

Worthington excused himself and exited the house.

"How's my only child?" asked Adams.

"I'm great," she replied, giving him a hug. "I see you're talking money again. Has he made you another ten million this year?"

"Actually, a little more. I trust very few people, and Charles has always been honest and discreet."

"I haven't a clue about the particulars of your investments, but your nose seems to be always right."

"If it's about my nose, then Charles Worthington would be the air," Adams responded. "He does the work. I just provide the funding. He's never failed me."

Megan had always found her father's friend to be a little unsettling. She didn't share her father's trust in the man.

Worthington could play the role of a highly sophisticated and extremely devious villain in a book or movie. He's my father's closest friend, but something about him troubles me.

Her footsteps echoed in the marbled tiled hall leading to the dining room. Besides her parents, a couple of staff personnel were present in the large house during days that didn't involve parties. On those weekends, the help would depart after food was prepared Friday afternoon and would return early Monday morning. Megan stepped into the massive dining room and considered her surroundings.

There will be three people eating here tonight. It would make far more sense for my parents and me to eat at the kitchen table. There's no need for this. However, it'll be nice to see them both.

Since moving into an apartment in Gwinnett County, she often enjoyed supper on her couch while watching TV. Away from the wealth of her childhood, she now enjoyed a life without pretense. Taking her father's advice, she had majored in finance in college. With Worthington as a reference, Megan easily found employment at a lending agency. Attending graduate classes at night at Georgia State, she lacked only three courses to obtain a Master's in Business Administration. From the time she was very small, her father taught her practical lessons regarding how money works. She was well prepared for a career in finance.

Seated alone in the eloquent room, Megan thought about the coming weekend. Saturdays were usually somewhat boring for her. She tried to imagine what her life would be if she had grown up in the apartments where Sam Blaylock lived. Despite the fact that he was relatively poor, Megan couldn't help liking him. Sam didn't appear to be intimidated by her social standing, and she found his confidence to be intriguing.

"I bet Sam could make a Saturday fun," she whispered to herself.

Reaching into her small handbag, she found the church bulletin on which he had written his cell number. She quickly entered it into her phone contacts list and sent him a text.

"Coming to church again this Sunday? – Megan Adams."

She heard footsteps in the hall. Megan shoved the phone in her purse as her mother entered the dining room.

"How have you been?" asked Michelle Adams.

Megan stood to greet her mother.

"Fine," Megan replied. "Nothing much new at work. School is a little boring."

"I don't know why you don't just ask your father for a position. Why do you insist on working for those people? If he wanted, Allen could simply purchase that agency."

"I think that's the point," answered Megan. "I want to see what life is like outside our family."

"Have you found them to be of interest?" asked her father, who had quietly entered the room.

"Not usually," answered Megan. "However, my church did something unusual a few weeks ago. We visited people in an apartment complex south of I-20."

"I have nothing against you attending that church," said Michelle. "However, I don't see why you should embark on every odd endeavor it comes up with."

"I agree," stated Allen. "I know a couple of people who attend there, but I doubt they took part in going to south Atlanta. Maybe you should use more discretion."

Kitchen workers began placing food on the large dining table, and the three seated themselves. Throughout the meal, Allen Adams repeatedly checked his cell. After a rich dessert, the three talked for another hour before being interrupted by the chimes of Megan's cell phone.

"I want to take this one," she announced, before rising to exit the room.

"He better have money," she heard her mother say.

Megan waved an acknowledgement, as she made her way toward the library. There she pulled the chain of an expensive small lamp on an end table, illuminating rich walnut shelving filled with books. She dropped onto a couch and answered the call.

"You could have just texted me," said Megan.

"I wanted to make sure it was you," replied Sam.

"Well, you told me to contact you via this cell number if I wanted to invite you back to church."

"Why don't you meet me tomorrow at the zoo on Boulevard?" asked Sam.

"I thought we were talking about church."

"You were talking about church, and I'm talking about the zoo. I like the monkeys best. They stink, but they're funny. What do you say?"
"Are you coming to church Sunday?"

"Go to the zoo with me tomorrow and I'll drive out to the church on Sunday. Deal?"

"How about a museum instead?" suggested Megan.

"What do you have against monkeys?"

"You said that they stink. A museum doesn't smell bad."

"When was the last time you saw the monkeys?"

"I'm not into monkeys."

"I didn't take you for a monkey hater. I'm not sure what to think about that."

"I dislike stink, not monkeys. I'll do gorillas, but you have to promise that you'll be at church Sunday."

"You drive a hard bargain. OK, gorillas it is."

"Church? Are you going to be at church?"

"I promise I'll come to your church on Sunday, but you have to meet me at the front of the zoo tomorrow at 11:30AM. If you're not there, forget church."

"OK."

Once the call ended, Megan found her mother sitting alone at the dining table sipping a glass of wine.

"Where's Dad?"

"He said that he had to return a couple of calls. Your call must have been important."

"Not really. Just a guy I met."

"Just a guy? I've not seen you move that fast since you were a kid on Christmas morning running to see what was under the tree."

"Just a guy, really," insisted Megan.

"Want to tell me about him?"

"Not really."

"I see," replied Megan's mother. "You're a big girl now, and I guess you're entitled to a little privacy."

"A guy asked me to go to the zoo tomorrow. That's all."

"The last time we took you to the zoo you were about ten. You said that you hated the smell."

"I'm sure they've made a few improvements over the years."

"You should have insisted that he go to the Cyclorama instead."

"It's no longer in Grant Park. They moved it."

"Nothing seems to stay the same."

"Some things stay the same," replied Megan. "You and Dad still have your adult parties, and I'm still not invited. Once I became in adult, I thought I might be included."

"You wouldn't be interested. It's made up of older people, like the Worthingtons. We only invite a select few friends."

"You might let me make the decision as to whether I would be interested."

"As you earlier said, you're entitled to your privacy. Your father and I are entitled to some ourselves."

"Yes, you are," agreed Megan. "I should probably be going. Tell Dad that I love him."

Megan stood and hugged her mother.

————·●·————

MEGAN FOUND SAM standing at the zoo entrance the following morning, wearing a grim face.

"What's the matter?" asked Megan.

"It's 11:28," answered Sam. "You like living dangerously, don't you? Two more minutes, and I was going to walk."

"What?"

"But you made it," Sam replied, reversing the morbid frown into a kind smile.

"You're ridiculous."

"Are you up for the gorilla feeding?"

"Sure."

"OK, but it turns out that they don't feed the gorillas until just after 2:00. So, why don't you and I go for lunch and come back?"

"I see how this works. I wasn't planning to spend the entire day with you!"

"Not the entire day, just lunch and the gorilla feeding. I know a great place that's not far from here."

"Great place? It just might be interesting to see what you consider to be a great place. What do they serve?"

"This restaurant has several things on the menu. But we need to get going if we want to get back in time for the gorilla feeding."

"My car is just over there," said Megan, pointing.

"You need to let me drive on this one," stated Sam. "I know where it is."

"Give me the address, and I'll enter it in my GPS."

"This lunch is supposed to be a surprise. I should

have known that you wouldn't have a sense of adventure."

"What made you think that I care to share an adventure with you?" questioned Megan.

"You agreed to go to the gorilla feeding. An adventure starts with one step at a time, right?"

"I just…"

"Enough talk. Time to go."

Sam took Megan by the hand and began leading her across the parking lot. After several steps, she pulled back.

"What do you think you're doing?"

"We're going to be late for the feeding if we don't get a move on. My truck is right there."

"Where?"

"The silver one with the toolbox in the bed," Sam answered, pointing.

"That!??!" You want me to get inside that?"

"Shhh! You're going to hurt its feelings, if you're not careful."

"You're crazy."

"Judging a book by its cover? You need to watch that. Come on."

Again, Sam led her by the hand toward his truck. Just as they were standing outside the passenger door, she pulled her hand free from his.

"This truck is…."

"Stop! Stop right there, before you say something that you might regret."

Sam opened the door to reveal an immaculate interior.

"Go ahead. Step up in there."

Stunned at the stark difference between the exterior

and interior of the truck, she silently obeyed. She ran her hands over the polished black leather seats.

"Now, see there. Book – by its cover? While I walk around to the driver side, I want you to whisper sweet loving words to my truck. She needs to feel appreciated from time to time, and she never knows what to expect from strangers. I'll walk slow, so that you have a little time to find the right words."

Sam closed the passenger side door, and slowly made his way around the truck. Opening the other door, he witnessed Megan fastening the seat belt.

"See," said Sam. "She's already giving you a hug. That's nice. I believe you two girls could become good friends."

He quickly entered the truck and started the engine. Megan sensed power beneath the hood, but the smoothness of the idling motor spoke elegance. He gave the engine a slight rev, and the mixture of sound and vibration produced a slightly sensual feeling within her. He dropped it in gear and started up the incline that led from the parking lot onto Boulevard. It crept for a second, before Sam gave the accelerator a punch. Within less than two seconds the vehicle was moving at forty miles per hour."

"Smooth, huh?" asked Sam. "She's a workhorse, but the shocks are designed for the street."

Megan answered with a polite smile.

Within fifteen minutes the truck moved into the crowded parking lot of a small diner. Megan became uneasy. She had no concept of the fact that Sam had denied himself his normal cooler of iced down soft drinks during the hot work week, just so he would have the money to treat her to lunch. He would have never told her.

This place looks like a dive. Oh god, he's taken me to some greasy dirty roach-infested dive. I'm probably going to get sick.

"I'm definitely not going to use the restroom in this place," complained Megan. "This place looks nasty."

"Book by its cover," reminded Sam. "Come on."

"Greek?" questioned Megan, as she entered the restaurant.

"You like Greek?"

"Normally," answered Megan. "The restaurant next door looks better. Why don't we go there instead?"

"That place is more of a bar than a restaurant. I'm just asking that you give this place a chance."

"OK," Megan said with a grimace.

"You've got to save room for baklava," advised Sam.

The two were seated at a booth by a window that faced the establishment suggested by Megan. They were given menus by a young Greek woman.

"Our special today has two keftethes, served with creamy sauce and basmati rice," the waitress explained. "It comes with pita bread and a feta salad."

"Please bring krasi," requested Sam. "We'll spend a few minutes looking over the menu.'

With a smile, the waitress turned to retrieve the wine.

"You must come here a lot," said Megan.

"I like to support small family-owned businesses. Our waitress is a daughter of the owner."

Suddenly, Megan was startled by the sound of two gunshots at the restaurant outside the window. With incredible speed, Sam leapt up and pushed Megan down so that she was lying across her seat.

"Stay down!" he shouted.

As he sped toward the front of the restaurant, two plain-clothed policemen with guns drawn ran out of the restaurant toward a man holding a handgun in the bar parking lot.

"Police! Put down your weapon! Put it down!"

As Sam turned to make his way back to Megan, she was sitting up and staring out the window. Her eyes wide open in disbelief, she watched as the two policemen approached the man with the gun. The man obediently bent over, laid the gun on the pavement, then stood with both hands over his head.

"Turn around and drop to your knees!" one policeman shouted.

One officer placed handcuffs on the kneeling gunman, while the other attended a bleeding man lying behind a parked car.

Sam tapped Megan on her shoulder.

"I told you to stay down," he whispered.

"I couldn't," answered Megan.

"When shots are fired, it's best to get down."

"And what did you think you were doing? Did you think you were going to run out there and take on that man? You don't have a gun. What did you think you were going to do?"

"I guess I thought I would try to stop him from retreating into this café," said Sam, still watching the scene outside.

"With what?" asked Megan, shaking her head.

"I don't know."

"I'll have to say that you can move pretty fast. I'll give you that. Why would you bring me to such a violent neighborhood?"

Sam glanced down at the table.

"This neighborhood is normally less violent than mine."

"I find that hard to believe," Megan replied.

"From my bathroom window, I witnessed a mugging the first day that I moved into the apartment. About three weeks later, I heard four gunshots at night just as I went to bed. There was a party in the apartment directly behind mine. A guy got mad at his girlfriend, and he shot her in the head four times. I clearly heard each of the four shots that killed her."

"I can't imagine..."

She stopped in mid-sentence, as she noticed that several customers had left food uneaten and were lining up at the register. The young waitress approached the booth where Sam and Megan were still peering out the window.

"I have your krasi," she said. "I hope you'll stay for lunch."

"I don't plan to go anywhere," replied Sam, glancing at Megan.

Megan silently pointed to the scene next door. Three police cars and an ambulance seemed to have come out of nowhere. A uniformed officer relieved the plain-clothed policeman of the person he held in cuffs. The wounded man was quickly placed in the ambulance, before it sped away with sirens blasting.

"I've never seen anything like this," Megan quietly said, turning her attention to the young woman standing beside her.

"Are you ready to order?" asked the waitress.

"Yes," Megan said.

"What would you like?" asked Sam.

"I think we should first say a prayer for the man who was shot," she replied.

Turning to the waitress, she found the young woman with eyes closed and head bowed.

THE FEEDING OF GORILLAS had just begun when Megan and Sam arrived. Females with babies ate a mixture of leafy greens and fruit. Megan's attention turned to a massive male.

"That one is huge," she said. "They've given it about twice the amount of food as the others."

"I think it's interesting to watch the interaction between the females and babies," stated Sam. "They're huge animals, but they can be remarkably gentle."

"I would be horrified if I were to be alone in the jungle with that big male," said Megan.

"He's a large lowland gorilla," informed an employee of the zoo. "He weighs about 450 pounds."

"Are they gentle?" asked Megan.

"Usually," answered the employee. "However, these large primates can be almost as unpredictable as humans."

As they left the zoo, Megan turned to Sam.

"You promised to come to church tomorrow. I expect to see you."

"Why do you go there?" asked Sam. "Did you grow up in that church?"

"My family only attended church on Easter and for weddings, and it wasn't at that church. No, I began attending because a neighbor invited me. You promised to show up tomorrow."

"I'll be there, but you have to promise to go out with me again."

"You keep adding conditions."

"Next time, you can pick the restaurant. I'm thinking that you would rather have a more peaceful meal."

"You sure know how to show a girl an exciting time, but you're right. I would like to have fewer bullets with my order."

"I'm guessing your family goes to expensive places to eat. I'm not sure that I can afford them."

"Believe it or not, I don't always eat at exclusive establishments."

"I've got to ask you a question," said Sam.

"Yes?"

"Does your father have a tall guy with sunken eyes who answers the front door – goes by the name of Lurch?"

"We aren't THAT Adams family!"

"I had to ask."

"Now, look who's judging a book by its cover!" she exclaimed, while poking him in the ribs with an index finger.

"Ow!" complained Sam. "You're really quick to inflect physical pain. I'll have to remember that."

"If you know what's good for you, you'll be at church this Sunday."

"Yes, Ma'am."

Chapter 8
Border

FBI AGENT JASON BAGWELL sat across a table from TJ Turner. A Royal Canadian Mounted Policeman had found the huge man walking down a dirt logging road near the US border.

"You've made serious trouble for yourself, Mr. Turner," informed agent Bagwell. "What possessed you to break your parole?"

"I've got more trouble than being locked up by the Canadians, or by you," answered TJ. "Speaking of my parole, please contact Russ Blevins in Atlanta."

"I've read your file, and I know about Mr. Blevins. I also understand that you were a decorated Special Forces veteran who served in Afghanistan. Looks like things haven't gone well since coming home. You've gotten yourself into a mess, and it's best for you to come clean. You came here for a reason. What or who are you running from?"

"I'll talk, but only if Mr. Blevins is present," replied TJ.

The agent rose from the table without saying

another word, collected his briefcase and walked out of the room. Down the hall, he knelt while opening the briefcase. After fumbling through a few papers, he entered the name and number in his cell contact list. He stood after shutting the case. Leaning his tall frame against the wall, he placed a call.

"This is FBI agent Jason Bagwell. Is this Russ Blevins?"

"Yes."

"The probation officer of a Thomas Jordan Turner?"

"That would be me. I take it that you've found him."

"A Royal Canadian Mounted Policeman found him hitchhiking on Provincial Trunk Highway 12 inside the Canadian border. Your parolee didn't possess a passport, so the Mountie radioed someone at the Canada Border Services Agency. He then contacted his commanding officer. Considering Mr. Turner's record, I'm a little surprised that he offered no resistance."

"Well, they say the Mounties always get their man," replied Russ. "Have they given him over to your custody?"

"That's being determined, at this point. The Canadian authorities got to be a little excited after they emptied Mr. Turner's duffle bag."

"How so?" asked Russ.

"They found a couple of handguns, ammunition, and a butt-load of cash."

"Crap!"

"Your big boy's in serious trouble. TJ dumped his car near the end of 410 Avenue in Minnesota and hiked north through forests to enter Canada illegally. He found a road leading north to Provincial Trunk Highway 12. TJ hoped to be picked up by truckers heading west. Instead, a local resident saw him and called the Royal Canadian Mounted Police. A few homes were recently burglarized in the small town of Sprague, and the caller was suspicious of the large man carrying a duffle bag. He broke a number of laws while entering Canada illegally. They allow entry at only a few entry points, and Canadian law enforcement gets a little concerned when someone with guns and cash enters the country on the sly."

"Listen. We need to bring him back to Atlanta. It's possible that he could lead the police to much bigger fish."

"You're talking about ongoing efforts of Detective Frank Reynolds?"

"Yes, but I didn't know that you were aware of it. I guess you guys at the FBI have connections. Has TJ started talking?"

"That's the reason for the call. He says he'll talk, but only if you're present. What's that about?"

"I don't know. Do you want me to come up there, or wait for you to bring him back here?"

"Like I said, the custody of Mr. Turner is being determined. When can you be here?"

"I'd like to leave immediately, but I need the approval from my boss."

"Give me your boss's name and number. I'll make sure that he sends you my way."

"Do you want me to notify Detective Reynolds?"

"This is no longer in the hands of local law enforcement; it's become a federal matter. I don't need Reynolds, just you."

RUSS BLEVINS STEPPED away from the car rental counter at the Grand Forks International Airport. Taking hold of his rolling garment bag, he reflected on the information he received from the agent.

The fact that he didn't have a passport wasn't what set off the Canadian authorities, it was the contents of the duffle bag mixed with his record. They were right to call in the FBI.

As Russ drove to the Highway/Land Border Office located near Sprague on Canadian highway 12, his thoughts shifted to Jason Bagwell.

One of my criminal justice classes in college was taught by a retired agent, but Bagwell is the first working FBI agent I've ever encountered while dealing with a case. He sounded reasonable, but I'm not sure what the Canadians will do. I'm afraid TJ's in big trouble now.

The FBI agent was standing outside the door of the Sprague office when Russ parked the rental car.

"I'm Russ Blevins."

"Jason Bagwell," the agent answered, displaying his shield while gripping Russ's hand. "He's inside. Mr. Turner hasn't said a word about what or who he's running from."

The agent informed a Canadian inside the office that Russ had arrived, and the two were escorted to a small room where TJ sat at a table. He seemed relieved at the sight of his probation officer.

"Thanks for coming," TJ said, slightly smiling. The big man took a deep breath. "Mr. Blevins, I need some kind of protection."

"We aren't talking deals at this time," interrupted Jason. "You said that you had information for us, and you demanded to have your probation officer present. He's here now. I've done my part, so talk."

"If I go to prison, I'm a dead man," said TJ. "If I'm sent back to Atlanta, I'm a dead man. I'll give you a confession and additional information - but at some point, I'll need an assurance of protection."

"Start talking," ordered Jason, his patience growing thin.

"I left two men dying on a street in DeKalb County. They would have eventually killed me. I saw an opportunity to stop them, so I broke the windpipe of one and I shot the other."

"I'm aware of them," said Russ. "The man with the broken windpipe lived, but not the guy shot in his car. An anonymous person called for an ambulance. Was that you?"

"That was me," said TJ.

"Now we're getting somewhere," said Jason. "That's a serious confession, and Mr. Blevins seems to be able to corroborate those crimes. In spite of the fact that you called an ambulance, murder and attempted murder could put you away for life. I can understand why you ran."

"That had nothing to do with why I ran. I wasn't running from the police. Tony Gallucci has connections. He would have found me and had me killed. My only chance was to find a remote spot and lie low so that he would have little chance of finding me."

"Who is Tony Gallucci?" asked Jason.

"This is where I think we should talk about a deal,"

whispered TJ. "I can give you a lot of information on Tony Gallucci."

"Protection for a murderer takes some doing," said Jason. "You've offered nothing that makes me even consider requesting a deal for you."

"Gallucci is really bad," replied TJ. "He's a killer – he's worse than a killer. Gallucci is why I had to take out those two guys. He had them on me, and I had to get away from him."

"You've already confessed to being a killer, yourself," sneered Jason. "I have no reason to offer a deal, based on a hypothetical statement about someone else."

"I confessed so that you would know that anything that I tell you about him is true," stated TJ. "I'm being straight up with you. I hurt those two goons in self-defense, and I now understand the fact that one of them died. I'm not asking to be set free, only for protection."

"I think we're done here," said Jason, rising up from the table.

"Gallucci's bad, and I've done some pretty bad things for him," said TJ. "I can show where he had me dispose of a body."

"You have my attention," said Jason, sitting back down. "Go on."

"Disposing of human remains can carry stiff penalties," cautioned Russ. "What else have you done for this Gallucci?"

"Believe me, there's more," said TJ. "If I give you everything without a deal, I'm a dead man."

"Let's talk about the location of this body," said the agent.

"Like I said, I need protection," reminded TJ.

"If you lead us to this body, and you can give us evidence that Gallucci had something to do with the death – then we may be able to work something," offered Jason. "Who was the victim?"

"I have no idea," replied TJ. "Somebody had done horrible things to her. I opened the container she was in, and I almost got sick. I've seen awful things in war, but this got to me. Her face was left untouched, but her shoulders and breasts were covered in burns. She also had bruises. I only saw the top half of her, but that was enough."

"What did you do with the body?" asked Russ.

"At first, I didn't realize that the box I was given contained a body. It was really heavy, and I couldn't imagine what could be inside. It took both of the two guys I hurt to load the container in the trunk of my car. I guess curiosity got the best of me. I drove to where I had been instructed to get rid of it – a really remote area. I figured no one would know if I looked inside. I keep an emergency box in the trunk of my car. It contained jumper cables, a few tools, and a small military shovel."

"Why a shovel?" asked Russ.

"I've driven down muddy roads when hunting, and a shovel is helpful whenever the tires get stuck," explained TJ. "On several occasions in the military, I found a shovel to be handy."

"OK, go on," advised Jason.

"Those two guys working for Gallucci told me to drop the container into a deep lake that had once been an abandoned quarry. After arriving at the spot, I decided to take a look inside. The lid had been fastened with screws, so I had to take them all the out. She was in there, packed in sand. It makes sense. If you want to make sure the container sinks to the bottom, weight has to be added. But once I knew that a woman was in that box, I couldn't do it. A person deserves a burial. I drove down the hill to a wooded area. The container was pretty heavy, so I removed a lot of the sand. That's when I saw the burns and bruises. Without so much sand, the container was light enough for me lift it from the trunk and carry it to a small clearing. I fastened the lid back on and used the shovel to bury her there. The place had plenty of large rocks. I placed several over her grave as a marker. I'm not much of a religious man, but I said a short prayer to God for her. Whoever she was, she deserved that much."

TJ dropped his gaze and stared at the tabletop. He wiped a tear from his cheek with the back of his huge right hand.

"You can give us the location?" asked Jason.

"I can," TJ sighed. "There's a lot more about Gallucci, but not without a deal."

Over the next hour, TJ gave specific details regarding the location of the body. Jason called in the location.

"That's enough for now," the agent pronounced. "Let's see what they find."

Russ and Jason left the building in silence. In the parking lot, Jason turned to Russ.

"Have you checked into the motel?"

"THE motel?" Russ questioned.

"If you're willing to drive, you might find something else."

"I'm good with staying wherever you are. It would make it easier to discuss this case."

"I'm going there now. I'm ready to take a load off."

Russ followed him back to the motel and checked into a room. Afterwards, he found Jason at the attached diner.

"Some story, huh?" Russ whispered.

"I've heard a lot of them, but this one ranks right up there," replied Jason.

"I doubt there's much that frightens him, but I think he's genuinely scared of this Gallucci. He's a big guy, has Special Forces training, and I'm sure he's seen more than we can imagine in Afghanistan. I think Tony Gallucci has him scared."

"He doesn't want to spend the rest of his days in a cell. I'm thinking that he's more afraid of going to prison."

"If Tony Gallucci is a big player with connections, TJ's right about not being safe in prison. Is there a chance he can get a deal?"

"He probably deserves whatever he gets, but if he can lead us to bigger people – maybe," replied Jason. "Several informants have helped take down big operations. We'll see."

* * *

THE FOLLOWING AFTERNOON, agent Bagwell received a call confirming the burial of the woman near the abandoned quarry. From a helicopter personnel spotted a pile of rocks in a small clearing in the forest. A team recovered the badly decomposed body.

"You were telling the truth about the body in the container," Jason told TJ. "They found her."

"What else do you know about this Tony Gallucci?" asked Russ.

"I'm in a bad situation," answered TJ. "What are the chances of a deal offering protection?"

"I'm working on something," said Jason. "But we aren't there yet. How do I know that Gallucci had anything to do with this? We know you've killed. You could have done it all on your own. You may have killed her, blamed it on Gallucci, and you're now looking for a deal. I can't submit a request based on this."

"I didn't have to tell you anything," replied TJ. "I've told you things that could put me away, because I hoped it would lead to you getting Gallucci. I could have left the entire matter with me crossing the Canadian border with a couple of guns. That's not nearly as serious as admitting to attacking those two. I'm looking at murder. I've been totally honest with you, haven't I? I've made serious mistakes, and I've hurt people. However, I'm not like Gallucci. I need protection from him, and innocent people need him to be put away."

"You were in jail for badly injuring a woman," said Russ. "I wouldn't call that just a mistake. There was also an unproven charge that you almost beat a man to death, leaving him in a side street."

"The situation with the woman was a mistake," said TJ. "A guy got in my face, and I tossed him into a wall. I didn't realize that the woman was between him and the wall. Her head slammed into a granite mantel over a fireplace. I don't intentionally hurt women. She was hurt pretty badly, and she rightfully pressed charges. I accept that. I have been telling you the truth.

I want no part of Gallucci. I'm not like him. I need protection. If I give you something that puts him away, he can still have people come after me…and he will. He has connections you wouldn't believe."

"Can you prove he had something to do with the death of that woman in the container?" asked Jason.

"No, I have no proof," answered TJ. "His guys loaded her in the trunk of my car. Take a look at the tips of my fingers. Those burns on the woman looked a lot like these cigarette burns he left on me."

"The body is in pretty rough shape now," explained Russ. "I'm not sure that bruises and burns can even be determined at this point."

"We need proof," said Jason. "Talk to me. What else has he had you do for him?"

"He had me rough people up, so they would pay him. I also kidnapped a woman, but I let her go. I think Mr. Blevins knows who I'm talking about."

"Misty Callahan," said Russ. "She's physically fine, but she's scared to death. I'm curious. Why did you let her go?"

"I was afraid she would end up like that girl I buried," answered TJ. "As soon as I took a good look at the waitress, she reminded me of someone I once knew."

"Why did you take her in the first place?" asked Jason.

"I was stupid," replied TJ. "Gallucci personally gave me the order and told me that it was just to teach her a lesson about something. I thought it was only about scaring her a bit. He's really good at instilling fear in people. Once I took a good look at her, it sort of hit me. I figured that the woman in the container had probably been kidnapped by someone else, and it was possible that Gallucci had the same intentions for the waitress. I couldn't let that happen."

"You left the military with an honorable record," said Jason. "How did you hook up with this Gallucci guy?"

"I wish to God I had never met the man," answered TJ. "I was a mess when I left the service - always on edge. My temper got me fired from jobs, and Gallucci made me an offer to work for him. It was like he came out of nowhere, and it seemed like his offer would help me get back on my feet. At first, it was just intimidating people to pay him what was owed. It was good money. Over time, it became more violent and weird."

"Can you prove any of this?" asked Russ. "So far, I'm not sure that you've given us anything that would concretely incriminate him."

"Didn't the police find drugs in that warehouse?" asked TJ.

"What warehouse?" asked Jason.

"The night I left Atlanta, I called Mr. Blevins about a warehouse with drugs," answered TJ. "It belongs to Gallucci. It's where he interrogated me and burned the tips of my fingers. He moves drugs using orange traffic barrels. They're transported on trucks, and nobody ever inspects a truck carrying traffic barrels."

"What's this about?" Jason asked Russ.

"I called 911 and gave them the information," replied Russ.

"What did the Atlanta police find?" TJ asked Russ.

"I'd forgotten about that, and I'm not sure what came of it, answered Russ. "I'll check into it."

"So, Mr. Turner previously mentioned a

connection with Tony Gallucci?" Jason asked Russ.

"TJ mentioned the name on that call," replied Russ.

"Tell me about the trucks," said Jason.

"The drugs are taped to the inside of the barrels, and transported by truck," answered TJ. "I know a couple of the trucks had New Jersey plates."

"Jason, I need to call Frank Reynolds," said Russ. "I believe it's time we told him that we located TJ. I'd also like to find out if something came out of the 911 call."

"OK," replied the agent.

Russ excused himself and stepped into the hall to place a call to Detective Frank Reynolds.

"Frank, Russ Blevins. I'm glad I caught you in the office."

"Did you locate your guy Turner?" asked Frank.

"As a matter of fact, I have. He's in the hands of the FBI now. He attempted to enter Canada illegally."

"Have they let you near him?"

"They have. TJ wanted me to be present when questioned. However, I need your help on a different subject."

"What's up?"

"I need to find out what happened to a 911 call I made about a tip on drugs in a warehouse owned by a Tony Gallucci. Can you tell me if anything was found?"

"I can search on your name, but it would help to have the address."

"I'm not sure. I think it was off Mooreland Avenue."

"When did you call it in?"

"Last month."

After several of minutes of scanning a database,

Frank found records of an unfruitful search of a warehouse.

"I found a call made by you. A few traffic barrels were found, but no drugs. It came up empty."

"Does it indicate how many barrels were checked?" asked Russ.

"They found about a dozen barrels."

"OK. I'm still in Canada. I'll get with you when I return."

Russ ended the call and stepped back into the room.

"The police didn't find anything illegal at the warehouse," Russ said. "They found about a dozen barrels, and none contained drugs"

"Mr. Turner, it appears you sent the police on a wild goose chase while you were busy skipping town," Jason accused.

"There was at least two hundred traffic barrels in that warehouse," replied TJ. "He must have been tipped off, and he cleared things out in a hurry."

"Who would have warned him?" asked Jason. "Now you're accusing the cops of being dirty?"

"I didn't say cops were dirty!" shouted TJ.

"So far, you've given us no evidence of any criminal activity by Gallucci," said Jason. "We have you wanting to make a deal for nothing. And now you're accusing cops of being in on this. You're just throwing crap on the wall and hoping something will stick."

"I'm not making this up," said TJ.

"You've been setting up this Gallucci from the get go, as a diversion," accused Jason. "You're a lot smarter than I first gave you credit. I think we're done here, today."

"I've told you the truth," insisted TJ.

Jason and Russ left the building. As the two approached Russ's rental car, Jason took the probation officer by the arm.

"When were you going to tell me about this 911 call involving Turner and Gallucci?" Jason demanded.

"It slipped my mind," explained Russ. "I had left it with the police. I don't think he's blowing smoke. It doesn't make sense that he would incriminate himself while falsely accusing Gallucci. What good does that do?"

"It's possible that he's telling the truth, but I need solid evidence."

"You're giving him the impression that you don't believe him, hoping he'll spill more information."

"Sure," replied Jason.

"Do you think there's a possibility that someone tipped off Gallucci?"

"I'm not ready to start accusing the Atlanta police of being dirty, if that's what you mean."

"No, not the police. It could have been someone listening to a police scanner.

"Mr. Turner said that a couple of the trucks had New Jersey plates," noted Jason. "If those trucks crossed state lines, that would be enough to pull the FBI into the matter. I'll do a little checking from my end."

"I have to get back to Atlanta tomorrow. Let me know if you find out anything."

— • ● • —

TWO DAYS LATER, Jason contacted Russ

Blevins.

"I'm not sure whether there's anything solid, but I've found something. We've checked video cameras in the vicinity of that warehouse mentioned in TJ's call. One captured a truck leaving the warehouse that evening."

"One carrying traffic barrels?"

"Exactly," replied Jason. "That truck left the warehouse in less than thirty minutes after the call."

"Someone tipped them off."

"Looks like it."

"Are we talking about a dirty cop?" asked Russ.

"You placed that 911 call at 2:13 AM, that night. It seems the police arrived at the warehouse at 2:51 AM. Since it wasn't an emergency, the reaction time wasn't what it would have been if someone had been in danger. During the lapse in time, somebody got those trucks moving."

"You believe TJ's claim about a tip off?" asked Russ.

"It's a stretch to think that the trucks leaving the warehouse immediately after the 911 call was a coincidence. The guy was painfully honest about things that would put him away for a long time. I think he's telling the truth."

"I agree," said Russ.

"In order to move those barrels in less than thirty minutes, someone had to be tipped off immediately. As you pointed out, it could be anyone listening to a police scanner. It's possible that someone with money could hire people to monitor a scanner 24/7, but I doubt the operation would point directly to Gallucci. I would expect that he would have a middleman handing things."

"I have the feeling that he's working with a light crew," replied Russ. "TJ mentioned Gallucci repeatedly using the same two guys. They picked him up for questioning, and later assigned to keep an eye on him. He said the same two guys loaded a body in the trunk of his car."

"You're right. Gallucci seems to be a hands-on guy. Still, somebody got those trucks rolling."

"What information does the FBI have on the man?" asked Russ.

"Gallucci owns a construction operation, but his main money comes from being a high-end art dealer. He often travels to Europe."

"Art dealer? How does someone go from construction to high dollar art? "Get this. Gallucci is a graduate of Politecnico di Milano in Italy, with graduate studies in fine arts at Carnegie Mellon University in Pittsburgh. He has a degree in architecture, and the guy knows art. In Pittsburgh, he was top of his class regarding fine art."

"He's definitely not just a construction guy. With that kind of education in architecture and fine arts, why doesn't he own an architecture firm? Why construction?"

"That is the question, isn't it? Maybe Mr. Turner is right. Maybe it's a front for moving drugs."

"What's going on with TJ?"

"I've worked with the Canadian authorities, and I'm bringing him back to the States."

"To Atlanta?" asked Russ.

"He begged me not to, so I'm taking him to our FBI office in Minneapolis."

"I don't blame him."

"Oh, get this. Gallucci's wife Mia is a graduate of the International Institute for Management Development in Lausanne, Switzerland. That's one of the top graduate business schools in the world. She's no slob, either."

"So, do you think she's the brains behind their money?"

"We estimate that they're worth more than a hundred million. However, those who deal in art have been known to hide very expensive paintings and sculptures. Then there are the trips to Europe. He could have money tucked away in European investment institutions. We honestly have no idea as to their true worth."

"With that kind of money, why take risks with drugs?" asked Russ.

"A number of successful people, who appear to be refined on the outside, also have a dark side."

"It's difficult to see into the soul of a man."

"True," replied the FBI agent.

Chapter 9
Connection

"HAVE YOU EVER HEARD of a man named Tony Gallucci?" Russ asked, when placing a call to Misty Callahan.

"I really don't want to be pulled into something. Unless you're calling to tell me that the guy who grabbed me is in prison, I want to be left alone."

"Please just answer the question," replied Russ.

"An old boyfriend mentioned running errands for a guy named Gallucci."

"What boyfriend? What's his name?"

"Why can't you leave me alone?" asked Misty.

"We found TJ Turner."

"Is he in jail?"

"The FBI has him in custody. He admitted to kidnapping you, and he said he was ordered to do it by Tony Gallucci."

"Crap! Oh, Crap!"

"What?"

"My ex-boyfriend sometimes did odd jobs for that guy. Why would he want me kidnapped?"

"TJ said that Gallucci told him that he wanted to teach you a lesson. At first, he thought it was to just give you a scare. But later, he believed that you might be physically harmed. TJ said that's why he let you go."

"TJ? You and my kidnapper are on a first name basis? Is he a buddy of yours now?"

"Of course not. I'm his probation officer, and I usually try to get to know parolees who are assigned to me."

"I don't want to get to know this guy."

"We're trying to obtain more information. Do you know Tony Gallucci?"

"No!" blurted Misty. "I don't remember ever meeting Gallucci. Oh God, I'm scared! Do you think he knows where I live?"

"I'm trying to find out what I can about the man. Can you help me?"

"I couldn't care less about helping you. I may need to find somewhere safe. That guy who grabbed me warned me that I might have to keep moving."

"I think you better just lie low, for now. The more that I can find out about him, the better it will be for your safety."

"I can't believe someone gave an order to have me kidnapped! This is worse than I imagined."

"What kind of work did your old boyfriend do for him?" asked Russ.

"I was never introduced to Gallucci. Ricky had done yardwork for him, and the guy paid really well. There were a couple of rich men that Ricky worked for from time to time. I told Frank about it. I did meet a rich guy named Adams once."

"Are you talking about Allen Adams?"

"Yeah, that's him. I found Ricky talking with Adams one evening on a street corner. Ricky introduced me to him."

"What makes you think he was rich?" asked Russ.

"Later, when we were alone, Ricky told me that he was one of the richest men in the Atlanta area. Do you know him?"

"I know of him."

"I'm really scared. Does Frank Reynolds know about this guy Gallucci?"

"We've talked."

"Do you think he would come out here and give me some kind of protection?"

"He's an Atlanta cop. Do you want me to notify the police in Colorado Springs?"

"I don't know any cops here, but I think I can trust Frank. I need a man with a gun, and I don't really know anyone out here that I can trust."

"Don't do anything rash. I'll call you if I hear anything that would put you in danger."

"Promise?"

"Yes."

The call ended. Russ Blevin's mind raced.

Allen Adams?!? Could there be a connection between him and Gallucci? Maybe it's just a coincidence that Misty's ex-boyfriend did work for both of them, but this is getting weird.

———•●•———

THE FOLLOWING MORNING, Russ placed a call to Megan Adams.

"This is Russ Blevins. Do you have a few

minutes?"

"What's up?"

"Does the name Tony Gallucci ring a bell?"

"He and his wife are friends of my parents. Is there a problem?"

"Do you know him well?

There was a silence on the call for several seconds.

"He's a regular acquaintance of my father and I've spoken with him on several occasions. My parents have adult only weekends from time to time, and the Galluccis come to the house on those weekends."

"What do you mean by adult only?" asked Russ.

"They're weekends without children. I'm sure a number of adult couples enjoy the company of other adults, without children under foot. When I was a child, my parents always made arrangements for me. I usually stayed with a relative or friend."

"Do you participate, now that you're older?"

"As an adult, I've never been invited. Those are very private weekends, shared with very select people."

"Select people? So, the Galluccis are very close friends of your parents?"

"I think so, but I've not heard of them getting together outside those adult only weekends."

"Ok, I've never been rich – so, I can't imagine that life. However, I've never heard of people having weekends like that on a regular basis. It seems odd."

"My parents are not odd. They've always been kind to everyone I know, and they fund a number of charities. They have a right to engage in private weekends."

"There's certainly no law against it. How often do they have these special weekends?"

"I would say, about half a dozen times each year."

"Would you recognize Tony Gallucci if you saw him out somewhere?"

"Sure. I would recognize both Tony and his wife Mia."

"I would suspect that these special friends of your parents would also be wealthy. Is this the case?"

"Mr. Gallucci is an art dealer. He travels abroad to buy and sell paintings. I'm sure he has money."

"An art dealer. Does he have any other occupations or investments?"

"I wouldn't know. Why all the questions about Mr. Gallucci?"

"I'm working with someone who is investigating something, and Tony Gallucci's name has come up. That's all."

"I'm not stupid. You called me because my father's name also came up – didn't it?"

"We're just trying to sort some things out, that's all."

"Now, you have me concerned. Maybe I should call my father."

"Your father isn't being investigated. Please don't call him. I need to make sure nothing interferes with the investigation. I didn't mean to upset you. I'm sorry."

"Who's being investigated? Tony Gallucci?"

"I can't tell you that," explained the probation officer.

"But you are asking me if I know about Tony Gallucci; and you don't want me to contact my father about this. I think you owe me an explanation."

"I have to be careful about what I say. I don't want to cause interference with the investigation."

"In case you forgot, you're my Sunday school teacher. I'm supposed to be able to trust you? You're not helping with that."

"Ok. We've questioned people, and someone threw out the names of your father and Tony Gallucci – mainly Gallucci. Your father is well known, and he isn't being investigated. However, I don't really know this Gallucci fellow. We're just trying to make sense out of it."

"Who is this person?" asked Megan.

"I can't tell you more, and I probably shouldn't have told you anything. You've known me for a while. I'm asking you to trust me."

"I'm concerned about my father's welfare. You said that my father is not being investigated. Can you assure me that he's not a concern of this investigation? Can you promise me that my parents are safe?"

"They are not being investigated."

"Promise?"

"I promise."

"I guess I can trust you."

"If it makes you feel any better, your information about Tony Gallucci's occupation has been helpful. When I heard your father's name, I hoped that you could shed some light. I sort of just jumped on the idea of calling you. I'm sorry. I didn't mean to cause you worry."

"Ok."

"Are we good?"

"We're good," answered Megan.

"Am I going to see you Sunday?"

"This was a disturbing call. You shouldn't do this to people. Yes, I'll be there to kick you in the shin."

"That's fair. I promise I'll stand still and give you the opportunity to kick away."

After the call ended, Megan scanned the items on her work desk. She picked up a report, but quickly found she couldn't focus. Dropping it on her desk, she placed a call.

"Yeah," Sam Blaylock answered.

"This is Megan Adams. Are you busy?"

"I have a couple of minutes."

"Would you have more minutes if you took me out to dinner tonight?"

"I think I could handle sitting across a table from you. Should I go out and rob a bank to pay for a high-class restaurant?"

"Meals are about twenty bucks at the place I have in mind. Does that require a holdup?"

"No. I can handle that."

"I'm about to text the address. Meet me at seven."

"Yes, ma'am."

• ● •

"DID SOMEBODY MAKE you mad?" asked Sam. "You look like you'd like to slap someone, and I happen to be the only person in arm's length."

"Later," Megan replied.

The two were soon seated. Megan's eyes silently scanned the menu; her eyes intensely darting across the items.

"What's this about?" Sam interrupted.

"The waitress will be here any minute, and you haven't yet picked up the menu," replied Megan. "We can talk after we've placed our orders."

"A little bossy, are we?"

"I'm sorry," Megan replied, peeking over the menu. "I'm just really uptight, and I need someone to talk to."

"Take your time, Your Grace" he replied with sarcasm.

After placing their orders, for the first time Sam understood that she was genuinely worried. Her countenance seemed drained. He reached across the table and took Megan's hand.

"What happened?"

"Have you ever really worried about your parents?"

"After my father left us, I worried about my mother a lot. You didn't answer me. What's happened?"

"I'm not supposed to tell anyone."

"What?"

"I don't want to explain."

"You wanted to meet me so that we have time to talk about something – but you don't want to talk about it?"

"I don't know."

"Tell me what you can. I won't press you."

"My parents have always engaged in special weekends, where a few select adult acquaintances are invited to the house. I was recently questioned about one of those acquaintances."

"Questioned? By who?"

"It seems to be a police matter. It appears that a friend of my father is being investigated."

"About what?"

"I don't know. I was asked if I knew the man. I said that he and his wife are close friends with my parents."

"If they're close friends of your parents, you must know them pretty well."

"These weekends are adult only. I've conversed with the couple a number of times, but I really don't know them all that well. As a child, I spent those weekends with relatives. I wasn't around."

"That's odd."

"Why does everyone think it's odd for adults to periodically want a kid free weekend? If you had children, wouldn't you want a break sometimes?"

"I don't know. My mother never had a kid free weekend until I left home. I think it's unusual, but that doesn't really matter. You're concerned about this friend of your father's. Do you think he's gotten himself in trouble, and that it may impact your father's life?"

"Yes – that about sums it up. You know – you really have a way of taking a complicated issue and stating it in simple straightforward terms."

"This friend visits your parents during the adult only weekends?"

"He and his wife, and another couple come on those weekends."

"Is it always the same? The adults consist of your parents, and these two couples? No one else?"

"I don't know of others."

"How often do they meet?

"About six times a year."

"So, this is a regular gathering of six?"

"Yes, they meet on a regular basis," answered Megan. "It's always the same six people."

"For what purpose? What have your parents told

you about it?"

"Nothing. It's just a time to get together with only adults. I'm not invited. I have no idea as to a specific purpose."

"People don't have regular events, if there isn't a purpose."

"I guess you're right."

"Is this some kind of private charity, or business interest? I assume that they're all wealthy, and they must have a common interest. Maybe it's a gathering of philanthropists, supporting a charity in secret."

"Do you really think this is what the meetings are about?"

"I wouldn't know; I'm just guessing. Has your father talked about charities?"

"He openly supports several foundations and the symphony. None of that is done in secret. If this is a charitable venture, why would a friend of my father's be investigated?"

"What I would like to know is, why are YOU being questioned? Why not just question your father, and leave you out of the matter?"

"I happen to know someone who is involved in the investigation."

"What can I do to help?" offered Sam.

"Nothing, unless you have a crystal ball that can tell me what goes on during those private weekends," Megan answered, forcing a smile.

"There's nothing mystical about me. You're the spiritual one, with your church and all."

"To be honest, I've always wondered about what happens on those weekends. As a child, I tried to imagine what those 'grown up' activities were. Now,

I'm really curious about those who attend."

"Maybe you should stay out of it. You don't want to be caught up in an investigation."

"If the police told you that close friends of your mother were being investigated, would you be inclined to stay clear of it?"

"Point taken. What do you plan to do?"

"I really want to find out what goes on during these weekends. I just don't know how to go about it without my parents noticing."

"Well, I have a telescope," replied Sam. "Do you think we could witness anything from a distance?"

"Oh, God! Are you some kind of pervy?"

"No! I bought it for the meteor shower, but it didn't really help. It's been in a closet ever since. Do you think I sit around peeping on people? Why would you even think that?"

"I don't know what you do in your spare time," Megan answered.

"I can't believe that even entered your mind. So, now you think I'm weird?"

"No…I really don't know you all that well, and the neighborhood that you live in…"

"You called me. You told me about something that was bothering you, and I'm just trying to help. Now you're talking down to me. I should have known the snotty rich kid would come out in you eventually."

Sam rose from the table, dropped his napkin next to his glass of water, and slowly walked away shaking his head. As he stepped from the restaurant, he felt a tug at his arm.

"Please," begged Megan. "I don't know why I said that."

Sam turned to her - his face stony.

"I don't need this," he replied. "I'm not going to be toyed with. I should have known better. I'm a poor working slob, and you come from one of the wealthiest families in the country. We just need to…"

She quickly threw her arms around his neck and embraced his lips with hers. Megan then buried her face in his chest and began sobbing. Sam placed his hand gently under her chin and lifted her face. Her eyes were filled with tears. Megan's small frame trembled.

"What's going on?" Sam asked.

"I don't know," she sobbed, burying her face again in his chest.

Sam's arms held her close. After a moment, he released her and wiped her cheek with his rough hand.

"Are you alright?" he asked.

"No. I've never behaved like this."

"I'm sorry I stomped out like that. You're having a difficult time, and you're fearful about your family. I shouldn't have been so self-centered and touchy."

"I think about you all the time!" blurted Megan, taking a step back from him.

"I think about you, too."

No. You don't understand. I think about you when I go to bed, and I think about you when I get up in the mornings. I don't even know you all that well. I don't understand it. When this came up, you were the first person I wanted to see. I don't really know you, but I feel at peace when I'm with you. I find myself trusting you, and you've given me no reason to do so. I've dated a lot of guys, but I've never behaved like this."

"So, are we dating?"

"I don't know. What are we doing?"

Sam stepped close. Taking her face in his callused hands, he looked deep into her eyes.

"You can trust me. Know that. I don't really know you all that well either, but I won't do anything to hurt you. I promise."

His hands moved from her face, his right hand taking her left.

"We have a nice meal waiting on us," reminded Sam. "Want to go back inside?"

"I do, but I'll need to wash my face before going back to the table."

"Yeah, you don't appear to be quite as uppity as you did earlier."

Megan wiped tears from her eyes with her free hand.

"I'm not what you call 'uppity' on the inside," she said, with a sniff. "There is something about you that causes me to be myself when I'm around you. I don't really understand it, but I feel that you and I have a special connection."

"I agree."

Chapter 10
Sniffing

"WE NEED TO TALK," began Frank Reynolds.

"You're calling me from a cell phone?" questioned Russ Blevins.

"Yes."

"That's a first. What's up?"

"We need to talk face to face, in a private setting."

"What's going on?"

"Can you meet me in Hurt Park at 11:30 AM?"

"I'll be there."

* ● *

"IT'S WORSE THAN I thought," said Frank, meeting Russ at the park. "We considered the possibility that Gallucci was tipped off by someone monitoring a police scanner, but I think there's another angle."

"What angle?" asked Russ.

"We have a new IT kid, and he found something."

"Yeah?"

"He found what he calls a sniffer program running on our 911 system."

"You're losing me."

"He says this program is hard to detect and searches the system for particular key entries," explained Frank. I told him to keep it quiet for now, and to let me know what the program was looking for. After a couple of days, he came by the office with a list of items that it searches for."

"Like what?"

"Like the name, Gallucci, for starts."

"What?"

"It also searches for several addresses, one being that warehouse off Mooreland Avenue. When we continued checking the list, we found several addresses belonging to property owned by Tony Gallucci."

"So, you're telling me that Gallucci has a hacker on the inside?"

"Maybe. I don't know for sure. What I do know is that this kid needs to keep this quiet until I know more."

"Do you think that's the right thing to do?" asked Russ. "Shouldn't you report this immediately?"

"Maybe not."

"Gallucci is a wealthy man, and your man Turner says that he's extremely well connected. It's possible Gallucci paid off people to turn a blind eye. If so, I don't know how high it goes."

"What are you going to do?"

"I'm not sure," replied Frank. "I told the kid that we should leave the sniffer in place for now, in order to continue monitoring activity. I instructed him to report things only to me, but I doubt I'll be able to keep him quiet for long. If there is somebody on the inside, would you think that kid is safe?"

"It sounds like you're in a tight spot."

"That's why I need your help."

"I'm no programmer!" objected Russ.

"I want you to call your FBI contact and tell him what I've told you. I also want you to pass him this list."

Frank handed an envelope containing the list of sniffer items to Russ. The probation officer looked at it as though he had been handed a disease.

"I don't know," said Russ.

"You don't know what? You don't know if you want to help take down Gallucci? Or maybe you don't know if you want to leave me and that kid in a mess? Which is it?"

"OK, I'll contact the agent."

"That's more like it. How about some lunch? There's a good café two blocks down."

— • ● • —

THAT EVENING, RUSS nervously placed a call to FBI agent Jason Bagwell.

"We may have something, and I need your help." Russ began.

"You need my help?" asked Jason.

"Not just me. There's an Atlanta cop and an IT kid who needs your help."

"OK, just tell me what you have."

"Ever heard of a sniffer program?"

"Go on."

"Detective Reynolds told me that a new IT kid

found a sniffer program on the Atlanta area 911 system, and the sniffer items have to do with Gallucci."

"That is interesting. Is the sniffer still running?"

"Yes. Frank told the IT guy to leave it there so they could monitor it, and to report only to him."

"Can you get a list of those items?" asked the agent.

"I was given a paper printout."

"I'm going to text you a FAX number, and I want you to FAX that list to me."

"OK, but you have to keep this quiet. Detective Reynolds is afraid there's a cover up, and he doesn't know who is involved. He says that he doesn't think he can keep the kid quiet for very long, and he's worried about it."

"If there's inside personnel involved, he has every right to be concerned. I'll have an agent contact both Detective Reynolds and the kid. That should give the young man confidence that someone is taking this seriously, and that he is a part of a confidential investigation. His secrecy will be stressed. Your man Turner may score big on his Gallucci story. Leave things with me. I'll be in touch."

Russ ended the call with mixed feelings. He was glad that he would soon be rid of the list, but he couldn't shake the genuine concern reflected in Frank's voice when they talked in the park.

He's genuinely worried. This thing could blow up, with Frank and the IT guy in the middle of it. We have strong evidence now that Gallucci is up to no good, and his close friendship with Megan's father will surely result in Adams being pulled into the investigation. I'll say no more to her about any of this.

DURING THE CHURCH service the following Sunday, Russ intently watched the interactions between Megan Adams and Sam Blaylock. He was hopeful that she might be distracted from asking him more questions about the investigation. As he continued to observe, he was somewhat stunned that she seemed to sincerely enjoy the company of the construction worker.

I never expected her to get tied up with Sam Blaylock. What is it with that guy? How in the world did a guy from that stinking neighborhood hit it off with a multimillionaire's cute daughter? Hormones never cease to amaze me.

Russ Blevin's marriage had lasted less than a year. The pressures of his job had contributed heavily to the breakup. His wife became more and more afraid of parolees under his care. The continued late nights at work also took its toll. It was after the divorce that he began attending that church, while in search for answers to personal questions. He watched older couples, who had been married for decades, comparing their relationships with his own failed situation. Some of them had been separated for periods of time, due to military service. Yet, they remained committed to one another. He wondered if he would ever figure it out.

After the service, he quietly moved through the door and into the parking lot. Hearing footsteps behind him, he turned to find Megan and Sam closing in on him.

"What are your plans for lunch?" asked Megan.

"No firm plans," replied Russ.

"Do you like Greek?" asked Sam.

"What do you have in mind?" questioned Russ.

Megan took him by the arm and told him about the place she and Sam had gone the day of the shooting. She then raved about the food. Within forty minutes the three were seated at a table.

"What have you found out about Mr. Gallucci?" Megan asked the probation officer.

"Not as much as I would like, but I can't really talk about it," Russ replied. "Why do you ask?"

"The more I thought about it, I remembered being a little creeped out at times while around him."

"How so?"

"As a teen, I noticed him eyeballing my body. As I developed into a woman, I sensed him checking me out more often. You know, goggling my body – even in front of Mia, his wife. It seemed to stop after I moved out on my own. Have you received complaints about weird behavior of his around teens?"

"I can't discuss the details, but that subject hasn't come up," assured Russ. "Did he ever touch you?"

"No, my father would have killed him."

The eyebrows of Russ raised; his eyes widened.

"That was just a figure of speech!" exclaimed Megan. "I just meant that my father would have put an immediate stop to that."

"I can't comment on the situation," replied Russ. "My conversation with you was in confidence. Have you been discussing this with Sam?"

Sam had been quiet during the conversation, until this point. He leaned in close to Russ.

"Megan can discuss anything she wishes with me," Sam interjected.

Understanding now that Sam and Megan had grown close, he quickly defused the matter.

"It was my bad," said Russ. "I should have never discussed an ongoing investigation with Megan. I don't intend to follow up along those lines."

"It's fine," said Megan, while reaching for Sam's hand. "I was curious to know if Mr. Gallucci had caused problems for other young women, that's all. I've been acquainted with him for several years, but I really don't know him very well. I just wanted to let you know that I've felt uncomfortable around him a few times in the past."

The subject was dropped from conversation, and Megan replaced it with the story of the man being gunned down at the restaurant next door. Russ listened intently, as Megan and Sam described the event in detail.

———•●•———

"DO WE HAVE ANY information about Tony Gallucci having problems with women?" Russ asked, while phoning Frank Reynolds.

"What brought that on?" asked Frank.

"Megan Adams told me that she caught Gallucci looking her up and down while she was a teen. She said that it happened several times, and that it made her feel uncomfortable."

"I see. No, nothing like that. What made her tell you that?"

"Since Gallucci is an associate of her father, a while back I had asked her a few questions about the man. After church today, she and another young man asked me to accompany them to lunch. That's when the subject came up."

"Gallucci must have really bothered her."

"What have you found out about this guy?" asked Russ.

"Not much. I may pay his warehouse a visit."

"Do you have anything that allows you to get a warrant?"

"No. I'm just going to watch activity from the outside. Let's just say, that I have a gut feeling about the story Mr. Turner told about Tony Gallucci."

"Yeah?"

"I think he's telling the truth," replied Frank. "The sniffer crap pretty much confirms his statements. I plan to check into it on my own. I haven't discussed it with anyone in the department."

"What can I do?"

"Let me know if you find out anything from your FBI friend. Something about this guy Gallucci really stinks. We have TJ telling us that he was dumping nude dead women, and now Megan tells you that he was scoping her out while she was a teen. And this creep is supposed to be one of her father's closest acquaintances? It fits. Pass what you've heard on to the FBI. It's possible that, on top of dealing drugs, this guy could be involved in human trafficking of women."

"If he is, it's probably a high-class operation. Both Megan and the FBI told me that he makes his money as a fine arts dealer, handling high value art."

"I wonder how much Allen Adams knows about this man," said Frank.

"Probably more than I would like to think, but I don't plan to question Megan more. She told me that

Tony Gallucci and Charles Worthington were her father's closest acquaintances. For years, the three families hold an adult only weekend several times per year. She's never been invited to attend, as an adult."

"If you haven't already, let the FBI know about this information. They have huge databases. Maybe they can tie it all together. I won't be able to sit on the sniffer situation for long, and I have no idea as what will happen after it becomes known."

———•●•———

"THAT IS A LITTLE creepy," responded Jason Bagwell. "The scumbag blatantly scoped out his best friend's daughter – a girl he's known most of her life? But she says that he never actually touched her?"

"That's what she said," replied Russ. "I believe Turner. I think Gallucci is responsible for the death of that woman, and I wouldn't put him past inflecting burns on her beforehand. If half of what TJ says is true, this guy is bad."

"Both he and his wife Mia come from fairly wealthy families in Italy. Visiting family members could be the basis of some of those trips to Europe, but we don't know that for sure. We're still in the dark about a number of things."

"What came from the sniffer list?"

"We're monitoring things. It's probably best for Detective Reynolds to stay out of it, for now. We'll contact him, if and when we plan to move in."

"So, you plan to move in on Gallucci."

"I'm not saying anything concrete, right now. I suggest that both of you lie low, for the time being."

"Alright. Will do. What do you know about Allen Adams?"

"On the surface, he seems to be pretty clean. He's a graduate of Scheller College of Business at Georgia Tech and has a graduate degree from the Wharton School at the University of Pennsylvania. He and his wife are patrons of the symphony, and he generously supports several foundations. He and his wife Michelle have spotless records in our criminal databases."

"What's the wife like?" asked Russ.

"She comes from a lineage of wealthy Americans, and a graduate of Wellesley College. We don't suspect her of anything, other than being a debutante and a snob."

"The daughter isn't a snob. She genuinely seems to be a compassionate individual. I see her almost weekly in the Sunday school class that I teach."

"You'd be surprised at some of the things members of Sunday school classes are capable of," replied Jason.

"You're talking to a probation officer. I've seen a few things myself."

"Out of the three couples meeting on those special adult weekends, I find the Worthington's' presence the most interesting."

"How so?" asked Russ.

"Charles Worthington paints a complete picture of what it means to be an elite in American society. He is a graduate of the MIT Sloan business, and he holds an MBA from Harvard Business school. He's not just a banker, he's a personal financial advisor to some of the wealthiest Americans. It's people like him who are tapped out to be Secretary of Treasury. He's graced the covers of several financial magazines. I don't see why someone like him would risk being associated with the likes of Gallucci."

"That is interesting."

"He doesn't seem to be the type to do dumb things, like risk his family's position in society. His wife is a graduate of the School of Business at the University of Chicago. He didn't marry a dumb and beautiful daughter of an aristocrat, or a bimbo. He's as solid as they come. I don't understand the connection."

"Maybe he's the financial advisor of both families."

"He's the advisor to Adams, but not Gallucci. Tony Gallucci isn't as transparent as Adams."

"In the Atlanta area, these three families are exclusively wealthy. Like the old saying, birds of a feather flock together. Maybe it's just a status thing. Who else in this area would they hang out with?"

"Maybe."

"Do you have enough to offer TJ protection?"

"You'll be the first to know, if it happens."

Chapter 11
Church

"I AM CRUCIFIED with Christ: nevertheless, I live; yet not I, but Christ liveth in me: and the life which I now live in the flesh I live by the faith of the Son of God, who loved me, and gave himself for me."

While Megan's minister recited Galatians 2:20 from the Bible, Sam whispered in her ear.

"Why do you come here and listen to this?"

"Later," she quietly replied, giving him a stern glance.

"Most of us like the idea that our sins died with Jesus when He died on that cross," the minister continued. "But Paul takes this a good bit further. He says that he views his sinful life to have perished with Christ's crucifixion, and that he now lives a new life based on faith in God's grace. Some people call this being born again into a new life. Paul viewed himself as having a new life, considering himself to be dead to his old life. This was a significant statement because Paul had been a very accomplished person. He was from Tarsus, the home of a famous university. Some believe he held a seat at that school. Paul was taught under Gamaliel, a recognized Jewish leader and a member of the Sanhedrin – a tribunal council made up of prominent Jewish rabbis. This meant Paul was very educated, and well respected in Jewish society. He was also a Roman citizen, which caused him to be respected among the Romans who ruled the Jews at that time. Before coming to faith in Christ, Paul personally took part in Jewish leadership's attempt to exterminate Christianity. Paul laid this out in Philippians 3:6-9, which states:

'Concerning zeal, persecuting the church; touching the righteousness which is in the law, blameless. But what things were gain to me, those I counted loss for Christ. Yea, doubtless, and I count all things but loss for the excellency of the knowledge of Christ Jesus my Lord: for whom I have suffered the loss of all things, and do count them but dung, that I may win Christ. And be found in him, not having mine own righteousness, which is of the law, but that which is through the faith of Christ, the righteousness which is of God by faith.'

In other words, he viewed his past accomplishments as crap, in comparison to having found faith in Jesus Christ."

"This sermon is crap," Sam scribbled across a church bulletin.

He nudged Megan and pointed to what he had written. Like a mother scolding a misbehaving child in church, she gave him a scowl as she wadded up the bulletin in her hand and crammed it in her purse.

She fumed as they departed the church and walked across the parking lot. Sam repeatedly stared at the side of her stoic face. As she reached for the door of her car, he blurted a question.

"Why are you so ticked?"

"Why were you behaving like a brat in church?" she responded.

"Why do you listen to that guy?"

"Because I believe what he says to be the truth."

"He's a rich preacher in a church of rich people."

"Do you hate people with money? I come from a family with money."

"You're different…"

"I'm different because of what I believe. The other day, you talked about 'uppity' people. To a large degree, it's my faith that causes me to not be 'uppity'. But that doesn't seem to matter to you. All you can do is ridicule the faith of those with money, simply because they have wealth. Why are you so hateful?"

"A lot of them look down on people like me."

"Who? Who in this church has treated you badly?"

"So far, they've treated me fine. I've been around rich church people before. Some helped me and my mother when I was a kid. I overheard them talking among themselves. They didn't really care about us. They looked on us as a kind of personal project. They did it so that they could feel better about themselves. They felt they were superior people, reaching down to inferior trash. Don't get me wrong. I appreciated the help; we needed it. I just don't want to ever have that feeling again. I don't care to be looked down on. I don't want pity because I'm nowhere near their income bracket, and I don't want to be made out to be inferior to that bunch. My mother was twice the woman than any of those people who gave us help. She struggled financially after my father left us, working two jobs until she was able to find work at furniture refinishing. Those rich families had no right to look down on her. They didn't really know her. I just don't like being around people like that."

"So, do you have a different church that you would rather attend?" asked Megan.

"I..." stammered Sam. He had been caught off guard by her question. "OK, I don't really go to church all that often. I've been honest with you. I told you that I came here only because I thought you were hot."

"You don't really know these people. You judge them just like those people judged your mother. They didn't really know her, and you really don't know these people."

"I can feel it; I don't have to personally know each one. I can see it in their eyes. They have the same manner of speech, and the same superior tone of voice."

"Really?" questioned Megan. "How about Dora? Does she act superior to you?"

"Did I hear my name being battered around?" interrupted Dora, who had just stepped into the church parking lot.

"We were just talking about the fact that you're a special person," said Megan.

"This is a church made up of rich people, but you're more down to earth," said Sam.

"There are a number of good people here," stated Dora.

"I would think that you know them better than I do," replied Sam.

"Young man, you've been coming here for a little while," said Dora. "When do you plan to join?"

"No offense, but I'm not really convinced that I

need to join a church," answered Sam.

"It's good for people of like faith to spend time together," Dora responded.

"My faith might not be exactly like yours and the others here," replied Sam.

"Faith is a very personal thing," said Dora. "My faith is probably a little different from some at this church, but I try to focus on what we have in common. I think too many Christians pick at each other about minor aspects of faith."

"Minor aspects?" questioned Megan.

"For me, if a man believes Jesus to be his savior, that makes him my brother in faith," Dora said. "A lot of the other aspects of Christianity are what I view as minor. We are finite beings trying to understand an infinite Creator of the universe. We really shouldn't have major wars over minor religious aspects. I don't think any of us have a complete picture when it comes to understanding God."

"I think you're right about most of us knowing less than we think," said Sam. "When I was a kid, my mother and I attended a church where the preacher talked often about being saved. I remember asking my mother if he was talking about being saved from hell. She said that was part of it, but that God was in the business of saving us from ourselves."

"Sounds like your mother is a wise woman," said Dora.

"Was…, she passed away," replied Sam.

"I'm sorry to hear that," said Dora.

"She tried to read the Bible to me, but I really didn't get it," explained Sam. "I mean, I understand the ten commandments. Those are fairly straightforward.

After she passed away, I tried reading the Bible from cover to cover. I didn't get far. I got about ten chapters into Genesis and stopped. I really couldn't get past the contradictions. It would seem like there wouldn't be so many, especially right off the bat."

"Specifically, what bothered you the most?" asked the old woman.

"Take the subject of Cain's wife," answered Sam. "What about that? Did he marry his sister? If Adam and Eve were the first humans, how did Cain find a wife? How can the Bible begin with something so confusing?"

"I have my ideas about that," said Dora.

"I'd be interested in hearing an explanation," said Sam.

"My ideas are based on my personal interpretation," reiterated Dora. "It's not really what the church thinks about it, and I doubt our pastor would appreciate my view."

"I want to hear this," said Megan.

"Do you promise not to get upset and run off to the pastor to lodge a complaint about me?" asked Dora.

"Of course, not," said Megan.

"Traditionally, most churches consider the second chapter of Genesis to be a retelling of the first chapter," began Dora. "For me, that doesn't really make sense. The third chapter isn't a repeat of second chapter, and the fourth chapter isn't a repeat of the third. I read the second chapter as a continuation of the creation story, not a retelling of it. This is how I see it. The first chapter gives the order of creation. The second chapter begins with God resting from that creative work, and then proceeds to tell of more work. In other words, I believe God created human beings in the first chapter and then created special humans in the second. The order of creation is different in the second chapter, so I don't view it as a retelling of the first chapter. Like you indicated, it wouldn't make a lot of sense to contradict the first chapter with accounts in the second."

"You believe that people were created before Adam and Eve?" asked Megan.

"Well, yeah," answered Dora. "That explains where Cain got his wife, and it explains the people who Cain was afraid to face when he was sent away for killing his brother."

"It says that God rested on the seventh day," said Megan.

"It does," agreed Dora. "It didn't say that God quit on the seventh day. Sam, when you get home from a long hard day's work, you rest – right? But the next day, you get back up and continue to work. Resting doesn't mean the same thing as quitting. It simply means ceasing for a time."

"I'm shocked that you don't believe that Adam and Eve were the first people! exclaimed Megan. "You, of all people."

"Keep your voice down," said Dora. "You promised not to get bent out of shape, if I explained what I believe. This is what I mean by getting twisted around the axle on minor aspects of the faith. It's not really that important, is it?"

"I don't know," admitted Megan. "I mean, you don't seem to believe some of the basic parts of the Bible."

"I believe them," Dora said. "I just don't interpret some parts of the Bible the same way you do. What matters is that both of us believe that when Jesus died, our sins were placed on him and those sins died with him. This is the heart of our faith, right?"

"It is," began Megan. "I just thought we believed the same about the first book of the Bible."

"Does this make you view me differently than before?" Dora pressed.

"I'm just surprised, I guess," answered Megan. "Why would God create humanity, and then have a second creation with Adam and Eve?"

"For me, personally, I think God created Adam as the beginning of the Messianic line of people leading to Jesus. The Bible talks about the Jews being God's chosen people. I think the Jewish people began with Adam. It doesn't mean there weren't any other people around beforehand."

"Wow! I never thought you believed anything like that," Megan said. "I thought everyone at our church believed roughly the same, and I thought the account of God creating Adam and Eve as the first people was an established belief of Christians – especially the people here at this church."

"The interpretation of Adam and Eve as the first humans has been widely accepted as the undisputable view of the account in Genesis," replied Dora. "When I read it, I just see it differently. After some research, I found that there have been others who interpreted creation the same way I do – we're just in the minority. To be honest, I really don't know how it all happened. I wasn't there. I'm old, but not that old. This is just how I see it."

"I may have to read those scriptures again," Megan said.

"It's difficult to read the Bible without preconceived ideas," Dora added, as she turned to walk away. "I just try to read it for what it seems to say, regardless of what anybody else thinks."

"Well, I didn't expect that," Megan whispered to Sam.

"That woman scares me a little," said Sam. "But I like her. She's certainly interesting. What she said kind of makes sense… you know, about where Cain's wife came from. I'm sure she listens to the preacher, but she thinks for herself. She's seems to be different from most of the people at this church."

"Dora is a widow. She was married to a brick layer, who later owned his own construction company. He left her money when he died, but she hasn't always lived in comfort."

"I should have known. Like I said, she's different from the other rich snobs at this church."

"You really don't know the other people at this church."

"I told you that I've been around rich people before. I told you about going to church with my mother, as a child."

"My parents took me to church when I was small, but they stopped attending," replied Megan. When I began college, I tried this church. I like it. I like the people."

"These people like you because your father has money. They either are impressed with you because your family is super rich, or they hope you'll share some of it."

"That's not true. They didn't find out about my father until two years after I began attending. I was afraid to tell them. I don't go around telling everybody about my family. You're right about people judging, and I don't want to be judged in light of my father. I want people to take me for who I am. When people find out about him, they tend to judge me and put me in a particular box. You're right about some people buddying up to me because it makes them feel good to hang out with the rich girl. Other people don't trust me and treat me like I'm some sort of alien."

"OK, I've never been in your shoes. I'm not sure that I would like it."

"Fortunately, I was able to get to know these people before they found out about my family," explained Megan. "Some of them are really good people. They might not even consider your income if you don't bring the subject up."

"They've seen my truck. Believe me, they know that I don't have money. I just don't fit in, and I doubt that I ever could."

"Would you like to get to know the pastor?"

"No, not really. I told you why I'm here. I want to be with you; and not because you have money."

"I know; you think I'm hot."

"No, I KNOW that you're hot," said Sam, with a smile.

Megan rolled her eyes and shook her head. Sam gave her a wink.

"What am I going to do with you?" she asked, looking into his eyes.

"Oh, I can think of plenty of things," Sam replied with a grin.

Megan poked him in the ribs. The tension between them eased. Sam gave her a hug. Standing in the church parking lot, she felt as if they were the only two people on earth – like her belief of Adam and Eve. A man in a silver sedan watched from across the church parking lot.

Chapter 12
Secrets

THE FOLLOWING FRIDAY afternoon, Megan stood on a top floor balcony of an exclusive hotel. Leaning over the edge, looking down at the cars parked twelve floors below, she called Sam with her cell.

"Do you still have the telescope?" she asked.

"It's in a closet," he replied. "Did you hear about another meteor shower, or did you decide to peek on your old man?"

"Peeking is the plan. His friends are coming to the house for one of those special weekends."

"So, you're using me just for my telescope."

"Actually, I want you to spend the weekend with me in a hotel."

"In that case, you can use me for my telescope any time you want," replied Sam.

"Can you fit the telescope in a suitcase?"

"I can put it in one bag, and the tripod in a second."

"The hotel is on a hill, about a mile from my parent's home. I'm about to text you the address. Be here tomorrow afternoon at three; and don't forget the telescope."

A BROAD SMILE beamed from Sam, as he rolled two large suitcases inside the hotel room. He shrugged his shoulders at the sight of two queen sized beds.

"We could have gone with a single king size," he remarked.

"Funny," replied Megan. "Come out to the balcony."

"I'm not crazy about heights."

"You work construction, and you're afraid of heights?"

"I just get a little queasy if it's more than a couple of floors. There was an incident about a year back."

"It's not like I'm going to push you off the balcony. Come on."

Sam held the railing in a death grip as he moved out onto the balcony.

"Can you see that large white house at the base of that hill?" Megan asked, pointing.

"Yep."

"That's the home where I grew up."

"Quant little place, huh? Must be only about nine thousand square feet."

"It has a basement."

"So?"

"Eleven thousand square feet, if you include the basement."

"As a kid I bet you got lost a lot."

"At dusk, I want you to set up the telescope out here."

"I can do that. Can we go back inside?"

"You're not kidding. You really are afraid of heights. Sure, let's step back inside. Tell me about the incident you mentioned."

"You probably wouldn't understand. It shouldn't have been a big deal."

"Just tell me."

"Leroy and I were placing a downspout for a gutter on the rear of a large house. The house was on a slope – two floors in front, and three in the back. It was such a long downspout that I had trouble lining it up with the hole in the gutter – too much play. Leroy decided that he should get on the roof to help guide it to meet the hole, and he went back to the truck for a ladder. It worked. On his knees, he leaned over the side of the roof and guided it with his right hand. Once the downspout was aligned, I began to fasten it to the wall of the house with metal bands. I got one band on, when I heard him scream. I looked up and he was hanging by one hand off that three-story roof. He had mud on his boots, and his feet slipped as he stood up. Leroy was lucky in that he slipped near an exhaust pipe coming out of the roof. He grabbed it with one hand."

"Oh, good Lord!" whispered Megan, placing a hand over her mouth.

"I yelled for him to hang on, and he yelled back that he couldn't. I kept yelling at him, as I ran to find the ladder he had used to scale the roof. I saw it on top of the garage. After reaching the top of the garage, he had pulled it up to the garage roof to reach the top of the house. I yelled to him again and heard him franticly scream back that he couldn't hang on much longer. I ran back to the truck for a second ladder. We kept yelling back and forth the whole time. I quickly placed that second ladder against the garage. After I reached the garage roof, I used the first ladder to reach the roof of the house. I ran across the peak of the roof and then slid down it to grab Leroy's weakening arm with my right hand. The roof was fairly steep, so I had to hold a second roof jack with my left hand. He's a lot bigger man than I am, and I quickly realized that I wasn't strong enough to hold on to the pipe with my left hand and pull him back onto the roof with only my right. I dropped my right leg over the edge of the roof and told him to grab my pants leg with his free hand. I took hold of his jacket, and we both pulled. It was enough to get him back onto the roof. With the adrenaline flowing, we scrabbled away from the edge and up to the crest of the roof. Shaking, he thanked me. We sat up there exhausted for some time before taking the ladders back down to the ground."

"Three floors – that's a long way to fall," stammered Megan. "You saved his life."

"He would have been hurt really bad, falling backwards that far. After that incident, I became queasy each time I reached the edge of a roof that was more than two floors up. I didn't expect it to get to me like that. It didn't seem to affect Leroy the same way it did me. I would have expected him to be afraid, not me. On future jobs, he was fine working heights. But then again, he drank a lot."

"You're a hero,"

"I'm actually a chicken, for it to have affected me the way it has. I didn't do anything that Leroy wouldn't have done for me. Cops and firemen are placed in stressful situations almost every day. I faced one occasion, and I let it get to me."

"If you hadn't acted in time, he might have been killed."

"I think maybe God helped out."

"What do you mean?"

"I haven't attended church regularly since I was small, but it doesn't mean that I don't pray from time to time. You know, when I find myself in a real jam. It seemed like it took me forever to reach him. I wasn't just yelling for Leroy to hang on; I was also praying the whole time that he wouldn't fall. I think God gave him strength. Afterwards, I've prayed to God that I wouldn't be afraid of heights – but it hasn't helped. I still get edgy. That's OK. If I'm to have one prayer answered, I'm certainly OK with the one where God helped Leroy to hold on. He held on for a long time."

Megan wrapped her arms around Sam's neck and kissed him on the check. He returned the kiss on her lips.

"Do we have to sleep on two beds tonight?" Sam asked.

"Yes!" Megan exclaimed, pushing him away.

"I need for you to hold me tonight, because I'm afraid of heights."

"Was that what that story was about – trying to get me in bed? Did you make all that up?"

Sam's face became serious.

"I would love to have you in bed, but I promise that I'll never tell you a lie. The story was true, and I am afraid of heights."

"In that case, you can have the bed the furthest from the balcony," Megan replied."

As the evening approached, the two set up the

telescope on the hotel balcony. Megan was amazed at the clarity of view, even of people inside the windows of her parent's home. The uneventful first hour consisted of Megan attempting to read lips of the guests during dinner. Suddenly, all six rose from the table and toasted the night.

"That's a little weird," Megan stated. "I would love to know what that toast was all about."

"Probably about some multi-million-dollar business deal," replied Sam.

"Everything isn't always about money. Hey! They just left the room! Where did everyone go? Help me readjust this telescope. I need to find them."

Sam loosened the telescope on the tripod, and gently moved it to view several other windows. He saw no one. Sam then zoomed back out to view the entire house and surrounding property. Lights in the back yard illumined a path leading from the rear of the home.

"You gotta see this!" blurted Sam. "They went outside the rear of the house."

Megan placed her eye against the telescope, just in time to see them move out of view.

"Find them again!" she exclaimed. "I can't see them anymore. They appeared to be headed for the hill behind the house."

"I have them now," confirmed Sam. "They're at a large gate, of some sorts."

"That has to be the cave!"

"Your father owns a cave?"

Megan nudged him aside and viewed the six standing outside the fully opened gate of the cave. A box truck had been backed up near the cave entrance. Her father motioned to the men inside the cab of the truck, and it slowly moved away.

"They must have unloaded something in the cave," said Megan. "My father must have had something of value trucked in and hidden away in there. I should have known that cave was being used."

She witnessed her father step into the cave. He brought out torches, which were soon lit. The six stood momentarily outside the cave, saying words in unison, before entering the cave in single file.

"That does it!" barked Megan. "I have to know what's in that cave."

"Your family owns a cave, and you've never been inside?"

"Never! My mother always told me that it was dangerous. What a load of bull crap!"

"Maybe it IS dangerous for a little girl."

"My mother is all about avoiding lawsuits, but them taking guests inside a dangerous cave? No way! That was all a load of bull crap! What's being stored in there?"

"I wouldn't have a clue. I played in caves some when I was a child, but this is a little odd."

"You think? You have no idea how weird this is. My mother is not a caver – not in the least. We need to get inside that cave!"

Megan and Sam took turns watching the cave entrance through the telescope. After about an hour, everyone but Tony Gallucci and Megan's mother exited. After another half hour, the truck was in view again at the entrance.

"No one is getting out of the truck," said Sam.

"Let me see," replied Megan.

After a few minutes, Charles Worthington was

seen talking with the men in the truck cab. He then entered the cave again. A half hour later, Worthington, Gallucci and Michelle Adams exited the cave. Megan witnessed what seemed to be a confrontation between Worthington and Gallucci.

"Charles Worthington is shaking his finger in the face of Tony Gallucci," Megan began. "Now, Charles and my Mom are heading back to the house. The two men from the truck are heading into the cave with Gallucci. What is going on in there?"

"Let me take a look," said Sam.

Sam replaced Megan at the telescope, and repeatedly told her that he saw no movement. Sam moved his face away to rub his eye. When he again viewed the cave entrance, he saw the two men from the truck carrying a large box from the cave.

"They're carrying a large box supported by poles resting on their shoulders," informed Sam.

Megan motioned for him to step aside. She placed her eye on the telescope to view the men put the box inside the back of the truck. Gallucci's finger was in the face of one as he spoke to him.

"I would love to be able to read lips," said Megan. "They must have unloaded items from the truck into the cave, and now they appear to be trucking something away. The truck moved out, and Tony Gallucci is now locking the gate to the cave. I have to get inside that cave."

"Do they always keep it locked?"

"Of course, it's kept locked. It's a liability. If some kid entered and was hurt, my parents would be sued like crazy. What are they storing in there?"

"Do you know where the key is kept?"

"No, but I plan to find it."

"You said that for years they've met and kept things extremely private," replied Sam. "That key won't be lying around. I'm sure it's well hidden."

"At this point, I'm so ticked that I'm ready to use bolt cutters to see what's inside."

"Maybe the cave has another entrance," suggested Sam. "Some caves have multiple entrances."

"If it does, I'm sure my father has them protected. Like I said, lawsuits."

"This thing really has you wound up!"

"I don't like to be lied to, especially by my parents. I'm tired of this crap! I'm not allowed to come to their special adult weekends, and I'm lied to about the safety of a cave owned by my family. I'm getting inside that cave. Are you coming with me?"

"One minute you're talking lawsuits, and the next minute you want me to trespass into a locked cave owned by possibly the richest people in the Atlanta area. Maybe you should think this through."

"Maybe you should stop being a chicken."

"That's not fair. I confessed to you about one weakness, and now you jump all over it. There is being chicken, and there is having a little common sense. For example: I avoid large mean and crazy guys, so that I don't give one an opportunity to stomp the living dog poop out me. That's common sense. In the same way, I'm a little uncomfortable about being thrown in jail by a rich dude, for doing something that isn't really all that necessary – breaking into his private cave."

"Forget it. I'll go in myself."

"You're really serious about this? This really means something to you?"

"All my life, I've been held in the dark about some things. Now, a lightbulb has suddenly been turned on. I'm ready to see what they've been hiding. I've had enough."
"OK."
"Are you going to help me?"
"Yes."

Chapter 13
Frank

"TELL ME EVERYTHING you know about Tony Gallucci," Frank Reynolds demanded, when placing a call to Misty Callahan.

"I told that probation officer named Russ everything I know," she answered. "An old boyfriend did some work for him. That's all. I've never met the man."

"TJ Turner, has admitted to taking you, and he says Gallucci ordered your kidnapping."

"That doesn't make any sense! I've never even met that guy. Just tell me that the Turner guy's in prison."

"It's possible that Turner may have saved your life when he let you go."

"Is he in prison?"

"He's been cooperating with the law, so he hasn't yet been tried."

"He's trying to save his own skin with that story about somebody else ordering my kidnapping. Why are you listening to him?"

"Most of what he's told us has turned out to be

true. The kidnapping may have been just the tip of what's really going on, and I need to hear everything you can tell me about Tony Gallucci."

"I can't imagine what that Gallucci guy would want with me, especially to have me kidnapped. I understand that he's super rich. Stupid women flock to men with money. He wouldn't have any need to kidnap a woman."

"How do you know Gallucci has money?"

"Ricky told me so while we were eating dinner one evening. He said the guy owned a construction company and was really rich. He pulled out an envelope from his jacket and opened it. It was filled with twenties."

"Gallucci paid him in cash?"

"Ricky did jobs for several people who paid in cash, but Gallucci seemed to pay heavy."

"Did your boyfriend tell you what kind of work he did for him?"

"He said yard work, but I'm not sure if that's the only thing. I didn't really press him about it. Ricky had a bad side. For that amount of money, I really didn't want to know how he earned it. Ricky told me that he had done yardwork for a few rich guys. But nobody pays like that for yardwork."

"Can you tell me where I can find your old boyfriend?"

"I don't have a clue. We weren't together all that long. We broke up a couple of months after he introduced me to that rich guy named Adams."

"Allen Adams?"

"Yeah, that's him. I really don't want to get involved in all of this."

"Just a few more questions. What's Ricky's last name?"

"Taylor. His name is Ricky Taylor."

"Describe him."

"He was tall; six foot three. Ricky didn't have big muscles, but he was really strong – you know, kind of wiry."

"Do you have a photo?"

"A few on my cell. I just never deleted them."

"Send them to me."

"If you find him, please don't mention my name. Just leave me out of it. I broke things off because he began to scare me."

"Scare you?"

"He was late for a date, and I pressured him about why. He grabbed me by the arm and told me not to ask questions. He hurt my arm, but it was what I saw in his eyes that scared me. I'd never seen that look from him before. He became moody and more secretive over the next few weeks. Anything could set him off. I decided it was best to break things off."

"Have you been in contact with him since?"

"He called a couple of times. Both times he told me that I needed a guy like him for protection. I was polite, but a little distant. I didn't want to start things back up. Maybe he was right. If he had been walking with me that night, that TJ guy would have never grabbed me."

Over the next few minutes, Misty sent Frank four photos of Rick Taylor. He assured her that the FBI had TJ Turner in custody, and that she didn't have to worry about ever running into him again.

—•●•—

FRANK REYNOLDS SAT in his car reviewing a file on Richard Allen Taylor.

The guy certainly has a criminal record. What a name! His initials spell RAT. What kind of mother would do that to a kid?

Stepping out of his car, Frank's eyes scanned his surroundings. Graffiti covered a nearby dumpster, and trash lay along the curb of the street. With his badge in hand, he knocked loudly on the front door of Ricky Taylor's apartment. Frank heard movement inside. The door opened slightly. With the chain still in place, the occupant spoke.

"Can I help you?"

"Are you Ricky Taylor?" asked Frank, holding his badge so that it could be read.

"I am."

"I need to ask you a few questions."

"I've done nothing wrong."

"I see that you missed your last meeting with your probation officer, but we can clear that up with a conversation."

"I'll come outside," offered Ricky, sliding back the chain and stepping onto the porch.

"Good," replied Frank. "After a few answered questions, I'll inform your probation officer that you met with me. In the future, you need to keep your appointments."

"Got it."

"Do you know a man named Tony Gallucci?"

Ricky's eyes narrowed, silently attempting to size

up the detective. Frank returned a cold stare.

"I did some yardwork for that rich dude a while back," Ricky confessed.

"How often?"

"Just a few times. What's this about?"

"When you were performing that yardwork at Gallucci's place, did you see people coming and going?"

"Naw, man. My head was down raking leaves and mowing the yard. I didn't see nothing."

"How did you come to know Mr. Gallucci?"

"Through word of mouth, I heard he needed help – and that he paid good. I had to jump on that."

"You were unemployed?"

"Just for a while. What's this about?"

"What else can you tell me about him?"

"Not much. He's rich and he pays good for yardwork. I understand he owns a construction company."

"Have you ever worked construction on one of his projects?"

"No."

"Tell me about your conversations with Tony Gallucci."

"There's nothing much to say. The place is like a compound. I told the guard at the entrance to the driveway that I heard there was yardwork that needed to be done. He called the house, and then waved me to drive inside. Gallucci was standing with another man at the front door of that mansion. He had that man show me the equipment. He then told me that he might have more work for me later, if I did a good job."

"How about the next conversation?"

"When I was finished, the other guy escorted me to where Gallucci was standing on the front porch. He handed me an envelope containing cash and told me that I had done a good job."

"Didn't he have a person who did that kind of work on a regular basis?"

"The other man told me that the regular guy was really sick."

"What else did Mr. Gallucci say?"

"The next time I worked there, I dealt only with the other guy. I didn't even see the rich dude."

"Did you have other conversations with Tony Gallucci?"

"No. I only worked for him a few more times. I'm guessing the regular guy got healthier."

"OK. I'll tell your probation officer that we had this talk. Don't forget to keep your appointments with him."

"OK, I'll do it. Thanks."

Ricky watched Frank drive away. Once the detective was out of sight, he pulled his cell from his pocket.

"Mr. Gallucci, I know you said not to call this number unless it's important. Detective Frank Reynolds paid me a visit, and his questions were about you ... No, I just told him that you paid me cash for doing yardwork for you...No sir, I don't know what it was about... You're welcome."

— • ● • —

TWO WEEKS LATER, Frank got a call from FBI agent Jason Bagwell.

"We've confirmed that Gallucci and TJ Turner had several conversations. TJ gave us his old cell number, and we pulled the records. There's no question about them having talks. Everything Turner told us has been true."

"Then, you believe that he's been telling us the truth about loading drugs in traffic barrels?" asked Frank.

"I believe him. I also believe that Mr. Gallucci is a busy man. Not only does he own the construction company, he buys and sells fine art – high dollar fine art. He travels to Europe and attends auctions."

"None of that is criminal behavior."

"No, it isn't. But using a construction business to distribute illegal drugs is. We believe his construction company may be a front for other illegal activity."

"Any proof or leads?"

"Not yet."

"I'm here in Atlanta," replied Frank. "I can check him out."

"I was hoping you'd be interested."

"I'll let you know if I spot something."

———•◆•———

FRANK REYNOLDS WAS known throughout the department for his ability to tail a car without being noticed. One Saturday afternoon, he followed Tony and Mia Gallucci for several miles. He was surprised to see the car enter the long drive serving the estate of Allen Adams. He drove to a vantage point on a hill near the property. Using a small pair of binoculars, he watched for further activity. Frank couldn't make out anything happening at the house because trees along the street blocked his view, but he could easily make out the driveway. He watched a box truck move up the long driveway, but he didn't see it leave. Soon afterwards, he spotted a large luxury car visit the home.

"Perhaps this is a party with a catering service," he mumbled to himself.

Within a few minutes, a black van with heavily tinted windows slowly passed by him. He watched to see if it turned into the driveway, but it passed by the estate. After about thirty minutes, the box truck left the Adams place. Frank followed the truck at a safe distance. Eventually, it pulled into a rear parking lot of a diner. Two large men exited the truck and entered the building. Frank parked his car several spaces away from the truck. He quickly exited his car and inspected the truck.

No markings. What catering service fails to advertise the business on the outside of a delivery truck? It's unusually clean.

Frank entered the diner and scanned the establishment for the men. Neither were seated at any table or booth.

"May I help you?' asked a waitress.

"First time here. Can I have a table?"

"Sure," she replied. "Take a seat wherever you want. I'll bring you a menu shortly."

Frank selected a table that provided a clear view of the parking lot entrance. His eyes darted from that entrance to various interior doors lining the walls of the dining area.

Men don't usually go to the restroom together. I'm sure they went to a back room.

The waitress returned, and Frank quickly ordered. After fifteen minutes, there was still no sign of the two men. One of the interior doors seemed to have a mirror instead of a window.

One-way glass. Someone from behind that door can watch every table. Some managers have this setup in order to keep an eye on the staff, but I have a feeling that it serves another purpose.

He finished his meal, topping it off with apple pie with ice cream. More than an hour later, he was still sipping a cup of coffee when he spotted the truck leaving the parking lot.

They've been in the back the entire time!

Frank left money to cover the meal and a healthy tip on the table and made his way to his car. Unsure as to whether the truck was in the process of serving another catering job or if it was returning to the Adams estate, he decided to make his way back to the estate. Speeding down streets, he later spotted the truck.

Looks like it's bound for the Adams place. Maybe the party's over.

Night had completely settled in as he reached the estate, so he parked his car down the street from the mansion. His binoculars were of little use to him in the dark. The truck departed the estate an hour later. Just as he started his engine to follow, the black van with tinted windows pulled in front of him. Frank came to a sudden stop. A large man stepped out of the van and approached him. The detective placed his right hand on his side arm, while taking his badge into his left hand.

"Can I see an ID?" the man asked.

"You need to let me pass," stated Frank coldly, as he displayed the badge.

"I'm sorry sir, I thought you might be someone casing the houses in this neighborhood."

"I'm clearly not. Now, get out of my way."

The man stepped aside and allowed Frank to pass by. Just after passing by the van, he glanced in his rear mirror. By the soft red glow of the van's taillights, he saw the man place a cell phone to his ear. Remembering the truck, Frank sped up.

I can't believe this! I may have lost that truck.

Two blocks down, he spotted the brake lights of the truck brighten as it made a right turn. Frank's car hurdled down the residential street in pursuit. Soon, he was following it from a comfortable distance.

He watched the vehicle stop at a warehouse off Mooreland Avenue. A tall chain link gate opened to allow the truck passage into the area of the building. Through the gate, he watched the vehicle stop in front of a large delivery door of the huge warehouse. The man on the passenger side got out to enter the code causing the door to rise open. After the truck entered the warehouse, the man used the code pad on the interior to lower the door. Frank placed a call to Jason Bagwell.

"What I thought was a catering truck serving the home of Allen Adams is now in a large warehouse off Mooreland Avenue."

"Sounds a lot like the warehouse Turner talked about," replied Jason.

"I agree. The truck left the Adams estate, and I followed to Sally's Diner. The driver and another man entered the diner, but I never saw them in the dining area. I believe they remained in the back. The truck later returned to the estate before moving on to this warehouse. It would make sense for it to be a catering service, but I can't imagine why a dinner catering truck would be left overnight in a warehouse that's probably owned by Gallucci."

"What do you suppose the people in the truck were up to at the home of Allen Adams?" asked Jason. "You said they went to the place twice."

"I'm at a loss. There are no markings on the truck. I would certainly like to see the contents of that vehicle and the warehouse."

"I wouldn't try holding my breath while requesting a warrant. Try to get some sleep. Ask a patrol car to keep an eye on the warehouse, and to notify you if the truck leaves."

"I'll do just that. But I want to take a closer look."

After the call ended, Frank called in a black-and-white to patrol the area and report movement of the truck. Frank stepped out of his car and approached the tall fence surrounding the warehouse.

This is dumb. That truck is parked for the night, and the two men may stay with it. There's no sense hanging around here.

Frank was exhausted when he reached his apartment later that evening. As he placed his key in the lock, a wire suddenly went over his head from behind and was pulled violently against his neck. Unable to breathe, he struggled against his attacker. He grabbed the wrists of the man behind him and kicked backward against the man's shin. He tried to wedge his fingers on his left hand under the wire, as he reached for his sidearm with his right. Suddenly, there were men on each side of him. They took control of his arms. His eyesight soon faded. Frank lost consciousness within fifteen seconds, and his body was lowered to the concrete front porch. He was held in the grasp of his attackers until they were sure he was dead. The large man from the black van pulled the wire from Frank's neck and motioned to the other two that it was time to leave.

The next morning, a neighbor spotted his body and called the police. A day passed before Russ caught wind of Frank's death. While looking through Frank's records, a fellow detective spotted several references to Russ Blevins and notified the probation officer.

Russ's first call was to Jason Bagwell. His second was to Misty Callahan.

"We need talk," Russ ordered Misty.

"Can you and that detective just leave me alone?

"That detective is dead."

"Frank?"

"That was his name, and you need to come clean on everything you know about your old lover and Gallucci."

"You called me to tell me they killed Frank, and you think that I want to be pulled into all of this? I don't want to be involved."

"I'm afraid you are involved. Under Gallucci's orders, TJ Turner kidnapped you. Frank Reynolds investigated Gallucci, and now he's dead. Frank told me about having a conversation with your ex-boyfriend about his relationship with Gallucci."

"What relationship? I told him that my old boyfriend, Ricky Taylor, did yardwork for Tony Gallucci a couple of times. That's not really a relationship."

"There's a relationship that you may or may not be

aware of. You're in the middle of all of this. Your boyfriend worked for Gallucci. TJ Turner kidnapped you, and he says that Gallucci ordered it. Both men have ties to this guy, and both are connected to you. I see Gallucci and the boyfriend, with you in the middle. You need to tell me what you know. For your own sake, you had better come clean with me."

"I never met the man. Everything I know is second hand. I told Frank everything Ricky said to me about Gallucci. Are you saying that you think Ricky had something to do with me being taken?"

"I'm saying that Ricky had something going with Gallucci, and that Turner abducted you. There is a connection. You're not stupid. How else would Tony Gallucci even know about you?"

"Ricky's mean, but not a killer."

"Frank visited Ricky Taylor, and now Frank is dead!" snapped Russ. "Your old boyfriend is bad, and a friend of mine is now dead. Cut the crap!"

"If you're right about Ricky, he may come after me if he finds out I told the detective about him."

"You won't truly be safe until we get to the bottom of what's really going on with this man. We need to focus on Gallucci, and I need to know everything you told Frank about your ex-boyfriend's dealings with him. I'm sure the Atlanta police will work off Frank's notes on this case, but Frank was my friend. Now, this is personal. I need to find out everything that you know."

"You're not a cop, you're just a probation officer. What are you going to do? Frank was a detective, and a smart one. They killed him. How do I know that you won't screw up and let the wrong people know that I've talked? You could have those people after me again!"

"I'm working with people outside the Atlanta police. I've been assured the FBI is going to squeeze TJ Turner like a lemon, and you're going to cough up everything you know to me."

"You're not listening. I want to be left alone."

"The sooner we put a lid on Gallucci, the sooner you'll be left alone."

"I can't believe Frank's dead. I liked him."

"Believe it. Believe it when I tell you that you'd better hope Gallucci gets nailed, and fast. TJ Turner and Ricky Taylor won't be a problem if Gallucci is put away. There was a reason TJ was ordered to grab you, and it has to do with Taylor. This can't be a random thing. If you want to be safe, you'd better level with me."

"I need to get out of here!"

"Where can you go? You're as safe where you are, as anywhere. Your best bet is helping us nail this guy."

"But…"

"Stay put. I'm coming out to Colorado Springs."

"When?"

"After Frank's funeral on Saturday. I'll fly out that evening."

"I'm scared."

"We'll get this guy, but you need to help me. Just lie low."

———•●•———

THE NEXT MORNING Russ placed a call to Megan Adams.

"I need to go out of town this weekend, so I won't be able to teach the Sunday School class. Can I depend on you to present the material to the class?"

"Me?" Megan responded.

"Sure. You're one of the smartest people in that class. I can email you the material. You'll be fine. Just look it over Saturday."

"I have plans for Saturday."

"I really need you to help me. A friend of mine has been killed, and I need to fly somewhere after the funeral on Saturday."

"I'm sorry about your friend. Are you sure that I'm the best one to handle the class?"

"Out of everyone, I trust your ability the most. It's all laid out. This isn't a lecture class. I need you to look it over and just lead the class in the discussion."

"Who was your friend?"

"A detective friend named Frank Reynolds."

"You think he was murdered?"

"I know he was murdered," replied Russ. It's obvious. He was investigating the kidnapping of a woman, and someone killed him. I've got to go out of town and check something out."

"Don't be concerned about the class, I'll handle it."

Chapter 14
Cave

"I'M BEGINNING TO THINK you were right," Megan told Sam.

"About what?" he asked.

"I'll never find a key to that gate, and the best alternative is to see if there is another entrance."

Referenced in old land deeds, I found a few unmapped private caves in the metro Atlanta area documented on microfiche in the library. After days of researching, Megan and Sam gave up and decided to ask the local chapter of the National Speleological Society for additional information. No maps were produced by members of the society, but a small list of elderly cavers was provided. After unsuccessful talks with several, the name George Conner was strongly suggested by one homebound man. Megan placed a call to him.

"My name is Megan Adams, daughter of Allen Adams," she began. "We have a private cave in the hill behind our home and I'm interested to see whether it was ever explored before my father purchased the property."

"I think most in the Atlanta area are aware that your father is an extremely wealthy man," replied Conner. "I would think he can afford to have a team map that cave. Why ask me?"

"To be honest, my father has no interest in the matter," she explained. "This is a personal interest of mine. I asked several older cavers, and your name was suggested as someone who might have knowledge about the cave."

"I'm familiar with the existence of the cave, but I've …. never been inside it," Conner replied. "I apologize for speaking in broken phases. Please be patient…. I'm suffering from lung cancer, and I require constant oxygen. My days of caving are over."

"I'm sorry to hear that, Mr. Conner," replied Megan. "I'm listening."

"Fred Lowery claimed to have explored it, but he's dead," Conner continued. "If he had any maps of it…. I'm sure they're long gone."

"I'm particularly interested in whether the cave has multiple entrances," Megan explained.

"Most caves do. Why are you asking?"

"The cave currently has a locked gate across the entrance, but I'm wondering if there may be another entrance."

"Your concerned with …. personal liability, and your father isn't?

"He's satisfied with the gate at the cave entrance and the ten-foot security fence surrounding the property. My interest is based on personal curiosity."

"If memory serves me, Fred mentioned a …. small entrance on the east side."

"How would I find it?"

"There's a lot of limestone in the area …. limestone caves are usually formed by running water. First … see if there are any small streams and look for an origin. Water … may not be currently flowing … so also look for empty stream beds… Older ones could be overgrown by forests."

"Anything else?"

"The advice I've given is your best bet. Experienced spelunkers … would have more insight, but without … that experience you wouldn't be able to pick up on other signs."

"If I were to find a second entrance and wanted to explore it, do you have recommendations?"

"Safety is … the primary concern. First, never go very far … inside a cave without at least three sources of light. Secondly… don't go inside if there is rain forecasted. A cave can … become quickly filled with water. For someone like you, I would suggest … taking a large roll of nylon string. Tie one end to something outside the cave … and unroll the string as you travel through the cave. Gather the string … as you make your way out. You may not notice other passages until … you attempt to exit a cave. You can become easily lost."

"Those are great tips. Thank you."

"People who have not explored unmapped caves … envision large passageways. Most caves have passageways that … require one to crawl and squeeze … through tight spaces. Are you claustrophobic?"

"No. I can't remember ever experiencing fear of closed areas."

"A cave can bring it out in you. For many … squeezing through an opening in solid rock can cause panic. Make sure you remain calm…. It's important."

"Thank you, so much. You've been a great help."

"Be careful. Be very careful."

Megan smiled at Sam, as she ended the call.

"Security fence?" Sam asked. "When were you going to tell me about a ten-foot security fence?"

"Not a problem," replied Megan. "I have access to the home, and sometimes my father is away on business. It's been a month since my mother went away, and he cancels the cleaning crews when he is away. Since she left, he only has the cooks come in for special diners. The place is empty when he is gone."

"I'm sure he has heavy surveillance."

"Sure. There are security cameras all over the estate, but I'm family. A sophisticated alarm system notifies a private security firm. I think he even has partial ownership of that firm. I know the code to turn the system off. I've visited there more often since my mother left. I think my father is lonely. That's a huge place for one person."

"That place could house an army," replied Sam. "At least, it seems so from the outside. I've only seen it from a distance, the night we viewed it with the telescope."

"That was fun, wasn't it? I'll show you the inside of the house, but I really want to focus on the inside of that cave. We can put our flashlights and other items inside a backpack, and we can make it look like we are hiking the woods on the property. The cameras will show me taking a guy into the woods for a hike or a picnic."

"So, you have this planned out?"

"I've been thinking about it for some time. I feel

somewhat comfortable knowing that you've had some caving experience. Mr. Conner said that most caves have narrow passages. Have you ever taken a tight passageway?"

"I would love to take a tight passageway," Sam said, with a wink.

"Stop! I'm serious. It sounds like it could be dangerous."

"I never went very far inside one as a kid. I do remember crawling through one small opening and finding a larger room. The room wasn't very big; about eight feet across. I found a jawbone of a horse in that room. An animal must have carried it in there. I brought it home and put it in the bottom drawer of a chest. My mother freaked out when she saw it while putting clean clothes in the drawer."

"I never experienced anything like that growing up. I was sent to boarding schools, and really protected. I wish I had been able to play in those caves with you."

"You probably wouldn't have enjoyed being poor. I remember moving once because we could no longer afford the rent."

"I would imagine that it was a little unsettling. No. I've never experienced anything like that."

"It was years ago," said Sam.

"I think we're going to have a blast exploring a second passageway. I'm so glad I'll have you with me."

"You can have me anytime you want me, Baby," Sam replied, giving her another wink.

"Can't you think of anything else?" she said, pounding his shoulder with her small fist.

"You can really be brutal!" exclaimed Sam. "Is that anyway to treat your caving partner?"

He pulled her close and kissed her.

"THIS HOUSE IS UNBELEVABLE," Sam said, stepping through the front door and onto the marble floors in the foyer of Allen Adams' home. "Are you sure no one's at home? How would you know? This place is so enormous that it would take a year to search every room."

"No one is here," answered Megan. "There, I've turned the alarms off. We're good. Let me show you around the first floor. The second floor is pretty much bedrooms and baths."

After the short tour, Megan stepped out the rear door donning a backpack containing a jacket and food items. Sam carried a larger backpack containing lanterns, flashlights, and the large roll of nylon string recommended by Mr. Conner. He had to make a conscious effort to keep up with Megan's eager pace.

"So, that's the metal gate in front of the cave entrance," he observed, taking her hand.

"We'll have to forget about that," she replied. "I wouldn't find the key in a million years. We have to find another way inside."

Three hours later, with the sun high in the sky, Megan sat on the trunk of a fallen tree. She pulled off her backpack.

"Time for lunch," she announced. "Sit down. I packed a thermos and sandwiches."

"What do you think about our chances of finding a second entrance?" asked Sam. "We've completely combed the east side of the hill and found nothing."

"Are we sure that this is the east side?"

"It's the east side," Sam confirmed. "What about if we go further around, toward the north side?"

"Why not? But let's have something to eat first."

After they enjoyed lunch, they hiked toward the north side of the hill. Within a few minutes, Sam spotted what seemed to be a small dry streambed. Trees grew within it, making it difficult to see when not in the direct vicinity. They followed it up the hill several feet before discovering a small opening in a rocky area.

"Let's check this out," suggested Sam.

"Do you really think we can go in there?"

"We would have to take off the backpacks and crawl on our bellies, but we can fit. Here, I'll take a flashlight and crawl inside. I'll let you know how far it goes back."

"Maybe you should also take the string."

"I don't intend to go far. I'll leave the backpack out here with you."

Sam made sure the flashlight worked before beginning his crawl. His progress was slow. At one point, he had to wiggle to force his body through a snug passage. Once through, it opened up to a larger room. He was able to stand, but decided this should be as far as he should penetrate without the string. He called back to Megan.

"It opens up back here!"

"It's not just a hole, it's actually a cave?" Megan yelled back to him.

By this time, she had taken a second flashlight and had crawled about ten feet into the opening. Seeing Sam's light heading her way, she squirmed back out.

Soon they were both back outside.

"We need to tie the string to that tree, and take my backpack with us," suggested Sam. "There's no sense bringing yours. I plan to shove the backpack with the additional light sources in front of me as I crawl. It will be a bit slower, but I think it's important to have the backup lights with us."

"I can come behind you with the string."

"Sounds like a plan," said Sam. "I have lights that strap around our heads. Let's put the handheld flashlights back in the backpack."

"That looks fine on you, but my hair is going look like crap."

The two inched their way into the passage, and eventually found themselves standing in the room of the cave earlier found by Sam. Megan stretched her body after the crawl, as Sam placed the backpack on his shoulders. They shined their lights on the walls of the room, examining every crevice in the rock for the best potential passage. They selected an opening on the left. After about fifty yards, the ceiling of the passageway lowered, and they were forced to crawl. Suddenly, Sam stopped.

"What's the matter?" questioned Megan.

"Are you willing to crawl through water?" asked Sam.

"How deep?

"It looks to be about six inches for the next few feet, but we have water for about twenty feet. We have a couple of feet of air between the water and the ceiling. There's little chance we'd be able to keep the backpack out of the water. It would need to be left here."

Lying on his side, Sam slipped the backpack from

his shoulders and placed it on the cave floor behind him. The passage being about six feet wide, Megan crawled beside him.

"I bet that water is going to be cold," Megan observed. "Are you sure that it's only six inches deep?"

"No. I have no way of knowing how deep it gets before we reach the end. You're right about the water being cold, but the distance is only about twenty feet."

"Let's go."

Under the low ceiling, the two moved into the water. Sam led the way. Within ten feet, the water rose to Sam's chest.

"It's a good thing that we're wearing the lights on our heads," said Sam. "We're almost through, and I can tell that this is as deep as it gets."

"Yuk!" responded Megan.

They were soon out of the water, and the ceiling rose so that the two could stand. Sam stretched his legs. He turned back toward Megan, who stood with both arms tightly crossing her breasts. He moved to her and took her in his arms.

"I'm freezing," said Megan.

"We need to get moving" he replied. "It's the only way to warm up."

He kissed her cheek, then led the way. The ceiling rose to about thirty feet above their heads, but the floor was covered in large boulders.

"Where did all these rocks come from?" asked Megan.

"From up there,' answered Sam, turning his face upward so that the light on his head illuminated the cave ceiling. "It's called breakdown. Caves like this were formed over millions of years, and things like earthquakes cause rock to break loose from the ceiling."

"That's not very comforting," Megan replied, staring at a two-ton boulder.

"Well, if you have to go – that would be a quick death. We need to get moving."

Sam rounded a bend in the large passage and stopped in his tracks. Megan quickly stood at his side.

"What the crap is this?" he asked, shining his light on the backside of a stone statue.

Moving around the statue, they looked into a large room. The ceiling was now about twenty-five feet above a smooth flat floor. Sam moved his light from the statue to another one standing about twenty feet away.

"I don't know," replied Megan. "I think we should be careful. "Maybe this is why the cave entrance is locked. It's possible my father has purchased ancient relics and has them stored in this cave. If that's the case, he may have a security system in place. I think we should scan the walls and ceiling for monitoring devices, like cameras or motion detectors."

Megan moved back into the passage a few feet and tied the string to a large rock, leaving the rest of the unwound spool on the cave floor. For the next fifteen minutes, the two used their headlights to examine the room that contained the statues.

"I don't see any sign of cameras," said Megan.

"I would think that your father has the money to have them hidden pretty well."

"He does, but I would bet that not many people have seen the items in this room. I think I see a third statue, just over there. I'm guessing that it's about forty feet away from these two."

"There's also a smooth rectangular stone block in

the center of the room. I'm not sure whether it's a stone box or a table made from rock."

"We should check it out," suggested Megan, stopping her progress into the room. "But first, I want to get a good look at these statues."

She moved to the first statue, slowly scanning it with her headlight. Sam stood beside her.

"This is strange," she whispered. "Really strange. It looks like it's Indian."

"I can't image the Cherokee making this thing."

"No, from the country India."

"It's definitely a statue of a woman. Those are probably the most perfect boobs I've ever seen."

"It's just like a guy to focus in on boobs!"

"The statue has carved naked boobs. You expected me not to notice? They're just right here in your face."

"Did you notice the four arms?"

"Now, that you mention it. That's really weird."

"I think it's a statue of an Indian goddess. Two hands hold what looks to be flowers."

"Why would your father hide this in a cave?"

"I'm not sure. Maybe it's really old. It could be extremely valuable."

"Or, maybe he bought it on the black market. If he obtained this illegally, he would certainly hide it."

"I've never known my father to be involved with illegal activity. It's probably really rare."

"What about this other one? It's of a guy, holding a pitchfork and wearing a weird hat."

"That's not a pitchfork, it's a trident," rebuked Megan. "It seems to be Indian, as well. I never knew my father had an interest in Indian art."

"I want to take a look at that stone block in the

middle of the room. I wonder if it has something engraved on it. Do you think it's also Indian?"

The two moved to the rectangular stone. The top and sides of the block were perfectly flat and smooth, and a carved stone bowl had been placed on top. Carved images protruded from both ends. Megan turned her headlight to the ceiling, directly above the altar.

"Oh, my gosh!" she exclaimed. "Look up!"

"That thing is huge!"

"I've never seen a chandelier that large."

Sam spotted a cable running from the chandelier which was neatly fastened to the ceiling. He followed it across the ceiling and down to a wooden wall built into the cave.

"Look at this," he said, poking Megan on the shoulder. "He's built a wooden wall inside this cave. It has a door in the center."

As they moved toward the wall, Sam continued to scan the cable with his flashlight. He found that it ran into a small box mounted on the wall.

"I bet that's a light switch for that chandelier," he said, reaching for it.

"Wait!" shouted Megan.

"I think this wall has been built to block light from that thing from reaching other parts of the cave. Don't you want to see what it looks like powered on?"

"Yes…" Megan, timidly replied.

Sam flipped the switch and the cave blazed with light from the massive chandelier. Megan's mouth dropped.

"What is this place?" she asked.

"It beats me."

Besides the two Indian statues they had examined

on the left side of the room, there were more.

"What's with that statue of an elephant?" asked Sam.

"It's probably Indian, like the first," replied Megan.

"I'm smart enough to realize that two of these on the right are Greek or Roman, but the next one is really weird,"

Megan quickly made her way toward the statue on the right side of a laughing man with a long beard. Sam followed.

"There's an inscription at the base that looks Chinese," she said. "Why have three Indian statues, two Greek or Roman, and one Chinese?"

"I can't get over that thing in the middle of the room. I understand storing rare statues, but that stone block right under that massive chandelier is really odd. It's almost like some kind of altar."

"That stone block looks to be made out of stone from this cave," observed Megan. "And there are plenty of large stones back there to carve something like this from."

"I think you're right. He had someone carve this block and place it in the center of the room. It's like he put an altar in the center of these statues. Maybe he's Hindu. You said that those are Indian statues."

"I can't see my father worshiping some weird eastern religion. This statue is Chinese, and the other two seem to be Greek. If this was set up to be a hidden Hindu temple, I can't see adding Chinese and Greek items. This has to be a collection of rare statues."

"So, what is the stone block for?"

"I don't know."

"I think it's an altar," stated Sam. "Looking closer, it's possible that the smooth cave floor was carved out – leaving the stone for this block. I'm thinking that stone bowl is used for some kind of ritual. It's like he and his friends are into some weird religious practice in here."

"You're being ridiculous."

"Why wouldn't he let you come in here? I think he wasn't just having an adult weekend. I believe he's a member of a close-knit religious group that meets in here."

"My father is anything but a Hare Krishna type. He used to tell me about those weird people banging on drums and wearing shaved heads, except for a ponytail. My father told me about them hanging out in airports. He made fun of them and called them a bunch of drugged out lunatics."

"Just saying… this looks like a shrine or temple. Without the altar and the bowl, I would tend to agree that it's a collection of stone statues. That stone altar has been placed in the center of all this for a reason. However, you know your father much better than I do."

"Thank you, I do. Before we leave, I want to get a good look at the Greek statues."

"I left my cell phone in my backpack on the other side of the water," said Sam. "I wish I could take photos."

"I guess we'll have to go off memory."

"I'll do my best," replied Sam. "It's going to be dark in a little over an hour. I suggest we turn out that huge light and start making our way back."

"The first thing that I plan to do when we get back to the house is to change into dry clothes. Next time, we'll have to bring a change of clothes."

"You plan to come back?" questioned Sam.

"We haven't even opened that door in the wooden wall," she replied. "I have to come back."

"In that case, I suggest we leave the string in the cave just as it was placed during this venture. We'll need it as a guide."

It took almost an hour to make their way back to the small opening. Darkness had engulfed them as they entered the home of Allen Adams. Megan gathered clean clothes for herself, along with a couple of clean towels.

"I'm going to take a shower in this bathroom," she announced, tossing Sam a towel. "Just down the hall to the right is another one. The laundry room is at the end of the hall. You're free to wash and dry your clothes."

"I think I'll take you up on drying my clothes while I shower."

"Suit yourself. There's no hurry."

In less than a half hour, they were clean and wearing warm dry clothing. Sam turned and walked toward the rear door.

"Where do you think you're going?" asked Megan.

"I need to gather the two backpacks before I leave."

"Who gave you permission to leave?"

"I don't live here."

"Neither do I. I need you to help me identify those statues before we forget them. What do you say about ordering a pizza?"

"A pizza sounds pretty good. Do they deliver all the way to the house?"

"Of course, they do. I'll tell the guy to call when he arrives at the gate, and I'll open it. He won't have trouble leaving. It opens by itself on the way out."

Megan called in a pizza, and then took Sam by the arm. She led him to her father's study and sat down in front of his PC.

"Do you think we ought to look this stuff up on your father's computer?" asked Sam. "He'll be able to tell that we were searching for those items in that cave."

"Actually, you have a point. You may not have an education, but there's nothing wrong with your mind. I'll use my cell to look things up."

By the time the pizza arrived, she found that the Indian statue of the elephant was of a god named Ganesh. Within an hour, they determined two more.

"Let's take a look at what I've written down," said Megan. Lakshmi, Lord Shiva, and Ganesh. We're still unsure about the Chinese statue. It should be easier to determine the two Greek ones. There's one of a woman holding a child, and the other is a male wearing a hat."

"I didn't know Greeks carved statues of people wearing hats," replied Sam. "It seems really odd."

"Lakshmi is the Hindu goddess of wealth, fortune and prosperity. She appears to be one of the main Indian goddesses."

"The one with really nice boobs," said Sam, smiling.

"Lord Shiva is the Destroyer, and some worship him as the destroyer of ignorance and the preserver of truth. He is also the god of safety and security. Ganesh is a god of wisdom, success and good luck. It says he's the son of Lord Shiva and Parvati."

"I'm interested in the Greek statues," said Sam. "Especially, the guy with the hat."

"I believe it'll be easier to find information on

them," said Megan. "I think there's still more to be learned about the Indian gods. None of them seem to represent evil. If I were to pick a Hindu god, wisdom and good luck would be appealing."

"I still don't understand why they are hidden inside a cave."

"You're right. I want to find out whether there are any missing priceless statues of each. I believe my father acquired them legally, but I want to know for sure. I would think that they're simply statues that my father was able to purchase. He'll probably hang on to them for a few years and sell them for a profit. That's what he knows how to do – make money."

"It's been an interesting day," remarked Sam.

"This has been a blast, but I have church tomorrow. We probably should be going."

"I'll grab the backpacks and toss them in the bed of my truck. We'll be at your apartment within the hour."

Megan talked non-stop, after she climbed into the cab of Sam's truck. Her voice was only challenged by the sound of the truck's engine coming to life. Exiting the gate of the estate, Sam silently listened as he snacked on a slice of pizza.

"I've never seen you so excited," Sam said as he licked his fingers with the last bite of the pizza.

Engrossed by the events of the day, the two never noticed a man following in a silver sedan.

Chapter 15
Departure

A NUDE WOMAN lay faced upward upon a smooth flat stone altar, which stood about waist high. She lay in elegant pose – much like a naked Sleeping Beauty. Her eyes closed, her body still, except for the gentle movement of her breasts with each silent shallow breath. Red roses lay at her feet, along with a stone bowl. Hidden inside the cave, six people clad in long elegant red robes gazed down upon the woman. Charles Worthington raised his right hand, and each robed person took three steps back. Under the glow of a half-ton chandelier, suspended about fifteen feet over their heads, they recited carefully memorized words. Powerful steel cables securely fastened the massive fixture to the cave ceiling. After Charles gave the indication that the gathering of the six had come to a close, Allen Adams turned to his wife Michelle.

"It appears that each of us were exceptionally generous tonight," Allen stated, pointing to the stone bowl filled with cash, all hundreds and fifties. "I'm sure this beautiful young lady could use the funds."

"The truck should return in about twenty minutes," stated Tony Gallucci. "She should remain unconscious for at least another hour, and her ride in the truck should last only about fifteen minutes."

"Maybe the money will help her to advance her station in life," Olivia Worthington said to her husband, warmly gazing into his eyes.

"I hope so," Charles replied.

Tony Gallucci's construction business was a smaller source of income, compared to his dealings in the some of the world's rare classical and fine art. Though he was not a painter or sculptor, his live presentations of nude female forms at the gatherings were truly masterful. Gallucci's demonstrations of exquisite taste hid much darker aspects of his personality.

"Michelle and I will join you soon," Tony promised the others.

The other four moved slowly toward a door stationed in the center of a finely crafted wooden wall that spanned the height and width of the cave's room. Inside that door was a dressing room where the robes were kept. Prior to entering this exclusive area of the cave, each time the six traded their clothes for the robes.

Tony Gallucci gathered the cash from the stone bowl, placed it in an envelope and sealed it. Michelle Adams snuffed each of the six candles that surrounded the naked woman and moved them to a smaller stone table. Michelle tossed Tony a smile as he retrieved a forty-foot strong hemp rope from a cabinet built into the wooden wall. He tossed the rope over one of the powerful cables that held the chandelier, and carefully tied a perfect noose on the other end. Michelle gently lifted the head of the unconscious woman, to allow the noose to be easily placed around the neck. It was a ritual they had practiced several times before.

Tony took a syringe from the pocket of his robe, and quickly removed the cap that covered the needle. Michelle kissed him as he gave it to her. Shortly after injecting the unsuspecting nude young woman, her eyes blinked. Still unable to control movements of her limbs, her confused eyes darted. Tony pulled the rope, lifting the woman into a seated position upon the stone altar. He tied his end of the rope to one of the stone gargoyles which protruded from each end of the stone altar. Michelle took a smaller rope from the pocket of her robe, and tightly tied the hands of the girl behind her back. Taking a second smaller rope from her robe, she tied the victim's ankles. Awareness of the situation began to set into the mind of the woman, and she attempted to speak. However, the tautness of the rope prevented any understandable words from her mouth. Only a muffled moan broke the silence within the cave. Tony had perfected the art of silencing a person with the rope around one's neck, allowing just enough breath to keep the victim alive.

Michelle's eyes were ablaze with anticipation. She placed her right hand on the unblemished skin of the woman's right breast. Then she slowly moved it upward, stopping just beneath the rope that almost choked the woman.

Tony lit a cigarette. He inhaled smoke twice, artistically blowing perfect smoke rings that landed such that they framed the girl's breasts. Sensing the right moment when the young woman was fully conscious, but still unable to control the movement of her body, he moved behind her. Taking the cigarette from his mouth, he touched it to the woman's exposed back. The victim's body jerked from the intense pain, as her muted moans intensified into muffled screams. He continued to inflect burns on the victim's back and shoulders, as Michelle looked on with pleasure. Tears streamed down the face of the unclad woman. As motor movements in her body began to be restored, she attempted to twist her body away from Tony's brutal game. However, the taut rope around her neck held her small frame somewhat steady.

Michelle moved close to Tony. Her eyes closed in rapturous delight as the smell of burning flesh reached her nose. She seductively slid the cigarette from his hand and gave him a nod.

Tony took hold of the rope and began pulling hard. The victim began to frantically twist while he raised her. The woman's body was fully suspended so that her bound feet were about three feet over the stone altar. Her body struggled for air in vain. Michelle's eyes were fixed upon hers, staring intently as the light from the chandelier faded from the young woman's brain.

When the two were satisfied that she was dead, Gallucci again tied the rope off. Michelle and Tony unfastened one another's robe, allowing the garments to drop to the cave floor. Now nude, they embraced. Tony lifted Michelle in his arms and placed her upon the stone altar. He joined her there. Under the dangling body, they were soon fully engaged. Afterwards, Michelle rested in Tony's arms. She turned her head and gazed in silent delight at the still form hanging above them.

Suddenly, Charles Worthington opened the door in the wooden wall.

"What the hell is going on?" he shouted at the two.

Startled, Tony and Michelle moved for their discarded robes. Charles's eyes were fixed upon the lifeless body of the woman hanging below the chandelier.

"You killed the woman?" the banker asked.

Charles moved quickly to untie the rope. Tony answered, as she was being lowered.

"You have to admit, that her beauty can be more fully appreciated in this suspended manner."

"Michelle, take her legs and guide her gently back upon the altar," Charles instructed.

"I'm through with her," Michelle coldly answered.

Gallucci stepped forward and assisted in the effort to lower the body. He carefully took her legs and positioned her in a less elegant fashion than earlier. Charles's face twisted when he caught sight of the burns on her shoulders. His eyes blazed like fire, as he spoke.

"You desecrated this poor woman. Our purpose is to appreciate and celebrate exceptional qualities in humanity. I would believe her primary quality to be her exceptional body, which she has voluntarily shared with us. But you have taken that one thing from her!"

"She's now at rest," replied Michelle. "Do you really think the money in that bowl would have done anything to change her pitiful life? Her purpose was to serve her betters, and she has. We've simply ended her miserable existence."

"You ...are in agreement with his actions?" questioned Charles.

"She served the group well earlier, and she later provided Tony and me with a little additional fun," Michelle coldly answered. "Doesn't a farmer have the right to do what he wishes with his livestock?"

"A good farmer doesn't abuse his animals. You two were trusted to see about her welfare. A woman who volunteers to do this is to be treated with care."

"What kind of woman volunteers to be rendered unconscious for a while, to be paid a minimum of a thousand dollars?" challenged Tony. "Do you really think this happens?"

"I now understand that you've been taking women against their will," said Charles. "You were not allowed to do this."

"I was to provide an attractive young woman, who would be rendered unconscious while participating in our ritual," replied Tony nervously. "You gave no further instructions. I performed as ordered."

"I suggest that you take care regarding how you address me. I expect respect and honesty. You both fully understand the rules, and I made your responsibilities clear to you. Torture and murder have no part in our group, and you've brought disgrace upon this place and upon our order. You were to make sure she was securely loaded in the box and placed on the truck. The money was to be placed with her. The men in the truck have been waiting outside. I returned because you were late. You two have created a situation."

"It's not a problem," stated Tony. "I carefully vetted this woman. She won't be missed. There are no living family members, and the body will disappear. There will be no evidence."

"You took an oath; we all did," replied Charles. "We are not to engage in physical violence upon another human being, except in self-defense. We are to be overseers of those less capable than ourselves, not brutes. Put her in the box and get her on the truck. You'll be dealt with later."

Charles watched, as the other two placed her inside the box. Tony returned the rope to the cabinet in the wall. Afterwards, Tony and Michelle exchanged their robes for the clothes earlier worn that evening. The three informed the men in the truck that it was time to retrieve the box. Two long poles were slid through openings in the box, and the men from the truck lifted the box upon their shoulders by use of the poles. Charles moved to the switch mounted on the wooden wall and extinguished the light of the massive chandelier. As he exited the cave, he found Tony waiting for him at the gate. Michelle had already returned to the house.

"Secure the gate," Charles ordered. "I issued you a warning when I found you placing another unconscious volunteer in a disgraceful position. These women are not to be toyed with, and they're certainly not to be harmed or killed. You've gone too far. You'll be dealt with."

"I have the painting you asked about," whispered Tony. "Silence can be golden. It will be a personal gift."

"Aren't you afraid you're digging the hole deeper by trying to buy me off?" asked Charles.

"Business is business," replied Tony. "Life consists of exchanges. I'm offering an exchange."

"These actions can't be ignored," stated Charles.

Silence filled the night air, as the two men made their way back to the house. They found the other four seated at the dining table. Glasses of expensive wine were being filled by Michelle. Her haunting eyes spoke seduction, as they locked onto those of Charles. The banker was having none of it and returned a cold stare. He and Tony took their places at the table. The rest of the evening proceeded as usual.

"We'll talk more about that painting," Allen heard Tony say to Charles, as the gathering ended.

Charles said nothing. From the open front door, Allen and Michelle watched the others leave the estate.

"What took you two so long tonight," he asked his wife.

"The girl began to move, and Tony had to administer more sedative," she lied. "We couldn't risk her becoming conscious inside that cave."

"I'm surprised Charles didn't mention it before leaving. A miscalculation like that is a real point of concern."

"I'm sure he's confident that Tony will make the necessary adjustments next time," Michelle replied.

———— • ● • ————

ALLEN ADAMS felt tired when he entered the home after returning from business meetings in Belgium. He found his wife silently sitting in the den, staring out a window.

"It's always good to be home," he announced.

"We need to talk," she replied, still gazing out the window.

"What about?"

"I want something different."

"Different?"

"I want to move to England, to be near my sister.'

"I don't think that's possible."

"I've spoken with Charles, and everything is arranged."

"You talked with him, before discussing this with me?"

"Charles leads the gathering. He's determined that I can go, and that you'll remain here."

"I'm shocked that Charles would agree to this."

"He is perfectly fine with it. Charles assures me that he has found another member who can take my place. Other than the gathering, you and I no longer have a personal relationship. I don't expect that to change. You should feel somewhat relieved. This should offer you more freedom."

"It's been years since we were close, but there is more to your move than the membership of the gathering. What about Megan?"

"Megan will never be a part of the gathering. You know that. She's smart, but she's soft."

"She's our daughter. You're willing to leave her?"

"She'll have you. The little imp still latches on to you like a baby monkey. I thought she would be strong enough to stand on her own, but I've come to understand that she's different. You and I are of the right stock, but it just didn't work with her. Maybe she was influenced by other kids while attending the boarding school. I'm not sure what went wrong, but she's weak."

"What brought this on?" Allen asked.

"I don't answer to you. I went through the proper

channels. I elevated my wishes to Charles, and he's good with it. It's settled. I leave next week."

"We need to have Megan over. We need to give her some kind of explanation."

"You can do that. I'm done with this place."

"I'm calling her tonight. I'll invite her to come for dinner tomorrow."

"Do what you wish. I've got plans for tomorrow night."

"Are you wanting a divorce?"

"That's not necessary. I'll still have access to the account. You don't have to worry. Charles oversees it, and he'll make sure it remains stable. He'll make the arrangements for the new member of the gathering. Everything will be fine. You know that married couples aren't a requirement for membership."

"I thought you were good with our current membership,"

"I'm tired of it, and I don't want to pretend. I'll be happier in England."

"You aren't even that close to your sister. What's this really about?"

"Like I said, I don't answer to you. Make whatever adjustments you need for your own happiness and let this go. You're perfectly capable of handling this with Megan. Tell her that we haven't been good for some time, and that I have elected to spend the rest of my life near my sister. That explanation is as good as any. She'll have to deal with it. Megan needs to grow up. This may be the thing that forces her to do that. It could be the best thing for her in the long run. But I doubt she'll ever become the woman we hoped for."

"This doesn't make sense."

"Stop with this!" Michelle blurted. "You're acting like a child. What's wrong with you? You're one of the most powerful men in the country. What's with this show of weakness? There's no need for you to pester me about this. I had planned to leave next week, but I've now decided to leave tonight. I don't want to listen to any more of your whining. I'll have the rest of my things moved to England next week, but I'm gone."

Michelle stormed from the room, went upstairs and packed an overnight bag. As she later reached for the front door of the house, she felt Allen's hand on her shoulder.

"I wish success for you," he calmly stated.

"That's more like it," she replied. "You were beginning to concern me. I'll let you know when I arrive in Europe. I wish you much success, as well."

Allen watched as she drove away. Besides the cooks and cleaning crew that were present during the day, he was now alone at the massive estate. He retreated to his study and placed a call to Megan on his cell.

"I would really like for you to come for dinner tomorrow night," he offered.

"I have a long day tomorrow," she replied. "I'm sure I'll be pretty tired."

"Would you mind it if I dropped by your apartment tonight?"

"Are you alright? This isn't like you. Did something happen in Belgium?"

"I'm fine. We just need to talk."

"Sure. I'll put some coffee on."

"That would be great. See you in a little while."

Within an hour, Allen Adams set foot in his

daughter's apartment for the first time. Megan threw her arms around his neck and kissed his cheek.

"What's wrong?" she pressed.

"How about the coffee?" he suggested.

Seated at the table, he told her of Michelle's departure. Tears filled his daughter's eyes, as he laid out a story about a failed relationship with his wife. He told her that they had stayed together for several years for her sake, but things were now over.

"She didn't even tell me goodbye," sobbed Megan.

"This was probably difficult for your mother, and she wanted to make a clean break. Your mother deals with things much differently than I do. Give it some time, and maybe she'll have you visit England."

"This is just so weird. Why so abrupt?"

He held his daughter tight and stroked her hair just as he had done when she was small. He thought about the loneliness he would face, and the impact Michelle's departure would have on his daughter. At that moment, he determined to spend more time with Megan. On Allen's drive back to the estate, he pondered the question asked of his daughter. *Why so abrupt?* He quickly placed a call on his cell.

"Charles, what can you tell me about Michelle's leaving?"

"What did she say about it?" questioned Charles.

"She acknowledged that our marriage has been a formality for years, but I'm very surprised that she has abandoned the gathering. Should I be concerned?"

"I don't believe she's your concern anymore."

"What does that mean?"

"Just that. If she leaves our group, she will be the concern of others."

"I'm not sure that I like the sound of that. We've been married for a number of years, and she's still Megan's mother."

"Does your daughter know?"

"I told her tonight that Michelle is leaving me and moving to Europe. She's pretty upset. I don't understand why Michelle wouldn't tell her goodbye. It's not right."

"I can't help you with that."

"Michelle told me that you have her replacement selected for the gathering."

"I do. I'm taking care of the group. Do you question whether things are in hand?"

"No. I guess I'm just a little frustrated with the situation. Why so sudden? Her behavior is baffling."

"She has the right to ask for relocation. She is free to do that."

"I'm talking about a relationship with her daughter. I thought there was more to it. I thought my wife had a deeper relationship with Megan than to simply run away without giving her a word. Don't you see that as odd behavior?"

"I've granted her relief from our gathering. What she does outside the gathering is up to her. Maybe this is for the best."

"For the best? I thought you were a friend."

"Allen, make no mistake. I am your friend. As your friend, I'm going to let you in on something."

"Like what?"

"Since Michelle decided to leave us, I've decided to do some reorganizing. I don't believe the Galluccis are a good fit for us any longer. I have replacements for them, as well."

"What? Good fit? They've been members for almost two decades, and suddenly they're not a good fit?"

"I've been observing them. I believe it's time for the change."

"What brought this on? You're talking about replacing half of the gathering. Has this reorganization been cleared?"

"You know that it has. Don't say a word of this to anyone before our next gathering. Your wife's departure is a significant personal change for you, but I view you as a pillar within the gathering. I'm providing this additional information to you because I trust you."

"Are the Galluccis leaving Atlanta, as well?"

"I can't tell you more about them. Each member has the right to know that they can share with me in confidence. You know that. The Galluccis are entitled to personal privacy."

"Thanks for telling me this before the next gathering."

"I can't tell you more. Be assured that I'm more of a friend than you know. Use the next few days to get some needed sleep. Change can be a little stressful for anyone, even someone of your credentials and capability."

When Allen reached his home, he found a bottle of very expensive bourbon on his front porch. It wore a red bow, and a card lay under the bottle. It read, "From your friend."

Allen carried the bottle and the card into the kitchen and poured some bourbon into a tumbler. The house was remarkably quiet.

Something has happened. I'm willing to bet it

occurred during the last gathering.

Tumbler in hand, he stepped into the night air surrounding his back porch. He flipped on the row of lights that led to the cave entrance. His brilliant mind raced as he made his way toward the locked metal gate. He unlocked the gate and entered the cave. In the dressing room he examined all six of the red robes. Moving through the door of the large wooden wall, he operated the switch of the massive chandelier. Stepping into the center of the chamber, he momentarily studied the patterns of light cast on the cave ceiling by the elegant fixture. He fervently examined every object in the room. Returning to the wooden wall, he opened three built in cabinets before opening the one containing the forty-foot rope.

Why a noose, and who would have left it tied like that before putting it in the cabinet?

He left the cave and exchanged the tumbler for a large zip-lock plastic bag from a kitchen drawer. Moving into the study, he took an old pocketknife from a desk drawer before returning to the cave. Carefully holding the noose over the opened bag, he scraped particles from the inside of the noose with the pocketknife.

Owning a lab can be somewhat handy. Let's see where this noose has been.

Chapter 16
Table

MISTY CALLAHAN WAVED goodnight to the manager of the bar as she reached for the door of the establishment. In route to her apartment, she placed a call on her cell to Russ Blevins.

"Hello…" he answered, attempting to clear his head from a deep sleep.

"I want to know if they got that Gallucci guy."

"What? Has something come up?"

"No. I was just wondering if they had him."

"Do you realize what time it is?"

"Of course. I just got off work. It's 2:00 AM."

"Well, my alarm will wake me for work in two hours. It's 4:00 AM here in Atlanta. This couldn't wait a couple of hours?"

"You said that I could call you any time. Right?"

"OK. No, Gallucci is still under investigation."

"Well, I remembered something."

"Like what?"

"Ricky told me once that he ran across a weird magazine while he was doing yard work. It was in the leaves he was raking."

"What kind of magazine?"

"A pervert magazine."

"I'm not following you."

"It was one of those magazines showing naked women being tortured. You know, a magazine for perverts."

"What did he do with it?"

"He tossed it in a bag with other trash that he picked up from the yard. I'm thinking that probably means the guy is a pervert."

"If it was found in the yard, it could have come from a number of places. It could have been dropped by someone else who had been doing yardwork. If there had been a recent storm, it could have been blown onto Gallucci's property."

"Are you trying to defend that guy?"

No. I'm just saying that there's no way anyone could prove it was his."

"Next question. Is TJ Turner in jail?"

"He's in custody, but he hasn't gone to court. The FBI is hoping they'll get more information out of him."

"Will you call me the minute that he's put in jail?"

"Sure - anything else?" Russ asked, trying to hold back a yawn,

"No. Go back to bed, sleepy head."

"At this point, I'll probably just go in early."

"Your boss should be impressed. See, I'm helping you get in good with your boss. You should be thanking me."

Russ tried in vain to get back to sleep. After twenty minutes, he showered and left his apartment. Two hours later, he called Jason Bagwell and told him about

Misty's call.

"If the magazine's his, it fits a pattern of burning young women before killing them," said Jason. "It's sort of just another log on the fire linking him to those women."

"So, you think it's important information?"

"Nothing that would hold up in court, but it helps eliminate others. It helps narrow the investigation's focus on Gallucci."

———•●•———

ALLEN ADAMS OPENED the elegant oak door of his home Saturday morning. Charles Worthington had arrived to discuss the new members and plan for an upcoming gathering.

"You look a little tired," commented Charles. "Maybe you should put on some coffee."

"It's already on," replied Allen.

"I look forward to the upcoming gathering."

"It won't be the same."

"I believe you'll find the three to be excellent additions," replied Charles.

"I've heard nothing from Michelle. Have you?"

"I've heard through others that she's fine."

"That's good to hear."

"Now, about the order of the gathering. To begin with, I'm changing the practice of having a volunteer placed upon the altar."

"I thought that might be the case, since it was Tony's duty to find a volunteer. I'm glad you didn't pass the responsibility on to me."

"It was Tony's idea, to begin with. I've decided it's

best to exclude those who aren't members. That practice carried risk and complicated matters."

THE FOLLOWING MORNING, Megan was pleasantly surprised to see her father take a seat next to her just before the church service began. She leaned her head onto his shoulder, placing her hand on his. A wide-eyed Sam sat speechless.

"Who is the young man seated beside you?" asked Allen.

"This is Sam Blaylock, a good friend of mine," answered Megan.

"It's nice to meet a friend of Megan's," Allen said, extending his hand in the direction of Sam.

"It's good to meet you, sir," replied Sam, giving the hand a firm clasp.

"Sam and I have become close friends, Dad," Megan said.

"Is that so?" Allen asked, his eyes shifting to Sam.

"Yes," Megan answered, giving her father's arm a squeeze.

"Do you two have plans after the service?" asked Allen.

"Nothing special," said Megan, giving Sam a glance.

"I would love to have you both come to the house for lunch," offered Allen.

"Thank you, sir," Sam said.

"I think we have some catching up to do," Allen said to his daughter.

"In that case, I believe the lunch should be limited

to you two," said Sam. "I've got things to look after."

"I would very much like you to come over, if you can make the time," Allen assured.

"I'll be there," replied Sam.

Sam's mind raced throughout the entire service. If pressed about the subject of the pastor's message, he would have been a total blank. It struck him that his relationship with Megan had taken on a new perspective.

Good Lord! Allen Adams just invited me to lunch.

Sam entered the front door of the home with Megan on his arm. Allen escorted them both to the kitchen.

"Recently, I've somewhat abandoned the dining hall," he told Megan. "Would you mind if we eat at the kitchen table?"

"These chairs are really nice," commented Sam.

"They're fairly old," replied Allen.

"I would say they're from the 1920's," said Sam. "However, the table's a lot newer."

"You seem to know something about furniture," said Allen.

"My mother refinished furniture," answered Sam. "The workmanship in these oak chairs is special. What happened to the original table?"

"Come with me," Allen said. Turning to his daughter, he added, "I'm going to steal Sam for a few minutes."

He led Sam downstairs that took them to the basement.

"The table is in pretty bad shape," said Allen, as he turned on the basement lights. "I plan to use it as a workbench."

"Do you have a flashlight?" asked Sam.

Allen walked over to a cabinet and brought one out. Sam took it, dropped to his knees and moved under the table. After less than a minute, he bounced back to his feet.

"Sir, this can be restored," announced Sam. "This is tiger oak, blackened by a hundred years of beeswax and dust. This is genuine tiger oak, made from a very large tree. You won't find oak tables made like this today. They now join smaller oak pieces to make a tabletop, sometimes covering it with veneer. This is made from one piece, and it's the real thing. Some cheaper furniture made during that time was made to look like tiger oak. It was an art form, but made from cheaper wood."

"The wood is almost black," said Allen.

"I can restore this," said Sam, his eyes beamed.

"What would you need?"

"I can pick up everything needed, but what I really need is ventilation. Do these transom windows open?"

"Absolutely. You're willing to work on this table?"

"I would love to. I believe I could knock this out in a weekend – or at most four days. This table deserves to be brought back to life."

"Brought back to life. That's a nice way of putting it. Sam, you're welcome to give it a try."

"Sounds good!"

"Hungry?"

The two made their way up to the kitchen, where they found Megan helping the cook set the table.

"What are you two up to?" she asked, catching Sam's broad smile.

"Sam thinks he can restore the table that goes with

these chairs," said Allen. "I told him that he's welcome to give it a try."

"I could start next weekend, if you wish," offered Sam.

"It will have to wait until another weekend, I'm afraid," replied Allen. "I'm having guests over next weekend."

"The Charles Worthington crowd?" asked Megan.

"I'm afraid so," answered Allen.

Acknowledging the meal on the table, Allen thanked the cook and asked that Megan and Sam take a seat. Before sitting, Sam ran his fingers over the hand carved back of the oak chair.

"Would you mind if I asked God's blessing on this food?" Megan asked her father.

"By all means," he replied.

All heads bowed. Megan asked for God's blessings on the food and for the cook who prepared the meal. She then gave thanks for time together with the men in her life, her father and Sam.

"Sam, it's obvious you know furniture," observed Allen. "What's your profession?"

Sam took a breath. He knew that the subject would come up and had resigned himself to experience a disapproving look from arrogant eyes.

"I work construction jobs," he replied.

"Honest work," replied Allen. "How did you come to that profession?"

"My father left us when I was about ten," answered Sam. "My mother got work refinishing furniture, and I helped her from time to time. I got a taste of working with my hands and found that there's something gratifying about seeing a thing made or improved."

"Instant gratification!" said Allen. "I look forward to seeing what you might do with that table. How is your mother?"

"She passed away," answered Sam.

"I'm sorry to hear that," said Allen. "My mother died when I was young. Megan never had a chance to meet her. Did your father come back around?"

"No sir."

"You don't have to be formal. You can call me, Allen, if you wish."

"How about Mr. Adams?" asked Sam.

"If that pleases you," replied Allen. "I'm interested in hearing about how you two met."

Megan stepped in and told him about her class from church visiting Sam's neighborhood, and how Sam took her up on the invitation to church. She told him that since that time, they had become close friends.

"What do you think about that church," Allen asked Sam.

"When a beautiful woman asks you to go somewhere, a man has to give it serious consideration," answered Sam.

Allen chuckled.

"As for the church, the people seem to be OK. To be honest, I like spending time with Megan. The place isn't all that important."

Allen watched his daughter's eyes when Sam spoke. He clearly understood that they were not just close friends. Sam became more at ease as the afternoon wore on. About 4:00 PM, Megan suggested that she and Sam leave. When she gave her father a hug, she noticed that he seemed to hold her tighter than he had in years.

"The table – I'll find a suitable weekend," said Sam, as they made their way to Megan's car.

"Sounds good," replied Allen, echoing the words Sam used while in the basement.

"Is he usually like that?" Sam asked, as they drove away.

"No! He isn't… not with my friends. Something is different. Maybe he's lonely since my mother left."

"Do you think he was sincere with me, or is this some kind of tactic he uses while sizing someone up?"

"I'm not sure what's going on with him. I'm as surprised as you are. He's normally like that when he and I are alone, but he's usually much different with other people. My father's always in charge of things when he has people around that he doesn't know well. He projects an authoritative air that intimidates most people. He treated you a lot like he treats me when we are alone. I've not seen him do this before."

"I'll take him at face value, unless he proves otherwise."

———— • ● • ————

"TJ HAS AGREED to wear a wire," Jason informed Russ, on a call.

"Really? Do you trust him?"

"I do. Somebody higher up in the FBI has approved him for witness protection if he gains useable information."

"He ought to be pretty happy about that."

"Oh, he's good with the witness protection – but he's pretty apprehensive about wearing the wire. I need for him to meet up with Tony Gallucci."

"That could be a dangerous meeting for him."

"We need the details on the drug transportation racket. He's perfect for the sting."

"Would you give me a call after things go down?" asked Russ.

"That's a promise."

<hr>

THE FOLLOWING FRIDAY evening, Tony Gallucci felt a strong tap on his shoulder as he exited a restaurant.

"Remember me?" TJ asked.

"TJ," Tony nervously answered. He glanced around; his bodyguards were nowhere in sight.

"I need work, and you owe me," said TJ.

"Owe you? You killed one of my guys and left the other one really messed up. You're nuts."

"You burned my fingertips. Didn't you understand that I would take that out on someone? When you put those two idiots on me, it was like an invitation."

"OK… so, you want to call it even?"

"My fingers hurt for a long time. You still owe for doing that to me. I need money, and I need it fast."

"If you're serious, I have something for you this weekend."

"I don't want to hurt people."

"It's nothing like that. It's just loading trucks. That's the best I can do, right now."

"How much?"

"Seven hundred and fifty."

"You owe me."

"OK, a thousand – but that's tops. That makes us

even – and it's just because it's you. Look at it as a down payment for future work."

"Cash."

"Of course. You know the warehouse. Be there at 11:00 this coming Friday night."

TJ dropped into the seat of his car and drove to an apartment. There, waiting for him, was Jason Bagwell.

"Did you get the conversation?" asked TJ.

"We got it," replied Jason. "We had the van parked just down the street. They got it loud and clear."

"So, I get witness protection now?

"You've got to finish this. If you don't show up at the warehouse, Gallucci might think something's up. We have to catch him at this stuff."

"I might catch a bullet."

"You'll have a vest, if you like. I'll personally see to it. As soon as the trucks are loaded, and you're paid – get in your car and come back to this apartment. If the bust is successful, the deal for witness protection will be in process."

"I'd like to propose another idea," suggested TJ.

———•◆•———

FRIDAY NIGHT, TJ wore a large winter coat as he walked through the familiar door of the warehouse. He knew that the vest only offered a fraction of the needed protection. Upon Gallucci's orders, a bullet could easily be put in his head. The man at the door of the warehouse was almost as large as TJ.

"Get a move on," the man ordered. "We need to be out of here in thirty minutes."

TJ and two other men quickly loaded the truck.

Packages of heroin were taped to the inside of several traffic barrels. After being stacked onto other barrels, it was impossible to spot those containing the drugs.

"You worked up a sweat with that coat on," said Gallucci, as he approached TJ.

"I don't plan to be in here long, and it's cold outside," he answered.

"Take the coat off."

"Just pay me, and I'm out of here."

"Take the coat off," ordered Gallucci.

The big guy at the door and the other two who loaded the trucks surrounded TJ. TJ removed the coat.

"Now the shirt."

"What is this?" asked TJ.

"Take off the shirt."

TJ removed his shirt, exposing the vest.

"You wore a vest?" bellowed Gallucci.

"I have things to do after I leave here. I need my money, and I need to meet someone. I don't like the thoughts of being shot. Can we leave it at that? Listen. I don't have a lot of time. Just give me the money. I can't afford to be late."

"I thought you were coming back to work for me."

"I have to settle some debt, that's all. In case, you didn't notice – I've had to find work in other places over the past few months. I just have to settle things, that's all."

"Do you need someone to go with you?" asked Gallucci.

"No, that would be a bad idea. I need to settle this myself."

"Put your shirt on."

TJ put his shirt and coat back on, and Gallucci

tossed him an envelope.

"After tonight, you work exclusively for me," Gallucci said. "Get it?"

"Got it."

TJ left the warehouse and got into his car.

"Follow him," Gallucci ordered the man who guarded the door.

The man followed TJ for more than two miles to a city park. He watched him get out of his car and approach two men. There was a short conversation, before TJ handed one of the men a stack of bills. One man held a flashlight, while the other counted the bills. The flashlight went off, and the man with the money slugged TJ in the face. After the two men walked away, TJ returned to the car and drove away. Gallucci's man who followed him placed a call.

"Tony, he was telling the truth. He met two guys at a park and handed them money. One of them roughed him up a little, but it wasn't serious ...OK, I'll be back soon."

Back at the apartment, TJ was greeted by a smiling Jason.

"We got him," said Jason.

"You arrested Gallucci?"

"We went after the trucks, and we confiscated an estimated twenty million dollars' worth of heroin. We left Gallucci alone."

"You're letting him go?"

"I wouldn't say that. It was loaded at his warehouse, and it was on his trucks. He'll be brought in for questioning, but he'll probably say that it was his guys who did this without his knowledge."

"But we have him on the wire..."

"We do, and the wire was used to plan the bust with the trucks. I've been instructed to use it only as a last resort."

"I'm not sure that I understand."

"Some people will be very disappointed in Tony Gallucci's failure to deliver. I expect people to come out of the woodwork. We've upset the apple cart, so to speak."

"You want to use him to take down the entire operation."

"That's the plan."

The conversation was interrupted by a call on Jason's cell. He excused himself and stepped out of the room. When he reappeared, he wore a look of shock.

"What's up?" asked TJ.

"That was about your witness protection deal."

"And?"

"And there are strings attached…"

"I knew it!" shouted TJ.

"Calm down, big man. Somebody must like you."

"Spell it out."

"You'll be given a new identity, but there's a condition. They want you to work for the FBI as a field agent."

"What?"

"That's the word I used when I was told. I asked, 'What the crap? TJ Turner, an agent?' Don't ask me. I don't understand it. If you want the deal, your training starts next month."

"You're really full of it. This isn't funny."

"No, it isn't funny. I'm being straight up. They want you as a field agent. The FBI is impressed with your military record, and they said you performed well in the sting. It beats the heck out of me, but this is for real. What do you say?"

"You're kidding me, right?"

"This is no joke. From what I understand, this came down from somebody way up in the FBI stratosphere. You caught the attention of somebody."

"You're serious. OK. I think I could do this. Yeah. Tell them that I'm in."

Chapter 17
Return

"'AS A PRISONER for the Lord, then, I urge you to live a life worthy of the calling you have received. Be completely humble and gentle; be patient, bearing with one another in love. Make every effort to keep the unity of the Spirit through the bond of peace,' as stated in Ephesians 4:1-3," said the pastor at Megan's church.

"So many people define unity among people as being one in thought," the minister continued. "Here we are told to have unity of the Spirit. The prior scripture gives us insight into what that means. We are to be completely humble, gentle, patient, and bearing with one another in love. This far surpasses finding people with whom you agree. It's a much deeper relationship. It's more like the relationship of family members, and it doesn't require agreement of thought."

Standing in the church parking lot after the service, the words of the pastor caused Megan to think about members of her family. Her eyes turned to Sam.

"The minister talked about a deeper love that is common in family relationships. How could my mother just leave me without saying a word?"

"I don't have an answer to that question," replied Sam. "I can't imagine my mother doing such a thing."

"I can't begin to tell you how that makes me feel. I'm fine when I'm busy at work, but it really eats at me when I'm alone in my apartment."

"You didn't deserve that kind of treatment."

"Maybe I do. Why else would she have done it? She spoke with my father before leaving, but totally ignored me. To be honest, I know deep down that I've never lived up to her standards."

"Who lives up to the expectations of a mother? Normally, a mother's love reaches beyond failures of a child. What your mother did wasn't normal. It wasn't right, by a longshot."

"I think my father's love is more like that. It's clear that I haven't turned out to be the person he hoped for, but I believe he still loves me."

"Your father is twice the father I had. It seems like he loves you the way a father should. Your mother…your mother has serious problems."

"You never met my mother. How can you know what she's really like?"

"I listen to you, and I compare her to other mothers I've known. I had a mother who loved me. I have no questions about her love. I had friends whose mothers loved them. I know what's normal, and any mother who leaves a child forever without seeing them first isn't normal. I don't need to meet your mother."

"She sent my father a letter. He let me read it. I know it was from her, because I recognized her handwriting."

"Did it say anything about you?"

"No. She didn't really have anything personal to say to my father. It was mainly about moving money from one account to another. I don't get it. She never behaved like that when I was growing up. This is a huge departure from the person I thought I knew."

"Have you talked to your father about it?"

"I mentioned it, but he told me that there's a lot about my mother that I don't know. He refused to elaborate on what he meant. My father won't talk about her, but I know he's troubled about it."

"Her behavior would trouble any sane human being," said Sam.

"So, maybe that's it. Do you think she's suffering from a mental condition? That might explain it."

"I'm certainly not a shrink, but her actions are nutty. I'm glad that you still have your father."

"He's pretty busy, but he often makes time for me. I think he's more like what the minister talked about. Bearing one another in love – I think he does that; at least for me. Why didn't my mother appreciate that in him? I don't understand why she left."

"Maybe one day you will, but you can't help what other people do. I can't explain your mother's behavior. There IS something that I do know."

"What would that be?' asked Megan.

"I know that we need to make sure Dora doesn't find out that your father is alone," Sam jested, attempting to lighten the conversation. "She'd be all over him! He might want to move in with you just to be safe."

Meagan chuckled at the thought of Dora hitting up on her father. However, the brief smile couldn't hide the deep sadness in Megan's eyes. Sam couldn't imagine what she was going through. She rarely talked about it, and he always made himself available whenever she wanted to. Suddenly, her demeanor brightened.

"I want to go back to the cave this weekend," Megan said. "My father plans to have that group of people meeting at the house again – you know, the adult only gathering."

"What?" questioned Sam.

"We need to find out what that group is doing inside the cave."

"There is a slim chance that I could have a stable relationship with your father, and now you want me to jeopardize that by sneaking around a place he's restricted by gating it off?"

"Our research gave us information about those statues," reminded Megan. "As we thought, the easiest were the two Greek gods. One is Hermes, and the statue of the woman and child are the goddess Demeter holding Plutus. I found out that the Chinese statue is a figure of Caishen. There were some who believed that he bestowed wealth on people who were devoted to him. It seems like most of these statues are of gods which have something to do with wealth. The real mystery involves what those people are doing in that cave. We know very little about what goes on in there."

"I've heard it said that a little knowledge is a dangerous thing."

"That's Alexander Pope," said Megan.

"I know. 'A little learning is a dangerous thing; drink deep, or taste not the Pierian Spring'."

"I can't believe you read Pope!"

"I don't really. I read that back in high school, and

it sort of stuck with me. The guy was right."

"Well, now I want to know more."

"What?"

"I want to drink deep, like the poem says. I want to learn more. I want to find out why those statues are there, and I want to find out what those six wealthy people are doing in that cave every other month."

"You honestly think that your father is in a cult that worships weird gods of wealth?"

"No. Not a chance. But I have to understand what is going on, and it means going back into that cave while those people are there."

"You're the daughter of Allen Adams," replied Sam. "He'll love you, no matter what. As for me… a powerful man like him could come after me with who knows what. If I'm caught inside that cave, it could turn out bad for me."

"Where's your sense of adventure?"

"It's an adventure each time I step into my neighborhood. I've got plenty of it."

"I don't want to do this by myself. Are you going to leave me to do this alone?"

"You're unbelievable," Sam said, burying his eyes in the palms of his hands. "OK, I'll go with you…. I must be out of my mind."

"It's going to fun!" Megan shouted, as she gave him a quick hug.

Unnoticed by the two, the man in a silver sedan watched them from a distance. He placed a call on his cell and followed as they exited the church parking lot.

———•●•———

LATE SATURDAY AFTERNOON, Megan and Sam positioned themselves inside the cave behind a rock resting just a few feet from the statue of the Indian elephant god Ganesh. Just after 5:00 PM, Megan, stood from her spot behind the boulder.

"What are you doing?" asked Sam.

"I've got to pee," answered Megan. "I'm going back behind that big rock over there. Don't look and put your hands over your ears. I don't want you to hear either."

"Good grief."

About fifteen minutes after Megan returned to her place beside Sam, they heard the door in the wooden wall creak open. Each of the six people coming in single file through the door wore a red robe and a mask, and each carried a torch. One held a small silver platter in the left hand and the torch in the right. They placed the torches in six fixtures mounted to the wooden wall. One of them opened a drawer built into the wooden wall and took from it a bottle. They all moved away from the wall. Each person opened the front of their robes. Warm light from the torches revealed nude bodies. There were three males and three females.

Five formed a circle around the one holding the bottle, who proceeded to pour a substance into his right hand and then rub it onto the skin of the others. A distinct smell of camphor oil filled the cave air. Megan was astonished when she recognized one of them forming the circle. She immediately turned her eyes away.

Oh God! That's my father's exposed body. I shouldn't be seeing this!

From physical mannerisms, she recognized the

man with the bottle as Charles Worthington. He then held the bottle high in the air, as the others rubbed oil from their own bodies onto his. Those surrounding him stepped back, and he returned the bottle to the drawer in the wall. Charles waved his arms, and the group closed their robes. He then moved slowly to the switch which was mounted on the wall. Suddenly, the place was ablaze with light from the massive chandelier. Megan and Sam froze momentarily, and then ducked behind a large stone. Sam slowly eased his head from the side of the huge rock. Reaching back, he took hold of Megan's shirt sleeve. She quietly placed her head beside his.

They watched six robed figures remove their masks and surround the stone altar. Somewhat like the church sacrament of communion, Charles served the people with what appeared to be dumplings with a spoon from a silver platter. Handing the platter and spoon to his wife Olivia, she served him before placing the utensils on a small stone table near the right wall of the cave.

A large bronze bowl containing a pile of cedar strips rested on the stone altar. Charles set the cedar strips on fire with a long match. As the small fire grew, the six took a couple of steps back. One removed a piece of paper from her robe, moved close to the altar, and placed the paper in the fire. She returned to her place. With hands pressed together over their hearts, and with each head gently bowed, the six chanted in unison.

"We remember men and women of excellence in times long past who reached exceptional levels of power and wealth. You are our brothers and sisters. We attempt to see with your eyes. Salutations to your gods and goddesses of wealth, food, property, children, health, happiness, power, beauty, luck and sacredness - who sit holding golden pots overflowing with grain and gold - who form the strength of the cosmos - whose eyes hold the promise of contentment and fulfillment - who are restless - but generous to all who appreciate these gracious gifts. We remember the yearnings of those with exceptional qualities and look to the day when those thirsts will be satisfied."

Another woman removed a piece of paper from her robe and placed it in the fire. Each time one of the six placed paper into the fire, the chant was recited in unison. They afterword stood momentarily in silence, watching as the flames diminished. Then small cups of red wine were poured onto the fire to extinguish it. Sam and Megan were almost mesmerized as they watched.

Suddenly, Charles Worthington shouted, "apscindo!" The six turned their backs to the altar. Charles then shouted, "apprecor!" The six walked away from the altar in separate directions.

Fear flowed through Megan, as a robed woman approached the nearby statue of Ganesh. Sam took Megan's shoulders and eased her down onto the floor of the cave. He curled himself in a spooning position just behind her and placed fingers from his left hand against her mouth. The person stood before the statue in silence for several minutes. A call from Charles rang out loudly, "reverto!"

The woman turned and slowly walked back to the altar. The six positioned themselves facing the altar with bowed heads. Sam and Megan slowly raised their heads just above the boulder to have a better view. Charles moved away and used what looked like a small iron pot fastened to the end of a wooden pole to extinguish the torches that lined the wall. Each person donned their masks and took an unlit torch from the wall.

Finally, Charles solemnly spoke, "finem sum." The group reverently exited through the door in the wooden wall. The light from the chandelier was turned off by Charles before he exited. The two, still hiding behind the rock, were left in utter darkness. Megan blindly reached out for Sam, taking hold of his shirt. He moved closer and took her in his arms.

"Was that weird, or what?" whispered Sam.

"I'll tell you something else that was weird," replied Megan. "For years, the same six people have met here. Tonight, I had no clue who three of those people were. I recognized my father, Charles Worthington, and his wife Olivia. I've never seen the other man and two women."

"You didn't expect to see your mother, did you? She's in England."

"No, but I expected to see Tony and Mia Gallucci. Neither attended. It seems a woman has replaced my mother, but it appears the Galluccis have two strangers standing in their place."

"Do you think they left the country, as well?"

"I'm going to find out, and if they haven't – I'd like to know why they've been replaced."

"How do you plan to do that?"

"My father will be out of town next weekend. I can't wait until he returns from that trip. I plan to pay him a visit Wednesday evening. I'll casually ask him if the Galluccis are still close friends of his. It's not an unusual question. When a couple splits up, friends often feel uncomfortable hanging around. I'll ask if they've been coming by to comfort him after my mother's departure."

"You need to be careful poking around with this stuff. I have a feeling these people have more secrets than just the ritual we witnessed tonight."

"Like you said – I'm his daughter, and he'll love me no matter what."

"Do you think it's safe to go over to that altar?" asked Sam. "I want to see what they were burning."

"I don't have a clue what this group does during the remainder of the evening. I'm a little afraid they'll return. We left sleeping bags and a change of clothes on the other side of the water filled passageway. My vote is to go back, put on dry clothes, and warm up in those sleeping bags. I think we should come back in the morning."

"Getting warm sounds pretty good, but I want to see what's inside that bowl," replied Sam.

"Now, look who's talking about taking risks! Where did all that talk about having a good relationship with my father go? What if he comes back?"

"Once I put on those dry clothes, I don't plan on crawling through water to come back to this room. I have to check out that bowl. I'll be quick."

Sam turned on his headlight. Before Megan could say another word, he was off. She heard the squish of water from his shoes as his made his way to the stone altar. He stood for almost a minute shining his light into the bronze bowl before reaching in and taking something. Megan became nervous.

What does he think he's doing?

Suddenly, he scurried back to the large rock where Megan hid. He dropped down beside her.

"Are you crazy?" Megan asked.

"You were the one talking about having a sense of adventure."

"What were you doing?"

"I found a note that wasn't completely burned," Sam said. "It's wet with wine, but I can read some of the writing."

Shining the small light onto a piece of partially burned wine-stained paper, Sam read out loud, "I wish for Mia's s." The sentence was unfinished.

"This has to be a prayer for Mia Gallucci," said Megan. "I told you she wasn't here, tonight. Something must have happened to her or Tony. Why didn't my father say something to me? I realize this is some bizarre secret ritual in the cave, but I've had conversations with the Galluccis for years. It's obvious that something has happened to them, and they and my mother were replaced by three others."

"The group didn't wait long to replace them," commented Sam.

"Apparently not. What is really going on here? For years, I was told that this is an adult only weekend – spent with close friends. Half the group of so-called friends have been replaced, almost overnight. I've always felt my father was honest with me, but this doesn't add up. What other weird things is he into? I can't believe he's mixed up with people offering prayers before stone images of ancient gods. What the heck?"

Suddenly, they heard muffled voices. Sam turned off the headlight just before the door in the wooden wall opened. Again, the giant chandelier illuminated the room in the cave with light. Allen Adams and Charles

Worthington dumped the burned sticks and ashes from the bronze bowl into a large trash bag. As Charles held the bag, Allen used a paper towel to remove wine drenched sand stuck to the bottom of the bowl. He closely examined the inside of the bowl.

"Looks clean," pronounced Allen.

"Pour in clean sand and leave the bowl on the altar," ordered Charles.

Allen exited through the door and returned carrying a bag of white sand. As he poured in the sand, Charles tied up the trash bag. Together, they left through the door and turned off the chandelier.

"I told you," Megan whispered in the dark. "You could have been poking around that bowl when they returned!"

"It worked out," Sam replied, again turning on his headlight. "Are you ready to get dry and warm? How about the two of us getting into one bag? A little snuggling would help warm things up."

Megan socked him in the shoulder with her small fist.

"Something about this cave turns you violent," teased Sam. "Then again, maybe this is just a pre-snuggle ritual. You must be getting into this stuff."

"Agghh!" exclaimed Megan.

Sam pulled her close and kissed her. Megan slugged his other shoulder and pushed him. He took her again into his arms, and then ran his right hand under her shirt. She shoved him backwards.

"What was that for?" Sam asked.

"Your hands are freezing!"

"Are you going to henpeck and beat me all the way back?"

"Maybe."

Sam grabbed her again, this time placing his right hand on her rear. She kissed him, and then ran her cold left hand under his shirt. "OK, you're right…cold hands." Sam said, stepping away. "We just need to be glad that it's not supposed to rain tonight. That passageway could fill to the top easily during a heavy rain."

"Lead on, Caveman," Megan replied.

With headlights bathing their surroundings, they made their way around the large rocks on the cave floor. The ceiling soon became low, forcing them to their knees.

"This water hasn't gotten any warmer," Sam said, crawling into the half-filled passageway.

"Stop being a baby."

Once they reached the sleeping bags and backpacks, Sam turned on a lantern. The two stripped out of the wet clothes.

"I vote that we forget the dry clothes and just get into a sleeping bag," suggested Sam.

"No way! Just put your clothes on, and hurry."

"We can zip the two bags together, and sleep in one big bag. Watch."

A naked Sam quickly unzipped both bags and then connected them by zipping them together. He stood and turned toward Megan. By this time, she had donned panties and a shirt.

"How do you like it?" he asked.

"I'm not getting in any sleeping bag until you get dressed."

"Body heat works better without clothes," explained Sam. "It's science."

"If you don't put on some clothes, I'm going to give you a lesson in science."

"Anatomy?"

"Yes, a dissection," Megan answered, pulling a knife out of her backpack.

"I can't get over how violent caves make you. Maybe this place causes you to revert to some kind of cave woman. Don't expect me to grab you by the hair and drag you around this cave. I'm not that kind of guy."

"Clothes. Now."

"If you insist. However, it's a fact that body heat is generated more effectively in a sleeping bag when you aren't wearing clothes. Just trying to be helpful, but am I appreciated?"

Sam reached for dry jeans and slid them on.

"Happy?" he asked.

"Shirt!"

"OK."

Sam slipped on a shirt, then got inside the expanded sleeping bag. Megan fastened her jeans.

"Waiting on you," he said, smiling.

"I'm too tired to make you separate the bags," she said, sliding in beside him.

Sam extinguished the light, and Megan rolled her body away from him. He then moved into a spooning position behind her.

"What do you think you're doing?" she asked.

"I'm telling you - this will warm us up pretty quick."

"Just keep your hands to yourself."

"Yes ma'am."

"Go to sleep."

"I've got to say, you're incredibly beautiful," Sam said, pressing his body against hers.

"We're in a cave. It's dark."

"Earlier, there was plenty of light. I've got to say that your body is as attractive as your face. I've got one word for what I saw before you put on those clothes."

"What?"

"Perfect," Sam whispered.

Silence filled the cave. In total darkness, Megan's eyes blinked. She reached for his hand, took it in hers, and pulled it to her abdomen. Within moments, she was asleep.

Chapter 18
Tony

TONY GALLUCCI PLUNGED his spoon into a decadent dessert at his favorite restaurant. Outside, a man waiting in a black SUV received a call on his cell phone. Once the call ended, he turned to the second man in the vehicle.

"We're done here; we've been told to leave."

As the SUV pulled away from the restaurant, the second man sat in disbelief. Sensing an intense stare from his right, the driver spoke.

"Yeah, it's what you're thinking."

Through a front window of the establishment, Tony's eyes caught the movement of the vehicle leaving. He nervously laid his spoon beside the half-eaten dessert and motioned to his chauffeur that he was ready to leave.

"I need to stop by warehouse six," Tony instructed, as he dropped onto the black leather rear seat of the car. "It shouldn't take more than thirty minutes. Just stay in the car until I come out."

Once there, Tony entered a code that he shared

with only those he most trusted. He rifled through several files in his office, placing some inside a black briefcase. As he opened a desk drawer, he heard the opening of the warehouse door.

"Is that you, Ricky?" shouted Tony.

Stepping out onto the warehouse floor, his countenance dropped. The huge door was now closing behind six men.

"I've been given some unsettling information," stated Tom Richards, a high-level drug distributor.

Tony tried to answer, but words were stuck in his throat. He quickly surmised that someone had given Richards the code to the warehouse door. Now the father of a girl he had tortured and killed was standing before him with five of the worst kind along-side him. Tony had lived on the edge, feeding his twisted appetites for violence and depravity, knowing that he was enveloped by the protection provided by the gathering. His greatest fear gripped his soul. Protection had been withdrawn. The five men accompanying Richards surrounded Tony Gallucci, and his face became pale.

— • ● • —

WEDNESDAY MORNING, Allen Adams glanced down at the gold ring on his right hand while seated in his study. With the index finger of his left hand, he rubbed the engraving of six intersecting sixes forming the shape of a flower. Smooth red rubies filled the circular non-intersecting portions of the sixes. On the right side of the engraving was the number sixty-three in small lettering. His gathering of six was the third residing in the United States, the US being the sixth region of the world-wide organization. His thoughts were interrupted by a call from Charles Worthington.

"I have bad news concerning Tony Gallucci. He was found dead in one of his warehouses this morning."

"Dead?"

"He was hanging from the rafters by a rope."

"Suicide?"

"Doubtful. He was also stripped of his clothes and his body had suffered multiple severe burns. I'm sure he was killed. It's apparent that he'd made enemies over the years."

"How's Mia taking it?"

"I paid her a visit before calling you. She has family in New York. I've made arrangements with a gathering in that region. She should be fine."

"Fine? Her husband was tortured and murdered!"

"She's a much stronger person than you may know."

"You're still involved with Mia's welfare. I take it that Tony was the real problem here."

"You're right."

"How about Michelle? Was she a problem?"

"It was her choice to move to England. I've released her from the gathering, but I made sure that she still has protection."

"Thank you. Who killed Tony?"

"I don't know who's responsible."

"I'm guessing protection was withdrawn from him."

"That's about the size of it. I don't really want to talk about it in detail. I'll tell you that Tony became messy, and he posed a risk. I told you that he wasn't a good fit. He became involved in things that he shouldn't have, and his murder shows that he wasn't living in a manner that's expected of a member of the gathering. This wasn't a random mugging; someone came after him for a reason. Indications are, this was personal."

"As a member of the national gathering, I'm sure you have access to more information about members than I would. I trust you. I'm sure the removal of protection was based on sound information."

"Protection is rarely removed. He no longer deserved the benefits afforded to members. Unlike you, he was a selfish man."

"What do you mean?"

"You know the rules concerning each member being assigned three protectors. A married couple can combine their six in any manner they see fit. Michelle kept her three, but you've shared one of yours to protect Megan. Tony wasn't the sharing type of individual. He insisted that he was to have four, leaving Mia with only two."

"I'm sure that the Galluccis had an understanding regarding the matter," noted Allen.

"Let me put it plainly. Tony felt he needed the additional protection because of his personal behavior."

"He also traveled a lot, purchasing and selling fine art."

"You always try to give our members the benefit of the doubt, and you present them in the finest manner. That's a quality that I admire about you, but it's also important not to be naïve about failings of fellow members."

"I don't know the details, but I often suspected that

Tony had a few shady deals on the side.”

“Shady deals on the side don’t usually result in someone being tortured and murdered.”

“Point taken.”

“With Tony’s death, will come investigations of his associates. I believe it’s best that we move our gathering to a new location. I’ll handle everything, including the removal of the statues from inside the cave.”

“Nothing is the same with our gathering,” Allen sighed.

“True. As the elite of the world, distractions like this should be embraced with strength and grace.”

“I plan to attend Tony’s funeral.”

The two discussed the funeral arrangements for several minutes. After the call ended, Allen wept. For almost two decades, he and Michelle enjoyed a friendship with the Galluccis. Now, everything was different. He understood that Tony had become a liability for the gathering, but the man’s sense of humor had helped Allen cope during the years when he and Michelle grew apart.

The guy could really be funny, and I can’t count the times when laughter eased tension. He helped me to not feel so alone. However, in truth, I had little detailed knowledge about his activities outside the gatherings.

Allen locked up the mansion and retreated to the bedroom. There, he pulled back the exquisite cover and sheet on his bed. The house was so quiet that he felt as if he was in a sealed tomb. He had every material thing a man could dream for. If he wanted the attention of a woman, there were plenty of beautiful women who would be willing to entertain his most vivid desires.

However, he was wise enough to understand the vanity of a playboy's life. He yearned for something real, something that money couldn't buy.

Megan. She's really all that matters. Without her, my existence would be a shallow and lonely monument to an idea. She doesn't have the cunning and ambition in which I've prided myself throughout my life, but she has something else. She has an eye for something that goes beyond words and deeds. Megan sees things in people. She saw something in that young man she brought to the house. When he talked about salvaging that table, I caught a glimpse of something deeper about him. If she hadn't seen it first, I would have never paid that young man any mind. He would have been just part of the scenery, simply an object among thousands or millions. Because he mattered to her, I took notice. Her mother counted Megan as unworthy, because her drive and raw ambition is nothing like hers. In truth, my daughter has insight that I never dreamt to be of value – until now.

Allen pulled the covers across his chest. He thought about Megan, about the fact that she had now become the only stable aspect of his life. Allen Adams understood the fragility of wealth and power. Members of the gathering could come and go. Protection of the most powerful in this world could be withdrawn in a heartbeat. His success couldn't guarantee that a woman would remain at his side, even the mother of his child. Megan was blood of his blood. She was more than that. She was dedicated to him; she truly loved him. Allen was more determined than ever to spend more time with her.

THE NEXT MORNING Allen received a call from his lab.

"Mr. Adams?"

"Speaking."

"The results from the examination of the contents of that bag are final."

"And…"

"I found a mix of fiber; like those of a hemp rope. But I also found human skin cells."

"What do you make of it?"

"The skin cells were from all three layers of the skin. The epidermis, the dermis, and the hypodermis. You can tell a lot from human skin cells."

"Like what?"

"I could tell that these are cells from a young woman."

"Interesting."

"The combination of all three cell layers, and the hemp rope fiber leads me to a notion."

"Meaning?"

"I would put money on this being evidence that a young woman was hung by a hemp rope."

"That's concerning," stated Allen. "What leads you to believe that someone was hung?"

"It takes a lot of pressure to force all three layers of skin to adhere to rope fibers. The most common is when someone is hung by the neck. Because the person struggles during the ordeal, the rope works deep into the skin. I'm sure this would be the conclusion if a police lab examined the contents of the bag you provided."

"Thank you," replied Allen. "I appreciate your discretion in this manner. You understand that these findings remain between the two of us."

"I do, sir,"

"You've been a big help. I may contact a member of law enforcement. Thank you."

Allen placed a call to Charles Worthington.

"Charles, I found something in the cave that bothers me."

"What would that be?"

"In one of the cabinets in the wall, I found the old hemp rope that we used to suspend the chandelier before we used cables."

"So, what concerns you?"

"It was tied to make a noose. Who did that? It had to be one of us."

"Mind if I come over for dinner tonight?"

"I would like that."

"Is six too early?"

"Six o'clock is perfect."

———•●•———

CHARLES WORTHINGTON stepped into the elegant foyer of Allen's home, at precisely six o'clock that evening. Allen excused the help for the evening as soon as dinner was served.

"What can you tell me about the rope?" asked Allen.

"Like I told you, Tony Gallucci posed a risk," explained Charles. "He tied the noose, and left it tied when he put it away."

"You know what I'm getting at – why was a noose tied?"

"You seem focused on things that may prove to be of discomfort to you."

"Please tell me."

"The reason your wife moved away, and the reason Tony was removed from the gathering, is because I caught them hanging that young woman who last lay on the altar."

"They hung her?"

"Yes."

"They killed her?"

"Yes."

"Dear God!"

"As your friend, I've attempted to save you further pain."

"The young woman volunteered to be sedated and was to be paid handsomely!" blurted Allen.

"It turned out that Mr. Gallucci wasn't always using volunteers. He had a very nasty streak that proved he was not the caliber of person who should be a member of our gathering."

"And Michelle?"

"I'm thinking that it wasn't her idea, but she was engaged in the activity."

"Why would she do something like that?"

"She's your wife. I'd think you'd know her best."

"Apparently, I've been oblivious. Murder! Cold blooded murder. They committed murder on this property. Who does this?"

"Allen, I've told you that I'm a better friend than you know," said Charles. "I hope you now understand. I could have made things very difficult for Michelle.

When I talked with her, she confessed that her relationship with you was badly damaged. She asked if she could move to England to be near her sister. I agreed to that arrangement. As I've told you, she has protection. That protection is a courtesy to you, my friend."

"Thank you. The move was difficult enough on my daughter. If something more serious happened to Michelle, Megan would be devastated."

THE FUNERAL OF Tony Gallucci seemed like something out of a Godfather movie. Mia, dressed in an abundance of black lace, took on an appearance of elegant gothic fantasy. Two refined older men, dressed in expensive black tuxedos, escorted her to the family seating area of a huge Catholic church. She looked as if she had stepped out of the pages of a fictional novel about a wealthy widow. Allen had never seen anything like it. The solid bronze casket remained open, and Mia paused at it before kissing her deceased husband. Tony's unburned face revealed nothing of the grotesque burns that scarred his body. After she was seated, several members of the Gallucci family placed small items in the casket before stepping before a lectern to tell stories involving Tony. Each was dressed in black. The priest performed rites, followed by a Catholic mass. The liturgy was conducted entirely in Latin.

In the back row of the church sat an older woman. Dora Hitchcock's late husband's construction business had caused him to be in connect with Tony Gallucci's when building large projects. Though the status of the

Hitchcock family was far below that of the Galluccis, the two men had formed a relationship. Enough so, that Dora understood that Tony was not a man to be trifled with. Out of love for her dead husband, she had come to pay respects.

As Mia was being led away at the conclusion of the mass, she stopped where Allen was seated.

"Please accompany us to the gravesite," she requested.

"Of course," replied Allen.

At the gravesite, the family gathered as the casket was lowered into the vault. Each member tossed a flower onto the lid of the casket, before walking away. Mia was the last to leave, and she again was escorted by the two older men. Allen stood a respectable distance from the immediate family. She spoke something in Italian to the two men, and then approached him alone. They gave Allen a nod before walking to an awaiting limousine. Mia moved close to Allen and took his hand. Her large dark eyes were almost mesmerizing.

"Out of everyone, you were the best friend to Tony," she said.

"He was special," replied Allen.

"Tony didn't show you the respect you deserve, but I took notice. He had potential, but you live as one of your standing should. I'm sure you've been informed that I am moving to be near family in New York."

"I have, and I wish you much success."

"You will always be a welcome visitor."

"As will you," Allen replied.

Mia kissed him on each check, and then kissed him on the lips. She gave his hand a quick squeeze before joining the two men at the limousine. Allen was somewhat puzzled.

I didn't expect that. Maybe it's an Italian custom.

Allen approached his own car and found a finely dressed Italian man waiting near it. The man gave him a nod, and then opened the front door of Allen's car. He stepped aside and motioned for Allen to take his seat. Positioned behind the wheel of his expensive sedan, Allen studied the man. The Italian nodded again, shut the door, and walked away to join a couple of other finely dressed men.

This is an interesting family. I'm sure there is much that I didn't know about Tony.

<hr>

RUSS BLEVINS PLACED a call to Misty Callahan.

"I hope you're calling to tell me that TJ Turner has been sentenced to life in prison," Misty began.

"Tony Gallucci is dead," Russ said.

"Wow! I didn't expect that!"

"He was murdered. Someone left him hanging from the rafters of one of his warehouses."

"Murdered?"

"I'm sure he crossed the wrong person. Anyway, you don't have to worry about him anymore."

"How do they know he was murdered? Maybe his conscience got to him, and he hung himself."

"The police are sure. I'm not going into the details. I just wanted you to know that you have nothing to fear from the man."

"What about that guy named TJ?" asked Misty.

"You don't have to worry about him either. If you

have further concerns, you're welcome to give me a call."

"If you're ever in Colorado Springs, drop by the bar."

When the call ended, Russ took a sip from his coffee, and then placed a call to his friend in the FBI.

"Jason, I told Misty Callahan about Gallucci."

"I bet she was glad about him being bumped off," replied Jason.

"I wish this case hadn't taken the life of Frank Reynolds. His killers are out there and they're probably killing for someone else now that Gallucci's dead."

"We're tracking Ricky Taylor. I think he's our link to Frank's killers. I plan to follow through."

"Do you think you'll get the guys that killed Frank?"

"I've made it a personal task."

"Call me if you get them."

"You know that I will, friend."

———— • ● • ————

A WEARY ALLEN ADAMS returned from his trip. Before unpacking, he moved down the stairs leading to his basement. A broad grin spread across his tired countenance, as he flipped on the light switch.

"Wow! Would you look at that."

His hand graced the top of the linseed oil finish that brought to life the ancient grains of wood that had been hidden under decades of blackened bees wax and dust.

This is incredible! That young man, Sam, knew what he was talking about. It's a shame that there aren't more like him, whose trained eye sees past what is hidden from most. Similar to his view of furniture, Megan sees hidden treasures in people. She has an unusual eye, and I should never forget it.

He pulled his cell from his jacket and gave his daughter a call.

"I'm back."

"I missed you, Dad."

"I saw the table."

"What did you think of the job Sam did?"

"It's beautiful. Your friend was right. He did a fabulous job."

"I'm glad you like it. I'll tell him."

"I would love to have you two over for lunch again this Sunday."

"We'll be there."

"Don't you think you should check with Sam first?"

"He's with me. I gave him a thumbs up, indicating your approval of the table. You should have seen him. The more of the black stuff he removed, the more excited he got. He worked like a maniac all weekend on it."

"I like your friend, Sam."

"He likes you, too," Megan replied, giving Sam a wink.

— • ● • —

WHEN SAM AND MEGAN entered the kitchen of the Adams estate, they found the refinished tiger oak table had replaced the one that had been there.

"Good job, son," said Allen, extending his hand

toward Sam.

"Thank you, sir"

"Stop with the sir stuff, OK?"

"Mr. Adams, it was a pleasure to reveal the grain in this table. You have something special here."

"I believe my daughter has found someone special in you. I would have paid more than a thousand dollars for work like this."

"Please don't try to pay me," replied Sam. "I enjoyed doing this."

"I had men from a moving company carry it up from the basement," said Allen. "It looks even better in the light that comes from the windows."

"Looking at the chairs placed around it, maybe I should clean them up a little," said Sam.

"You're welcome to do whatever you want to them," said Allen.

"The table looks perfect in here," added Megan.

The cook placed the last item on the table, and the three took their seats. Soon, they were eating, talking, and laughing.

"This is such an unusual table," Sam said. "There is so much detail in the carvings on the sides and legs. Where did it come from?"

"It was given to me by an old friend," replied Allen. "I'm not sure of its origin. In his line of work, he ran across a number of items found at auctions."

"Which friend?" asked Megan.

"I recently attended his funeral. Tony Gallucci."

Chapter 19
Removal

THREE WEEKS AFTER Megan and Sam last entered the cave, they returned while her father was away on business. While examining the stone altar in the center of the room, they were startled at a loud pounding on the other side of the large wooden wall.

"Quick! Cut the light from the chandelier!" warned Sam.

Megan hastened to flip the switch. With their headlights beaming, the two rushed to hide behind a large rock.

"Turn off your light," whispered Sam.

In darkness, they placed hands over their ears to lessen the sounds of heavy beating on the wall. A section of the wall dropped to the cave floor, and a ray of light painted one of the stone statues. Sam's head rose to view the activity.

"Get down," whispered Megan.

"Somebody is breaking down the wooden wall," replied Sam.

A muscular man burst through the door in the wall

and flipped the switch that caused light from the chandelier to fill the room. With crowbar in hand, he began removing the interior portion of the wall. The loud pounding was replaced with a steady creaking of wood loosened by crowbars. Soon, light from outside the cave added to that of the chandelier. Megan and Sam carefully watched four men busily converting pieces of the dismantled wall into wooden crates. From a trailer that had been pulled behind a truck, a gasoline powered forklift roared to life. It slowly rolled down a ramp and lumbered toward the gaping mouth of the cave. Men used crowbars to lift the base of a statue to enable the forks of the machines to slide under it. The statue was secured to the forks of the forklifts with straps.

Megan and Sam watched in amazement as statue after statue were placed in the crates. Plastic wrap was placed around each stone image of an ancient god, and then a compound was poured into the crates. The compound created a foam that rose and hardened, filling the gaps between the statues and the inner walls of the crates. As the crates were sealed, they were gingerly tipped onto their sides. Carefully, the men loaded them using the forklift. Padding was used to fill the gaps between the crates and the truck sides. The engine of the forklift became silent, and the men abandoned it to approach the stone altar.

"I'm not sure what to do about this!" spouted one of the men, throwing both hands in the air.

"Maybe one of those quarry saws could be used to cut it from the cave floor," suggested another.

"Those saws are huge." added a third. "Those machines couldn't be moved into this cave."

"We'd have to bust up a good bit of the bottom of this thing to break it loose." said the first man. "I'd better make a phone call."

As he walked to the cave opening to get a strong signal, the other three continued to offer up ideas about removing the altar. After several minutes, the one with the phone returned.

"He said to come back later with a jackhammer and break up the cave floor beneath it."

As the discussion continued, Sam and Megan quietly crept further back into the cave. Suddenly, one of the men extinguished the light from the chandelier. In the immediate diminished light, Megan tripped over a rock on the cave floor and let out a scream.

The chandelier became alive with light again, and the men rushed toward the direction of her voice. They found Sam escorting a limping Megan. One of them grabbed her arm. Sam immediately, slammed his right fist into his nose. Two other men took hold of Sam, while another moved to hold Megan in his powerful grasp.

"I'm going to break your neck!" shouted the man with blood running from his nose.

Holding his broken nose with his left hand, the large man grabbed Sam by the neck with his right hand – lifting him off his feet.

"Not here, man!" yelled the one holding Megan. "We're going to put them in the truck and deal with them later. Put him down."

"You better not let go of this little piece of crap!" blurted the wounded man, still with a hand on Sam's throat.

"You know I don't call the shots," the other one

replied. "We're paid well, but not to make the big decisions. Go back to the truck. Get rope and find something to blindfold these two."

The man reluctantly released Sam to the two who held him and headed back to the truck. Megan and Sam were forcefully taken to the area of the stone altar by the other three men.

"You have no idea what you're doing," warned Megan.

"Bring some duct tape!" the leader called out to the man still collecting items from the truck.

Megan let out a loud scream, and the leader stuffed a huge hand over her mouth. Sam twisted in vain, failing to free himself from the hold of the two men.

"If you hurt her, I'm going to break your face!" Sam shouted.

"I'm the one who stopped a guy who is twice your size from choking the life out of you," the leader stated calmly. "You both should shut up, or I may decide to let these guys shut you up permanently."

The man with the damaged nose dropped ropes and a roll of duct tape at the feet of the leader. Megan's mouth was taped first, and then Sam's.

"I've decided against using a blindfold, but I'm going to secure your hands behind your back," said the leader. "If you cooperate, I'll leave your feet free."

He tied their hands and ordered that they be placed in the back of the truck carrying the statues. They were positioned with their backs against opposite interior sides of the truck and were tied to metal rings fastened to the sides.

The doors of the box truck were closed, and the forklift was loaded on the trailer pulled by the second truck. Two men entered the cabs of each truck.

"These men are robbing my father of his statues," Megan thought in the darkness of truck. *"What's going to   happen   to   us?"* The diesel engines of the trucks started almost in unison. Her thoughts were interrupted by the lurch of the truck moving forward. The bodies of Sam and Megan trembled with the vibrations of the vehicle. As the trucks moved down the driveway of the estate, a silver sedan met them headlong. A tall lean man stepped from the car and stood in front of the lead truck.

"Deal with this guy," the leader told the man seated beside him.

The large man excited the truck cab and moved toward the fellow standing before them.

"I think you had better move your car," the muscular man told him.

The lean man caught the eye of the leader, and then raised his right fist – displaying a gold ring sporting a green emerald. The leader cut the truck engine, stepped out and approached the man standing between the truck and the silver car. Viewing the emerald and gold ring at eye level, the leader instructed the big man to move back and stand beside the truck.

"I'm sorry sir," the leader spoke to the man standing in his path. "Do you have something for us?"

"I have something for you, idiot," replied the lean man. "You have two people tied in the back of your truck, and one of them is the daughter of Allen Adams."

The mouth of the leader dropped.

"I'm going to tell you what is about to happen," the lean man stated. "I'm going to move my car to the street, and I'm going to watch you release these two people from this truck. You're to untie them, and you are going to apologize to them both. I need to see them freed and your lips moving before I'll move on. You will then be on your way. If I see further disrespect given to these two people, I will immediately place a call to Mr. Adams. Do you understand?"

"Yes, sir," answered the leader.

The man returned to his silver sedan and moved it to the street. The two men raced to the rear of the truck and opened the rear door.

"There's been a mistake," the leader announced to Megan and Sam. "This man is going to quickly release you. I apologize. I am sincerely sorry."

As the other man climbed into the back of the truck and began to release Megan, the man with the wounded nose jumped out of the cab of the second truck. He stomped up to the leader and shouted.

"What are you doing?"

"Shut up, and get back in that truck," answered the leader. "This is the daughter of Allen Adams."

"You can let her go, but not that little jerk!"

The leader slammed his large right fist into the already damaged nose of the furious man. Blood gushed from his face, and he dropped to his knees.

"Get back in that truck," the leader instructed.

Megan and Sam were untied, and the duct tape was gingerly removed from both. The man helped Megan to the ground, and Sam jumped to the ground from the truck.

"I apologize to you, too," the leader told Sam. "Please step aside, sir, and we will be on our way."

"What, and let you steal from my father?" accused

Megan.

"We were under orders to remove the contents of the cave," replied the leader. "We made a mistake. We didn't realize that you are the daughter of Mr. Adams, and I'm sorry."

Megan and Sam stepped onto the lawn beside the drive. The silver sedan slowly moved down the street. The trucks moved down the driveway of the estate.

"A penny for your thoughts," said Sam.

"I'm not sure!" blurted Megan. "I'm confused."

"I think it's really weird, and I also think we need to get the heck out of here."

"Regardless of weirdness, I've always felt secure at this house. I've never even considered being attacked at my father's estate."

"Let's talk as we walk to my truck. We left it at the park down the street. I'll feel a little better once I start that engine."

"At first, I thought my father had found a buyer for the statues. I became suspicious when they began talking about removing the limestone altar. That isn't an artifact. It's obvious it was formed from the rock in that cave. Who would want that?"

"I don't want to be near any of it," replied Sam. "We should pick up the pace."

"I'm not convinced that my father ordered them to take those statues. But if those men are stealing, why would they let us go and issue an apology? None of this makes sense. Why would someone who steals from my father be concerned about offending his daughter?"

"If they are removing these items for your father, do you think there's a chance that they thought we were trespassers on your father's property? Maybe they thought we were thieves?"

"How do you do that?"

"Do what?"

"Make sense of things so easily and present it in such a simple and rational manner. How do you do that? You have to be just as weirded out as I am, but you seem to still be able to keep a clear head."

"That explanation just seems like the only one that makes sense. But I could be wrong."

Chapter 20
Josh Wells

TJ TURNER WAS given a new identity as Joshua Andrew Wells. The granting of the new identity had to wait for an optimal situation; part of which was the death of a vagrant man with no family who roughly matched TJ's size. Such a homeless man in New Jersey was burned to death while sleeping in an abandoned building that caught fire. The FBI swapped the identity of the dead man with TJ's, and records were altered to better fit the situation. The dead man became TJ Turner, and Joshua Andrew Wells was born via the magic of manipulated databases.

TJ had only one sister. The two siblings had experienced a difficult childhood. Now living in Seattle, she was the polar opposite of him. She viewed his choice of going into the military with contempt and was even more disgusted when he was arrested. TJ's sister perceived him to be another version of their violent father. This father left them when TJ was ten and was now serving a life sentence in a maximum-security prison for murder. She permanently broke off all relations with both men.

His sister was informed of his death, and falsified records indicated that he died after rushing into a burning building. The FBI told her that a witness stated that her brother mistakenly thought he heard screams inside the place. Even with the false story of TJ's heroism, she seemed uninterested. No one attended the cremation of what remained of the unrecognizable body.

TJ's mother had passed away from a drug overdose while he was serving in Afghanistan. He learned of her death a week after she was buried. When back in the States, he had asked his sister to visit the gravesite with him. She wanted nothing to do with him. After his separation from the military, he found himself to be alone. In this new identity as Josh Wells, he began to form relationships with those in law enforcement – particularly with agent Jason Bagwell and his former probation officer Russ Blevins. They knew him better than anyone – as both TJ Turner and Josh Wells.

Josh felt somewhat saddened by the fact that someone had to perish in order for him to gain a new identity. Nevertheless, he focused on his newfound opportunity and completed the FBI field training in twenty weeks. His first assignment was in Denver, Colorado, and he welcomed the relocation.

"Agent Wells, how do you like your first assignment so far?" asked Jason, while the two stood outside a Denver restaurant.

"Six months ago, I would have never envisioned this," Josh answered. "It's like I've lived two lives, and I like this one better."

The ringing of Jason's cell interrupted the

conversation. Raising his hand to the big man, he indicated to the new agent that he needed to take the call. When the call ended, he spoke to Josh.

"I have a surprise," said Jason.

"What?"

"Turn around."

Josh turned to find Russ Blevins standing behind him. The huge new agent wrapped his powerful arms around his old probation officer and lifted him from the ground.

"Easy, boy!" Russ shouted.

"I can't begin to thank you for standing by me in Canada," said Josh.

"Are you used to the name, yet?" asked Russ.

"The last twenty weeks helped," answered Josh. "No one knew me by any other name. After having an instructor scream the name 'Wells' at me for weeks, I believe I may be programmed."

"It may take me a little more time, but I've been hammering myself with the new name while you were in training," replied Russ.

"It is so good to see you," said Josh. "Both of you."

"Hungry?" asked Jason. "I'm buying."

"You FBI guys must make a buttload of money," said Russ. "There's no way I could afford to feed this big lug."

"This 'big lug' scored the highest in a decade on the written exams," informed Jason. "Josh has a big brain to go with the body."

"Who did you threaten to beat senseless if they didn't give you the answers?" Russ asked the new agent.

"I'm telling you, this guy is one of the most

intelligent candidates coming through the program in a decade," said Jason.

"For real?" asked Russ.

"You can call me Professor Wells, if you wish," jested Josh, while jabbing the shoulder of the probation officer.

"Several titles come to mind, but none of them contain the word professor," replied Russ.

"How long are you in Denver?" asked Josh.

"Just a for a couple of days," answered Russ. "I have to get back to Atlanta. Gallucci wasn't the only bad apple in the area."

———•●•———

THE FOLLOWING WEEK, Josh decided to pay Misty Callahan a visit at the bar. As soon as the huge man caught her eye, he motioned for her to come over. Misty approached.

"I would like to talk with you about a fellow named Ricky Taylor," Josh said.

Josh showed her his FBI credentials, being careful not to let anyone else see it. Misty pulled him aside.

"He's ancient history," she informed Josh, rolling her eyes. "I really don't want to talk about him."

"Gallucci's gone, but the people working for him aren't. I just need a few minutes of your time."

"Why are you people determined to pester me while I'm at work?"

"I understand that you get off at 2:00 tonight. I can come back then. I'll walk you to your apartment."

"Whatever."

After Josh left the bar, another waitress took Misty

aside.

"Who was that guy?"

"A big lug who thinks he can give me a hard time," replied Misty.

"That guy's a hunk! I wouldn't mind him giving me a hard time."

"Shut up. You're ridiculous."

As Misty left the bar, she found Josh standing on the sidewalk about fifteen feet from the door. She pretended she didn't see him and tried not to make eye contact. From her left, an inebriated customer approached her.

"Hey, sweetheart – can I walk you home?" the man offered.

"I'm tired, and I don't need you to walk me home," she replied.

"You don't really want to be alone do you?" he persisted.

"Yes. I do want to be alone."

The man grabbed her rear end with his right hand. Misty spun around and kneed him directly in the groin. The man groaned and doubled over.

"Go home," she wearily instructed.

"That's some move you have there," said Josh.

"It's an acquired skill," Misty replied, still not making eye contact.

"I'll walk with you, but I won't hold you up."

"I saw the badge," she replied. "Wells, is it?"

"Josh Wells. When was the last time you spoke with Ricky Taylor?"

"It's been months. I've already talked with the law about that. Why are you pestering me?"

"We strongly believe that he's been in contact with

Tony Gallucci, and Gallucci had something to do with you being kidnapped."

"I hear that guy is dead.… Wait…are you saying that you're sure Ricky had something to do with me being grabbed?"

"We believe there's a connection. You knew Ricky, Ricky knew Gallucci, and Gallucci wanted you kidnapped. There are connections leading right to you."

"I've heard that line before. I don't believe Ricky would do that."

"You broke it off with him, right? I also understand that he had become more violent."

"Yeah, but he still wanted to get back with me. I'm tired. We need to call it a night. My apartment building is right here, and I'd like to get some sleep."

"Here's my card. If you hear anything that would cause you concern, please give me a call."

"It says you're in Denver," she said, reading the card.

"I work out of the Denver office. I'm in a lot of places, but plan to keep an eye on you."

"An eye on ME? You're serious. What's going on?"

"I'm just trying to put a few pieces together concerning you and Gallucci. I'd like to know why he was interested in you."

"No reason! We had no relationship! Why can't you people understand that? Hold on…you seem familiar. Have we met before?"

"Not to sound egotistical, but I'm not one of those guys that people tend to forget."

"I can buy that. How tall are you?"

"Six-six."

"You look like you work out."

"I try to keep my weight around two-sixty."

"Well, you're not fat. You carry two-sixty pretty well."

"At six-six, I sort of stretch it out."

"I need to get to sleep."

"I won't take any more of your time. If you think of something, or if Taylor contacts you, please give me a call."

———•●•———

THE CHIMES AT the front door of the estate belonging to Allen Adams announced that he had a visitor. Charles Worthington stepped into the eloquent foyer to share news with his friend.

"I've just purchased a hundred acres of mountainous property in northeast Georgia, and I want you to look over my building plans."

"I'd be glad to," replied Allen. "Let's step into the kitchen, where I can pour us both a glass of wine."

Charles spread out blueprints showing the elevation and interior views of the planned house. The two sat in chairs on one side of the oak table, each sipping wine.

"It will have a basement that requires the removal of a substantial amount of limestone rock. As you can see, I'll also have them chisel out an additional sixteen by thirty-four room coming off of it. The builder believes that it will be a storm shelter, but I plan for it to be our new gathering place."

"That looks to be a little over an hour from here," said Allen.

"It's a beautiful place. It'll be a perfect getaway for me to share with my wife Olivia, but it will also accommodate the needs of the gathering."

"You're taking all of this expense on yourself?"

"We've used your hospitality long enough. I'm the leader of our group, so it's time I provided the place for gathering."

"It looks really nice."

"The basement will have what appears to be a built-in safe, the door being well over six feet tall. A spin dial will unlock a the steel door, which will actually be the entrance to the back room. They'll have to bring in a jackhammer type of machine to carve out the limestone, and I plan to have the room reinforced with decorative concrete pillars and beams."

"Will it accommodate the statues?" asked Allen.

"Those statues have been relocated to a different site. The ceiling of this room will be only twelve feet in height, so I've ordered new statues to be made from bronze. Each will be six feet tall and will rest on two-foot-high polished granite blocks."

"Are you sure the current stone statues won't fit?"

"Esthetics. The room is much smaller than the cave, so the larger stone statues would overcrowd it. I'm glad to do this. As you can see from the plans, a large oak wardrobe will be placed right here to hold our robes and other ceremonial items."

"I'm sure the room will be eloquent."

"Bronze oil lamps will illuminate each of the bronze figures. An altar will be made of the same granite. On it will rest our bronze bowl for offering thoughts and wishes on paper. You understand that, at some point, the practice of rituals involving statues will cease."

"I understand," replied Allen. "We're paying homage to those who came before us. When the time is fulfilled, we will be focused on the future. What is the purpose of the rest of the basement?"

"As I'm sure you've assessed, most of the structure will not be associated with the needs of the gathering. This portion of the basement will be used as a wine cellar. I want to move a significant amount of my collection there."

After Allen watched Charles drive from his estate, he moved to his personal computer in the study. Within twenty-five miles of Charles's property, Allen found three other large properties for sale.

I have no intention of making such a long round trip for this gathering. I should build a cabin in the vicinity.

———•●•———

AGENT JOSH WELLS WAS quickly thrown into the deep end, as he was placed on a team planning a human trafficking raid. During the execution of the raid, he was shot in the left shoulder while taking out three criminals and freeing several sex slaves. The wound required surgery, and during his recuperation in the hospital he was decorated. Jason Bagwell was present for the presentation and stuck around after the others left.

"I thought you aced your training," said Jason. "You know, the training about how not to get shot."

"Funny," replied Josh. "But not that funny."

"All joking aside you did a great job. Those girls

may now get a taste of freedom. I'm proud of you."

"I took out two before catching a glimpse of the third out of the corner of my eye. I was a bit too late. I'm fortunate that he wasn't a better shot."

"He won't be taking any more shots at agents. You put four rounds in him after you hit the floor. Your composure was remarkable."

"I'm grateful for the training," replied Josh. "I've been heavily trained by both the military and the FBI. Looks like it paid off."

"Remember to stay quiet about Afghanistan," reminded Jason. "Your new records don't contain that information. That went away with the old TJ."

"The training didn't go away, and it's a good thing," said Josh.

"Agreed. Listen, I dropped by Colorado Springs to check in on Misty. She asked about you, and I told her about what you did in rescuing those girls. She said that she wants to cook you a meal when you feel up to it."

"Trying to get me set up with her?"

"Hey! She's the one who dropped your name into the conversation. I was checking to see if she had been contacted by Ricky Taylor. She said that she hadn't, but she asked if you were still on that case. That's when I told her about you getting shot."

"If she ever found out that I was the guy who put her in the trunk of my old car, it wouldn't be a good idea for me to eat her cooking. I'm not in a hurry to be poisoned."

"She has no idea. You have to admit that she's cute. Most guys would be all over the idea of her asking them to come to her apartment for dinner."

"Cut it out."

"By the way, I'll be there to eat as well. She wants us both to come by."

"Good! I'll be almost defenseless with this arm in a sling."

"Defenseless is not a word that comes to mind when I think about you."

"You haven't seen how she handles herself. I saw Misty leave a guy bent over and moaning after he grabbed her butt outside that bar. I'm telling you, she's a dangerous woman."

— • ● • —

THE FOLLOWING MONTH Josh received a call from Misty. She was frantic.

"You told me to call if I heard from Ricky! How did he get my new number?"

"What did he want?" asked Josh.

"He said that he wants to get back together with me. How did he find me?"

"Someone has probably hacked into your credit card use. That would be my bet. I'm guessing that Ricky Taylor gave them your old address, and they found your number and a credit card in your name. With a credit card number, he may even have your new address."

"That means that he knows where I am! That card was switched to my new address. That was stupid! I should have simply gotten a new card. That was stupid! Stupid!"

"Where are you right now?"

"I'm at the bar."

"Stay there. I'm coming. You're safe there. I'm

heading your way right now."

Josh jumped in his car and left for Colorado Springs. He called Jason Bagwell to tell him the news.

"You're right to go there," said Jason. "Stay with her. I'll get in touch with the folks in Atlanta. How's the shoulder?"

"A little stiff, but it's getting better."

"Don't let her out of your sight. Tell her to continue with her same routine, but I want you there with her. Do you understand?"

"Got it."

It took just over an hour for Josh to reach the bar in Colorado Springs. He found Misty busily serving customers. Her left hand rose to her mouth, as she saw him enter the establishment. Walking past two customers holding up empty glasses, she quickly made her way to him.

"You came…" she whispered.

"Of course," Josh replied. "And I'm not leaving."

She wiped tears from both cheeks with shaking hands.

"What should I do?" she asked.

"I'm here. Try to relax and go about things as normally as possible. I'll still be here when you get off tonight."

"Promise?"

"Absolutely."

She motioned for the hostess to seat Josh and turned to handle those with empty glasses. He wasn't seated at one of her tables, so another waitress took his order. Throughout the evening, Misty glanced in his direction to make sure he was still there.

"You plan to stay at this table all night?" asked the

irritated waitress.

"I do," Josh replied. "Keep the coffee coming and let me see the menu for pies."

Before walking out with Misty for the evening, he handed his waitress an extremely large tip. "You were great. I'd like to make up for holding your table all night."

"I don't know what to do," Misty said, as the two walked away from the bar.

"You're going home and you're going to get some sleep."

"There's no way I'm falling asleep tonight."

"I'll be in the apartment with you."

"What?"

"I have orders not to let you out of my sight. But I'll have to separate myself for a few minutes after we reach the apartment. I've been downing coffee all night, and I'm about to explode. I really need to visit your bathroom."

She took in a deep breath. It was the first time since his coming that he noticed the tension briefly slide from her countenance.

"Well, your orders stop at my bedroom door," she said.

"Agreed."

"I hope you have a gun."

"Of course."

"Let me see it."

"Right here in public?"

"It's not like taking a pee. I want to see it."

Josh moved his jacket back to reveal a shoulder holster.

"Finally, a guy with a gun," she said.

"I usually don't hear that statement from a woman."

"How many kidnapped and hogtied women do you know?"

"Point taken."

Reaching Misty's apartment building, Josh stood close behind her as she slid the key into the door. Before opening the door, she turned to face him.

"So, you plan to stay with me 24/7?" she asked.

"That's what I was instructed to do. Got a problem with that?"

"I have one demand."

"What's that?"

"You have to put the toilet seat down – understood?"

"Got it."

"Another question."

"Yep."

"Do you plan to change clothes anytime soon? Where's your luggage?"

"My car's parked down the street, and I keep a bag with clothes in the trunk…along with other things."

"Other things?"

"A shotgun, for starts."

"OK, good. I can deal with a guy stinking up the bathroom… I have a can of air freshener. But I am not as keen about hanging around a man who hasn't changed clothes for days… not happening."

"Do you want to go for the clothes now, or let it wait until tomorrow?"

"It's already tomorrow, and I'm beat. Daytime sounds fine."

Stepping into the apartment, Misty flipped on a

light. As she watched him step through the door, she fully realized his huge size.

"If you were any taller, you'd have to duck to step through a door," she commented.

"Yeah, and I don't drive small cars," he replied.

She pointed to the couch and informed him that she would provide him a blanket. Josh removed his jacket and hung it over the back of a chair. The gun in the holster was clearly visible. Misty glanced at the couch, then back at him.

"You'll never fit on that couch," she observed.

"It's fine," he replied. "I need to be between the exterior door and you."

"Do you think he's going to break in, or something?"

"Just taking precautions."

She turned and made her way to a hall closet. Returning with a blanket, she found Josh sitting on the couch while removing his shoes. Still in the holster, the gun had been placed beside him on the couch.

"Thanks," Josh said, taking the blanket.

"How's the shoulder?" Misty asked.

"Doing well. Not quite there, but doing well."

"I wish I had a bigger couch."

"It's fine. Go to bed and get some sleep."

— • ● • —

MISTY AWOKE TO THE smell of coffee. Slipping on a robe, she stumbled into the kitchen.

"You found the coffee," she said, holding back a yawn.

"I have a nose for it," replied Josh.

"I see you're wearing the same clothes."

"We'll take a walk to my car in a little while. How do you take your coffee?"

"Black, with a couple of packs of sweetener. Thank you."

Suddenly, there was a knock on the door. Misty's eyes widened.

"I've got that," said Josh, moving to answer it.

With a hand on the holster, he opened the door just wide enough to confirm his suspicions. His hand then moved to his pants pocket, and he handed the person a twenty.

"Thanks," he said, as he took a bag from a man's hand.

"A couple of donuts, and three muffins," he announced to Misty while closing the door.

"What kind of muffins?" she asked.

"Blueberry, banana bread, and the third is apple and raisin. The donuts are just plain donuts. Pick your poison."

"My favorite is blueberry, but the apple and raisin one sounds interesting."

"Have them both, if you like. I'm good with banana bread. You like muffins, right?"

"Yes, but you didn't have to call in an order for them."

"Besides the coffee, the contents of your kitchen are a bit bleak."

"Sorry."

"No need to apologize. I doubt that you expected someone to be hanging around the apartment. Have a muffin."

After breakfast, Misty excused herself to take a

shower. From time to time, Josh peeked out the window to the street below. Soon, he heard a blow dryer. While it was in operation, he inspected the apartment more closely. Josh quickly scanned her bedroom in hopes of finding a photo of Ricky Taylor. Finding nothing of consequence, he returned to the couch. When she exited the bathroom, she was fully dressed and her hair was done.

"Your turn.., anytime you wish," she offered.

"I'm not crazy about that chain on your front door," he replied. "It offers little protection if someone intends to come in. Would your landlord object to me putting in a deadbolt?"

"I'm not allowed to alter the apartment."

"Let's go for that walk. I need to grab my bag."

Stepping onto the sidewalk in front of her apartment, Josh and Misty were bathed in morning sunlight. His car was parked two blocks down and on the opposite side of the street. Just as they stepped into the street, they heard a vehicle accelerate toward them. Josh pushed Misty down between two parked cars. As she fell, she felt his massive body cover her. Josh was careful not to cause his full weight to come down on her, catching himself on the asphalt with the palms of his hands.

Still positioned between the parked cars, they heard the whining sound of a car engine in reverse. Josh flipped his body off of her, quickly moving to his feet in a squatting position. Duck walking a couple of steps, he moved in front of her. Just before the car stopped in front of them, he drew his gun from the shoulder holster with remarkable speed. A fraction of a second after spotting the barrel of a gun move out the window, he fired two shots. The car sped backwards down the street.

As quick as a cat, Josh turned and scooped up Misty into his arms. Even while carrying her, his speed and gate were that of professional running back. At the first alley, he bolted into it. Finding a dumpster, he gingerly placed Misty behind it. Before she could speak to him, he sped down the alley like a cannonball being fired. He peered down the street from the entrance of the alley and spotted the car three blocks down. He cautiously moved towards it, taking cover behind parked cars. A small crowd of people were gathering near the vehicle that had earlier been used as a weapon.

"Stay back!" Josh yelled.

Startled, the people momentarily stopped and slowly backed away from the car. Seeing the huge man with a gun in his hand moving in their direction, people began screaming. They ran in all directions. Arriving at a parked car near the offending vehicle, Josh understood why the people had approached it. The car had crashed into a parked car, and the driver inside was motionless. A closer look provided him assurance that one of the shots he fired had met its target. The man's face was covered in blood. Josh reached inside the window and found no pulse.

"FBI!" Josh shouted, holding up his badge. "FBI! Everything is under control. FBI!"

He quickly called the incident in, and then assured the people gathering that they were now safe. Suddenly, he remembered Misty. Looking in the direction of the alley, he saw her slowly walking in his direction. He flashed his shield at the first local policeman at the scene, and temporarily excused himself. He ran in the direction of Misty.

"Are you alright?" he asked.

"It was you, wasn't it?" Misty replied.

"What?"

"It was you who took me. You're in the FBI. That must be why you let me go. Why didn't anyone tell me all this time?"

"Are you alright?"

"A couple of scrapes, but I'm fine. Why didn't you tell me?"

"I'm thinking this guy is Ricky Taylor, but maybe you shouldn't look right now. You can identify him later."

"My eyes were closed when you picked me up from the street. It was like being lifted out of the trunk of that car all over again. It was the same. It was you."

She stepped closer and began beating his chest with her firsts.

"Why didn't you tell me, you bastard?" she screamed at him.

He wrapped his huge arms around her, calming her. He released her and began looking her over.

"If you're really unhurt, maybe you should go back to the apartment. But first, I need to brief the police for a few minutes."

"I'm not going anywhere. You're not talking to anyone else until I hear an explanation as to what the hell has been going on for the past few months."

If Misty's eyes had been lasers, they would have burned holes through the huge agent. She glared at him; her arms were crossed in front of her.

"Why was I questioned about my kidnapping, when the person who grabbed me was an FBI agent?"

"OK," he said. "Give me a minute."

He handed the local policeman his card and instructed him to call him in an hour. He explained that the woman standing next to him was a key witness and for her safety he had to remove her from the scene.

"OK, we can talk in your apartment," he suggested.

"Your clothes."

"What?"

"We came out here to get your stinking clothes from your car, and we're going to get them."

"The bag can wait," he said.

Misty slapped him hard across the face.

"Why is it that men like you don't listen to me. Are you deaf? Did I stutter? Get your stinking bag and get it now!"

"OK, OK… if it makes you happy, I'll get the bag."

Within a couple of minutes, they reached his car. Josh popped the trunk and snatched the bag.

"Happy now?" he asked, taking Misty by the arm and leading her back toward her apartment.

"Let go of me!" she warned.

"Or what, you're going to start beating on me again? I wasn't the guy who tried to run you down. What is it with you?"

"You know exactly what is wrong with me! You're the guy who grabbed me."

"What makes you think an FBI agent would kidnap you?"

"Shut up!" she shouted.

"You slapped the crap out of me, because you wanted me to talk…and now you're ordering me to shut up? Are you listening to yourself? That incident back there was a nerve-racking event for you. I need to get you back to that apartment, and you need to rest. I can call a report in from there."

"When we get back there, you're going to level with me," she demanded, pointing a finger in his face.

Stepping back inside her apartment, Josh dropped the bag near the couch. As he raised his cell to his ear to call in his report, Misty viciously slapped it out of his hand.

"What the…?" he stammered.

"You're going to talk to me first."

Chapter 21
Allen Adams

THE FOLLOWING YEAR, Allen Adams gave his daughter away in marriage to Sam. It was a bitter-sweet event for Megan. Her mother's only participation involved sending a half-hearted card of acknowledgement from England. Because Michelle Adams notified her that she would not be present, the wedding was a small affair conducted in Megan's church by her pastor. A few friends, along with Allen's sister, attended. Just before the ceremony, Megan was surprised to find her father and the pastor in a jovial conversation. As she later waited in the church vestibule to be escorted down the aisle, she turned to her father.

"What was that all about? You and the pastor looked like old friends."

"There was a time when we were," replied Allen. "Years ago, when you were much younger, we rather enjoyed the company of one another. Your pastor and I don't agree about a number of things, but I still like the man. He's an intelligent fellow, and I've always respected his honesty."

"We didn't attend this church when I was young," replied Megan.

"Your pastor was once a brilliant financial analyst before going into the ministry. His assessment of stocks was rarely wrong."

She squeezed her father's hand as the organist began to play *The Wedding March*, by Felix Mendelssohn. At the appropriate time, Allen released her to her husband to be. In planning the ceremony, Megan and Sam purposely avoided the traditional question from the pastor asking who gives the bride away. Michelle's stinging absence was gracefully played down. Standing with Sam, Megan caught a glimpse of her father wiping a tear as he sat in the first pew of the church.

At the reception, Sam told Megan's father that he was still amazed at Allen's acceptance of him. The older man first held out a hand, then gave Sam a sincere hug followed by a gentle pat on the back.

"You're a good man, Sam," Allen said. "I've found you to be a surprising individual, and I'm not often pleasantly surprised. I'm glad Megan has you."

"So, you're the famous Allen Adams," said Dora Hitchcock, stepping to the right of Megan.

"Dad, this is Dora Hitchcock, a dear member of this church," introduced Megan.

"It's nice to meet you, Dora," greeted Allen. "I've heard your name from both Megan and Sam. I understand that you're a widow. I'm sorry for your loss."

Megan and Sam excused themselves to mingle for a few minutes before leaving.

"I understand that you too know what it's like to live alone," said Dora.

"True. Over the past two years I've spent more time with my daughter. I wish I had not been so absent when she was younger."

"You and I both know that there are perils associated with wealth. There's a tendency to neglect family. Priorities are sometimes misplaced while attempting to maintain control over endeavors. At some point, we all come to realize that control is something that is fleeting."

"So true."

"Pursuit of money can drive our lives, and so can the fear of losing it. We think that we are in command, but some of us find ourselves to be servants of one thing or another. What do you serve, Mr. Adams?"

"Something that's based on good intentions, but may or may not be directly beneficial to my daughter. I'll leave it at that."

"Even for your daughter's sake, you're unable to abandon that thing, aren't you? You don't have to answer. I see it in your eyes. I believe you have a leash about your neck. There are limits to your personal freedom, and you never realized it until it was too late."

Allen's eyes were silently fixed on hers, searching for more information. His exceptional mind churned, analyzing the elderly woman standing in front of him. Finally, his eyes scanned the fingers on her hand.

"You won't find rings on my fingers, Mr. Adams. You were correct in saying that I'm a widow. I'm bound to no human or to any organization – only to my God, whom I intend to meet shortly. If I were you, I would carefully examine my priorities. Unlike others of immense wealth, deep down you know better. You know there is more to the universe than the things we accumulate and the power we temporarily grasp. It will all fall from your hands soon. You should decide to willingly release it before it is taken from you."

She then reached for his hand with both of hers, rubbing her thumb across the ring he wore. She looked up at him and smiled.

"This isn't you, Allen Adams. It never was. Not in your heart, it wasn't. Do what you can to make things right. Deep down, you're a good man."

With that, she turned and walked away. Allen felt something that he hadn't experienced since he was a child. His mother had passed away years prior, but he felt as if she had paid him a visit. Only there was something more, much deeper than even the loving touch of his mother. He couldn't help watching the old woman as she slowly moved away from. Dora blended into the small crowd. Allen searched the room for his daughter, and he made his way to her after he spotted her leaving a restroom. Allen intercepted Megan before she could reach her husband Sam. He took her in his arms and gave her a deep and long hug.

"Dad, are you alright?" whispered Megan.

"I've just given you to another man – a good man," he replied. "I wish I had given you hugs more often. I wish I had not sent you away to boarding school. I missed so much of your life."

"Daddy, we plan to visit you often. I promise."

"Good," he said, releasing her.

As Megan and Sam were about to leave the reception, Charles and Olivia Worthington surprised her with the gift of five thousand dollars.

"I hope this will help make your honeymoon even more special," Olivia said.

"Thank you both, so much!" Megan replied, giving her a hug.

— • ◆ • —

WITHIN SIX MONTHS of the wedding, Megan's father revealed to his daughter and Sam that he suffered from Creutzfeldt-Jakob Disease. His massive wealth could do nothing to reverse the impact. Doctors had given him less than a year. He asked that Megan and Sam spend a weekend with him in a cabin he had built in the mountains of northeast Georgia.

"This is really nice," said Sam, as he entered the cabin.

"Let me show you around," said Allen.

"I really like the stone fireplace," commented Sam.

"I'm glad," replied Allen. "There's more."

Allen escorted Megan and Sam to the master bedroom and two smaller bedrooms, each having a smaller stone fireplace. As Allen led them both to the kitchen, a smile spread across Sam's face.

"The refinished tiger oak table!" blurted Sam. "You brought the chairs, as well. Perfect."

Allen invited them to take a seat at the table. Reaching into a drawer, he pulled out a couple of envelopes.

"This is a certified copy of my latest will," Allen said, handing one envelope to his daughter.

"I see that it was witnessed by Charles Worthington," observed Megan.

"You'll see that the bulk of my fortune, a little

more than four hundred million, goes to Michelle in England. When she dies, that money will be placed in a World Bank account. You can also see that I'm splitting up a million between the help at the estate. Those who cooked and cleaned for me over the years deserve to be appreciated. I'm leaving the same for the two nurses I hired to care for me at the estate until my death. Besides Charles's signature, you can see that the seal of a notary public has been placed. This is official. I wanted to do this while I'm deemed to still be of sound mind."

"I've always known that you have a good heart," said Megan.

"Megan, outside of this will, I've placed fifteen million dollars in a trust under your name," Allen continued, as he handed her a second envelope. "I believe fifteen million should allow you both to live as you wish, but it's not so much as to cause you to be isolated from society."

"Dad…" Megan said, her eyes filling with tears.

"I set it up where the interest is paid on a monthly basis to a credit union account in your name," Allen explained. "The trust has an option of allowing you to take the full amount – but you would lose some of it to taxes. It's your choice."

"You've set this up in this manner, and I trust your judgment," said Megan.

"Sam, I've deeded this cabin and the surrounding one hundred acres to you," stated Allen.

"I don't deserve this place," said Sam.

"You certainly do," Allen said. "I'm so glad Megan found you."

"Mr. Adams, no one has ever been this generous to me," said Sam.

"I believe your mother to be the most generous to you; she just had little wealth to share," Allen replied. "But what she gave you will last you a lifetime. You carry that gift inside of you, and no one can ever take it from you."

The cabin sat on the side of a wooded hill, overlooking a pasture with a spring-fed stream running through it. Allen asked that they go outside. Standing on the front porch, he explained to Sam the boundaries of the property.

"Beginning forty yards beyond the stream, that pasture belongs to someone else, and that person's land ends about halfway up that wooded hill," Allen said. "As you can see, I recently had a small bridge made of weather-treated wood built over the stream."

"It's an incredible view," Sam replied.

As they walked the pasture, Megan asked him about the gathering of adults at the estate. Allen paused, stared at the grass beneath his feet, and then answered.

"It's a gathering of six people," Allen began. "It's part of a larger organization, and members are sworn to secrecy. I can't say much about it."

"Is the group something like the Masons?" asked Sam.

"A little different," replied Allen. "This organization is much more exclusive. It has very few members, but it's not limited to the United States."

"Have I ever heard of it?" asked Megan.

"I doubt that very much," answered Allen. "There are six of these gatherings within the United States. The US is one of six nations, each having six similar gatherings. Then there are six people who gather, each representing one of the six nations, to make a world gathering. It's a type of pyramid structure."

"Three sets of six," commented Megan. "Six gatherings, in six nations, with a world-wide gathering of six."

"There really aren't many people participating," said Allen. "Two hundred and twenty-two, sometimes less."

"I'm sure there's a purpose to all of this," she said. "Is it a philanthropic organization?"

"Most members contribute funding to a variety of institutions and organizations," Allen answered.

"Is there a goal to make the world a better place?" she asked.

"Actually, one of the goals is world peace," Allen stated.

"Why do this in secret?" asked his daughter. "There are a lot of people who strive for world peace. Maybe you should openly join up with the United Nations."

"The UN has become corrupted, in my opinion," Allen replied. "We are very selective when it comes to membership, and we personally hold every member to extremely high standards. We believe that this select group, meeting in secret, can accomplish much more than the United Nations."

"I might be interested, if it wasn't so secretive," said Megan.

"There's enormous pressure and responsibility on members, and I sense that you and Sam wish to live your lives free of major complications. To be honest, I truly believe this group is not for you. It demands sacrifice, and those demands sometimes make family life difficult. My wish for you and Sam is that you'll be happy, and that your family be more successful than the one I brought you into. You should daily appreciate life with each other and be free to have friends from various walks of life. I allowed my affiliation with that group to separate me from you. To some degree, it played a part in your mother and I sending you away to boarding school. I regret not spending more time with you. My advice to you would be to not become involved in these types of organizations."

"How did you become involved in such a group?" asked Sam.

"The organization has a strong focus on success," he answered. "My personal quest for excellence caught the attention of this group, and I found those like-minded people to be of interest to me. The objectives are to help solve some of the problems the world faces, and I found that appealing."

"I still don't understand why the group is so secretive," said Megan.

"That's all I'll say about it," said Allen. "I've answered enough questions about that part of my life. Live your lives doing what is best for your family, regardless of the opinions of other people and groups. Back to the matters at hand. Sam, what do you think about this property?"

"It's astounding!" remarked Sam. "This place is incredibly beautiful."

Allen refrained from telling Megan that his marriage to Michelle was heavily suggested by the gathering after he became an integral part of the group. She aspired to the same power and wealth he desired. Their prominence grew quickly within the gathering. However, for Allen, everything changed with the birth of Megan. He had never experienced such love for anyone. Allen truly hoped that his daughter would experience a much fuller life than he experienced. In Sam, he observed a richness that can't be purchased.

Shortly after lunch the following day, Megan and Sam departed for Atlanta. On the way, Megan reflected on what her father shared about the secretive group.

"Three sets of six. It reminds me of the six-six-six mentioned in the book of Revelations in the Bible."

"Don't start getting weird with stuff in the Bible that nobody understands," said Sam. "All that talk about a secret organization is weird enough without adding religious speculation. I'm more concerned about the possibility that your father is beginning to have serious trouble with his health. Do you think maybe his brain is already being affected by the illness?"

"I don't think so, but I'm not sure that I could recognize the early signs of the sickness. He talked about having nurses care for him. I'm sure he must be seeing a specialist regularly."

"You're right. If his mind was being affected, I'm sure he wouldn't be allowed to drive."

"It's certainly been an interesting time in the mountains," said Megan.

"Fifteen million dollars! I know that kind of wealth seems normal to you, but I can't really imagine living like that."

"It certainly won't change me, but I'm a little afraid of the impact on you."

"I'm for leaving all of it in your name and in your account," said Sam. "I doubt I'll take another construction job, but I don't feel that I'm ready to have that kind of money at my disposal. However, I certainly have plans for that property. I want to have a garden, a fruit orchard, and maybe we could have a few cows."

"Cows?"

———•◆•———

BACK AT THE CABIN, Allen placed a call to Charles.

"I did as we decided. I gave them a copy of the will and told them about the fifteen million I put in trust. They understand that the rest will go to Michelle, and upon her death it goes to the World Bank account."

"I'll make sure they have protection," promised Charles.

"Thank you."

"Did Megan ask you about the weekends?"

"She did. I told her that several people across the country meet like that, and that there are groups that make up a world organization."

"That's it?"

"The gathering isn't for them. I want a life of peace and simplicity for Megan and Sam. I've acquired a great deal of wealth, but I want my daughter to be able to enjoy a normal life. They deserve to enjoy the mysteries of life."

"So, you've entirely given up on your earlier hope that she would one day become a part of our effort. She's smart, and I've always seen potential in her."

"She's plenty smart, but she doesn't share the same vision of sacrifice required by the gathering. It's my wish that Megan and Sam have nothing to do with our organization. Maybe it's because I'm dying, but I've found myself wanting nothing for her except her happiness and peace."

"You haven't given up on our objective of bringing peace to the world, have you?"

"No, absolutely not. I'm somewhat saddened to realize that I won't live long enough to see that vision fulfilled. I know that it isn't my place to know the timing of things, but do you see this beginning in the near future?"

"I do," answered Charles. "The world has always suffered wars, poor health, a lack of education, and hunger. Until recent years, capabilities of mass communication haven't been available on a large enough scale to make a difference."

"The difference being today's technology," said Allen.

"That and the ability to connect the technologies so that everything is intertwined. That combination is becoming mature enough to soon facilitate our vision. People of various nations are almost ready for us. They've had their fill of international and domestic terrorism, expensive health care and education, fear of war, depletion of natural resources, and frustrations with the various political factions. They're almost to the point where they'll appreciate what we have to offer."

"I'm sorry that I won't be around to be a part of it."

"You have been a significant part of it. You've helped move us to where we are. Your personal vision has been purer than the vast majority of our members. I've always seen it in you. Most catch the intellectual or material aspects of the gathering. But you've carried what I would call the spiritual heart of the vision. You're a good man, Allen. You're exceptionally rare, and I personally hate the fact that we haven't found a cure for your affliction."

After the call ended, Allen reflected on the secret society.

We've paid homage to a variety of religious beliefs and rituals that have been exercised by the leadership of cultures for centuries. It's right to honor and respect those elite members of societies who've come before us. No person making up the 222 members of the gathering is so arrogant and ignorant to believe we are smarter than the elites of older times. There's much to be learned from those who went before us. They saw something of value in past rituals and beliefs, we share with them the understanding that they reveal the yearning of mankind for fulfillment of needs of individuals and societies. Humanity has always looked to something greater than itself for help. Religion, the worship of gods, is at the core of humanity itself. We place images of those gods in the places of our gatherings to remind ourselves of the longing of mankind. Soon, our efforts will replace any need of humanity to wish for unseen gods to aid their lives.

———•●•———

ALLEN ADAMS DIED. The man who drove the silver sedan placed a call to Charles Worthington.

"Twelve years ago, I promised Allen that I would look after his daughter, and her welfare has become a significant part of my life. He's now gone, but I would like to continue in that effort."

"I realize that her safety has been a personal concern of yours, and you've exceeded everyone's expectations in your efforts over the years," replied

Charles. "You've earned a gracious retirement. I want to assure you that her protection will personally be a priority of mine, but the duty will be assigned to someone else. If you wish, you're welcome to look in on her – but make sure that you don't come between Megan and her new protector."

At the visitation of Allen Adams at the funeral home, a tall thin distinguished man in his early fifties approached Megan.

"Megan, I'm Peter Hastings. I was a friend of your father's. We often enjoyed golf outings. I'm so sorry that you've lost him."

"Thanks for coming," replied Megan.

"Allen has told me so much about you over the years. I almost feel that I know you. He had me in stitches when he talked about your first date. Allen said the young man was so intimidated by him that he brought you home thirty minutes early, and that he never asked you out again."

Megan rolled her tear swollen eyes and issued her first smile of the day. She nodded agreement as she took his hand.

"Who is this fellow standing beside you?" Peter asked.

"Sam is my husband, and his support has helped so much," answered Megan.

Peter extended his hand to Sam. Glancing down, Sam noted the emerald mounted gold ring he wore.

"I sense that you're the kind of man who would look after Megan," Peter said to Sam.

"Yes, sir," Sam replied.

Peter Hastings excused himself and left the funeral home. Dropping into his silver sedan, he wiped away a tear before driving away.

When Megan planned the funeral, Allen's sister was emphatic that there be no religious aspects. She lived in the Tampa area and had rarely visited while Allen was alive. Her aunt wasn't well known to Megan. For the sake of maintaining peace with her father's only living full blood relative, Megan put her own wishes aside and agreed. Seated in the family area between her aunt and Sam, Megan stared at the bronze casket surrounded by large flower arrangements. Classical pieces were played softly on a baby grand, as photos displaying Allen's life were projected on a screen behind the casket. Pictures of Allen and his parents, while he was a child in Atlanta, were replaced with those of Megan and her two parents. This was the only showing of Michelle, for she was not in attendance. Like the wedding, she had sent a card to Megan containing a simple statement concerning the loss. Other photos were placed on easels, one being Allen's face on the cover of a business magazine. Megan silently wished that her pastor would have been allowed to share a few words.

At the end of the speechless service, a note was projected on the wall inviting people to the gravesite. Besides the three family members, there were only a dozen other people watching the casket being interned in the large white marble mausoleum. As the door of the crypt was sealed, Megan buried her face in Sam's chest. As those in attendance began to leave, she quietly spoke to her husband.

"The estate will soon pass to my mother. For the last time, I want to sleep tonight in my childhood home."

Sam escorted her to the car. As he started the engine, she suggested that they cook supper at the house rather than go to a restaurant. In route to the estate, they stopped at a food store to pick up steaks, baking potatoes, spices, and French bread. Sam also purchased pastries for the following breakfast. As he later cooked the meal, Megan brought out an expensive bottle of her father's red wine.

"OK, so you plan to get me drunk and take advantage of me?" Sam jested.

"Absolutely," Megan answered.

They thoroughly enjoyed the meal and each other's company. Sam even caused her to laugh a couple of times. By ten o'clock, the bottle was empty. She took Sam by the hand and led him to her old bedroom.

"You want me to sleep with you in your high school bed?" Sam asked. "Kinky! I'm afraid that I'll wake up tomorrow morning finding that I've been molested in my sleep!"

"I believe that I have a license to molest you any time I want," she replied.

———•●•———

THE FOLLOWING MORNING, Sam and Megan enjoyed the pastries with coffee. Sipping his cup of brew, Sam viewed the cave entrance from a kitchen window. He remembered their adventures, especially the first time that he'd seen Megan standing in the light of the lantern without clothes. He smiled.

As they later walked out the front door of the estate, bound for Megan's car, Charles Worthington pulled up in his.

"I saw your car parked here and thought I would drop by to see how you're doing," Charles said.

"I wanted to sleep one last night in the home of my childhood," explained Megan.

"I'm sure you have a number of memories," Charles replied.

"Not all of the memories have been good," said Megan. "Sam has been a source of strength."

"I'm glad you have him," said Charles. "I believe your mother will stay in England, even though the place will be hers. Please know that you can always call on me at any time."

As Sam and Megan drove away, from car side mirror Megan spotted Charles enter the Adams house.

"Charles didn't stop to check on me," she told Sam. "He's interested in something in the house. I don't care anymore. Charles can have anything he wants."

Inside the Adams estate, Charles stood before a safe that was hidden behind a bookcase in the study. He reached into a pocket of his jacket and took out a pair of thin gloves. Charles carefully spun the dial of the safe until he heard the tumbler click. He slowly opened the safe door. Inside, he found several bars of gold, a mahogany box containing stock certificates, and a brown leather bag that Allen Adams had placed there after his wife left him. Charles reached into the bag and examined a sample of the contents. After taking a deep breath, Charles returned the item to the bag. He reached into the box of stock certificates and took a handful. After careful review, he returned the certificates to the box. Taking only the leather bag with the contents, he shut the door of the safe.

Charles spun the dial and shoved the bookcase

back in place. In order to move the bookcase aside earlier, he had removed most of the books. He replaced all but three books. After locking the front door of the house, Charles placed the three books and the brown leather bag in the trunk of his car.

———•●•———

THE FOLLOWING WEEK, Charles placed a call to Megan Adams. He made arrangements for her to come the next day to his office. It was on the eighteenth floor of a building in the Buckhead Business District. At the appointed time, Megan and Sam entered the large office. On the right side of the room stood bookcases, a couch, two chairs, lamps, and a coffee table. To the left, the two saw Charles's massive desk with two elegant chairs placed in front of it. About ten feet behind the desk was a floor to ceiling set of windows spanning about sixteen feet in width. Crown molding graced the top of the walls, on which hung expensive original oil paintings.

"Megan, come in," invited Charles, looking up from documents on his desk. "I have personal matters of your father's that I wish to discuss with you. I see you brought your husband, Sam. Perhaps he should leave the room for a few minutes."

As Sam turned to leave, Megan caught him by the arm.

"No, I would like for Sam to stay," Megan informed Charles.

"Very well, would you please take the chairs in front of my desk?" requested Charles. "Megan, I have some things which belonged to your father; things he personally requested that I give you.”

Charles opened a bottom drawer of the desk and took two books from it. He gingerly placed them both on the desk before Megan.

“The first of these books is the Adams family Bible, going back to 1811,” Charles began. “The first page contains names, birth dates, dates of marriages and of deaths. Allen wanted you to have this.”

Megan ran her slim fingers over the page, examining the elegant and aged script written long ago. Sam’s eyes were drawn to the fine binding and eloquent artwork that framed the page.

“This next book is a photo album,” said Charles. “Not only are there photos of you, Allen and Michelle; there are photos of some of the people listed in the family Bible. There are names below each photo in the album, and you should be able to match some of these people to those noted in the Bible.”

“Why didn’t my father show these to me himself?” asked Megan.

“I can’t answer that,” replied Charles.

“The question that I have is, why did you invite us to your office?” asked Sam. “You could have brought these books to Megan.”

“Megan, over time I’ve come to understand some of what you see in this man,” stated Charles. “Sam is very astute. He’s absolutely right. This brings me to that very point. I have something else of your father’s.”

Charles opened another drawer and revealed the brown leather bag. After slowly placing the bag on the desk, he reached into it and pulled out three large diamonds.

“Good Lord!” exclaimed Sam.

"If you want, I can assist you in placing these at auction," offered Charles to a wide-eyed Megan. "I suggest that you sell them over a period of time, or save them for a future significant investment. I also advise you to keep them in a safe deposit box. I can arrange that, as well."

"What would you think these are worth?" asked Megan.

"I'm not an appraiser, but I knew your father well," Charles answered. "I would say that these are of the highest quality. I'd be glad to help you have them appraised and assist you in selling them. I understand investments, tax laws, and the market. I suggest that you take your time, if you wish to sell. Please feel free to call on me anytime. Here, take them."

Megan held each one up to the light.

"I'm certainly no expert on diamonds," she said. "Do you think I should take all three to be appraised?"

"You could," answered Charles. "In this bag, there are twenty-seven more."

"What?" Megan shouted. "Are you telling me that my father left me thirty diamonds?"

"They're cut differently, but they're roughly about the same size," Charles answered. "During his last months, your father observed how well you managed the fifteen million. Allen determined that you should have his diamonds. He acquired them after your mother left him, and she doesn't know about them. He left her the estate, but he wanted me to make sure you were given these."

"They're absolutely beautiful," Megan replied.

"Diamonds are always good to have," said Charles. "They can be used as emergency funding, if the market drops. I suggest that you have them certified by a professional appraiser."

"What do you think, Sam?' she asked.

"This is the first time I've ever seriously discussed what to do with a bag of diamonds," Sam answered. "Charles is the expert on investments. I would go with his recommendation. Put them in a safe deposit box, for a rainy day."

"Charles, please have my rainy-day diamonds placed in a safe deposit box," declared Megan.

"I thought this is what you would want," said Charles. "I have the paperwork prepared. My present to you is an insurance policy to cover them the first year. If you'll sign these forms, I'll take care of everything."

Megan signed the papers, and then dashed around the desk to give Charles a sincere hug.

"You've been such a friend to my father," Megan said. "Thank you."

"I'm honored to call your father my friend," Charles replied. "Allen was a great man on so many levels. He loved you very much."

From his office window, Charles watched Megan and Sam cross the street to the parking deck. They walked hand in hand. Charles pulled his cell phone from his pocket and made a call.

"This is Charles Worthington. The wishes of Allen Adams have been fulfilled. You may now turn his estate over to his wife Michelle Adams."

Seated in his chair behind the desk, he opened a drawer and took out the third book he had removed from the estate.

This is the ledger of every secret account of the late great Allen Adams. Most of it will go to the Six Princes, but Allen wished that I be given a sizable cut. We take care of our own.

Standing at the window again, he looked down at the wet pavement below that had received a brief rain during the meeting with Megan.

Like a small area of water pooled on a sidewalk after a rain, at some point a man's life evaporates and is gone. The wealth accumulated during a lifetime is left to others. In the case of Allen Adams, the only true essence left of his life in this world is his daughter. If there is an afterlife, possibly this fact will give him peace. Perhaps, there are riches of a different kind beyond this realm. I wish it to be so for my friend.

Chapter 22
Prince

SEVERAL MONTHS AFTER Allen's death, Megan and Sam spotted a smaller cabin being built at the base of the hill that rose on the other side of the stream. The two decided to meet their new neighbors. Crossing the footbridge at the stream, Sam spotted a huge man standing in front of the unfinished cabin.

"Maybe that worker can tell us who the owners are," he suggested to his wife.

"I earlier saw a woman going inside the place," replied Megan. "I would bet that she's the owner.'

As Megan and Sam neared the unfinished home, they watched the woman come out of the house and address the large man. The two were in conversation when Sam and Megan arrived.

"I'm Sam Blaylock, and this is my wife Megan," he called out to the two. "We live in the cabin just across from here."

"Are you the owner?" Megan asked the woman.

"That would be us," interrupted the big man.

"You have a beautiful place," added the woman.

"My name is Misty, and this is my husband Josh."

"Josh Wells," said the huge man, reaching out to shake Sam's hand.

"What brings you out here?" asked Megan.

"We have a real story!" exclaimed Misty. "People hear of lottery winners. Well, you're talking to two."

"You won the lottery?" asks Sam.

"Not the Powerball, just a smaller one worth five million," explained Josh.

"That's fantastic!" blurted Sam.

"What did you do before you won?" asks Megan.

"I was a waitress, and my husband was in the FBI," said Misty. "If you two ever have trouble over there, Josh can come in handy."

"Thanks, but I try to avoid trouble," replied Sam.

"That's the best way to be," said Josh.

"I bet you have a few interesting stories," suggested Megan.

"He can't talk about some of them," answered Misty. "The FBI can be pretty tight-lipped."

"We won't pry," said Sam. "We were just curious about the owners. It's great to have neighbors who are roughly our age."

"Same here," said Josh.

"Listen, it's probably none of my business," said Sam. "But I just noticed that this front gutter doesn't have the right pitch. I've worked construction jobs and spent some time hanging gutters."

"Stop!" warned Megan. "This isn't our home. Let them build it the way they want."

"No, I want to know if something isn't right," said Misty. "I've never had a house built before, and I wouldn't have a clue."

"So, what's the problem?" asked Josh.

"The esthetics are nicer to have less pitch, but you may end up with water settling inside the gutter instead of completely flowing from the downspouts. Standing water is a great place to breed mosquitos. That end should be about an inch lower, and the gutter should gradually fall to that level."

"I'll suggest that to the contractor when he comes by this afternoon,' replied Josh. "Thanks."

"We'd like to have you over sometime," offered Megan. "That way you'll have an opportunity to complain about our place."

"I welcome his knowledge of building," said Josh. "You certainly have no beef from me."

"I would love to come over," replied Misty. "Not to complain about your home, mind you. I'd love to get to know you."

Before parting, the four exchanged cell numbers. As the new neighbors watched Sam and Megan cross the stream enroute back to their cabin, Josh told his wife that he needed to make a phone call. He stepped about thirty yards away and leaned his tall frame against a tree.

"Charles, this is Josh. We just met our neighbors, and they seem like nice people. I almost feel guilty about being paid to live out here. This is really nice."

"I have all the confidence in the world that you'll do a fine job," replied Charles Worthington. "The way you handled the Gallucci mess was brilliant. He needed to be placed in the crosshairs of the FBI, and that stunt where you crossed the Canadian border did the trick. I commend you again."

"I didn't count on getting shot while spending time

in the FBI.”

“I believe I’ve made it worthwhile. Are you enjoying the lottery winnings?”

“Absolutely. I still don’t understand how you could influence a lottery.”

“It’s probably best that you don’t know. Just enjoy it.”

“I sincerely appreciate the lottery money, and the job of looking out for that fine couple. This should be the easiest job of my life.”

“You deserve it. I understand that you’re still in contact with that probation officer. Have you observed any indication that he suspected you in setting up Tony Gallucci?”

“Not a clue.”

“What did he think about your winnings?”

“He believes that I’m the luckiest man alive, and I’m inclined to agree with him. Russ Blevins is a good man, and I see him from time to time. He was shocked at the lottery thing, and so were the guys at the FBI. Especially, Jason.”

“You three should remain in touch. We don’t need the FBI poking its nose where it doesn’t belong, and that relationship could give you an inside view. I have confidence that you’ll redirect them if they start snooping. I have faith in you.”

“It’s unfortunate that the detective was murdered. I didn’t really know him, but it was tough on Russ.”

“Once I began to understand what type of man Gallucci was, I realized that he couldn’t be left out there. He was hurting people.”

“He sure burned the crap out of my fingers!” exclaimed Josh.

"Think about what would have happened to Misty, if you hadn't stepped in? And you two are married now, for God's sake!"

"How did you know that he would pick me to do the job of kidnapping Misty?" asked Josh.

"I've known Tony for years. Remember how I coached you to step up and be eager to take on more responsibility with him after effectively handling smaller tasks? I was sure that he would send someone he felt he could rely on, and you positioned yourself to be that man. He totally fell for the story about her reminding you of your sister. That was brilliant. You're pretty quick on your feet."

"I sometimes have a knack for making things happen, when needed. When I was in the military, I remember reading a sign on the wall of an office. It said that there are three kinds of people; those who make things happen, those who watch things happen, and those who wonder what happened. I intend to be the first kind of man."

"You certainly made things happen. I saw something special in you, and that's why I selected you to personally handle things for me. You've done an exceptional job, and you deserve the life you now have."

"Winning the lottery is out of this world. But I have to say, Misty's the best thing that's ever happened to me."

"Like I said - you deserve this life, Josh."

When the call ended, Charles thought back to the original intent for bringing TJ in as his personal angelus of the local region.

His IQ is off the charts. That and his military

success made him a perfect fit. TJ Turner has been one of my best successes. He was brilliant, extremely capable, and willing to make sacrifices in his handling of Tony Gallucci. He's stellar at what he does, and he's good at cleaning up mistakes. Mistakes like Gallucci can't be allowed to tarnish any aspect of our order. I've had to make sure that unnecessary risks are quickly rooted out. His duties as my angelus are behind him. Turner has earned his simple life as Josh Wells, now having the singular duty of providing protection for Megan Adams. He'll never understand where he fits in the overall picture, but he's an impressive individual. He could never be one of us, but he's probably the best tool I have.

Josh Wells will never know what he has actually been a part of. Unlike protectors, those who serve in the capacity of angelus have no knowledge of the organization. They are given no rings, and they are not told of the gatherings. They are selected by the regional leader, and they remain unknown by the regular membership. It's important that the identity of an angelus remains secret. I could have never handled Gallucci if the identity of my angelus was known.

Soon, everything will be in the open. For many years, we've positioned both corporations and governments to be where they are needed – usually without either of them realizing our influence. It's amazing how we've gone unnoticed. The secrecy will soon pass because there will no longer be any need for it.

That afternoon, Charles received a call from a member of the highest level of the order. He was first congratulated for orchestrating the exit of Gallucci.

Then the conversation moved to the subject of another expelled member.

"Should I be concerned about Mrs. Adams?" asked the voice on the line.

"Michelle Adams behaved very unwisely, but I believe she understands the necessity of discretion," Charles began. "I place the greater blame on Tony Gallucci. It was not understood in the beginning, but the man was poison. Michelle's husband Allen was an exceptional member. It is out of respect for him, that I allow her to retain a degree of protection."

"You allowed her one of your protectors, leaving you with only two. The three protectors of an expelled member are to be reassigned. Yet, you've elected to take additional risk by giving her one of yours. Do you consider this to be wise?"

"By giving her one of my protectors, I continue to have eyes on her," explained Charles. "If she is seen to be foolish, I'll know about it. She understands that I can withdraw that protection at any time. Michelle is aware of Tony's fate. She understands, that should her behavior warrant, words can be put out against her which would be understood by the angelus in the London region – just as I did with Tony Gallucci. Regardless of what she does, I believe my risk is minimal."

"What about the daughter?"

"I have eyes on her, and I'm not using protector resources needed by the order. I'm handling her protection on my own, without creating a burden for the order."

The call ended, and Charles stood at the windows of his office. From his vantage point, framed between two tall buildings in the district, he had an incredible view of the skyline of downtown Atlanta in the distance. The day was coming to a close. As the sun moved below the horizon, the sky was painted with reds and oranges. Lights within skyscrapers became visible. His thoughts were interrupted by the sound of rapping on the office door made by his administrative assistant.

"Come in," Charles invited.

"I'm leaving for the day, and someone just dropped this envelope off for you," she said. "The young man told me to give it to you immediately. Being hand carried, it must be important."

"Thank you," replied Charles. "Go home to your family and have an enjoyable evening."

Charles continued to stand at the window, watching as the brightest stars became visible. His ears strained to hear his assistant exit the outer door of the suite. Moving to the desk, he turned on a small lamp. There was no writing or typing on the envelope, but he easily recognized it to be from the order. The cream-colored linen envelope had a distinctive embossment on the flap. Taking a letter opener from his desk, he meticulously sliced it open. Inside was a card with a single symbol elegantly stamped by an ancient tool. It was the symbol of six connected sixes in the shape of a flower. Charles now understood that those above him saw the wisdom and intelligence he had displayed over the past few years. He had kept his pledge to his old friend, Allen. Now, it was time to focus on his own future. His mind drifted.

There are six world figures in our order, known as the six Princes of the World. It is they who actually rule the world, and I've now been assigned to become one of them. The Princes determine who exercises global power – and through lower level gatherings their collective genius shape world events. The gatherings of six operate in a separate economy, one which is above visual economies of the world, and are directed by the Princes.

Charles received a call on a disposable cell that he kept only for those from members of the order.

"Yes, I received the card," he spoke into the phone. "No, I don't see Allen's daughter to be an issue. She's turned over most of her inherited wealth to me for handling. Megan's busy enjoying her simple life. Besides, I have someone looking after her and her husband ... Yes, I'm free to do whatever is necessary. Olivia will understand. We're of the same mind.... I'm honored to have been recognized, and I look forward to establishing the final phase with the other five. I wish to address them on Tuesday."

Once the call ended, he glanced down at the ring he wore on his right hand. This ring would be passed to someone else, as he was to receive a different one. He imagined placing the new ring on his finger.

———•●•———

THE FOLLOWING MORNING Megan received a call from her pastor informing her that Dora had been hospitalized from a stroke and was in grave condition. Since arriving at the hospital, she suffered further strokes. The doctors didn't expect her to live much longer. The drive from the cabin in north Georgia consumed more than an hour before Megan and Sam entered Dora's hospital room. Monitoring machines had recently been turned off, and a nurse was in the process of disconnecting them from the deceased patient. The pastor rose from a chair beside Dora's bed to address Megan.

"She passed away just minutes ago."

"If we lived closer, we might have been there for her," Megan sadly replied.

"She was unconscious when I called," said the minister. "You wouldn't have been able to communicate with her. When I arrived, she was alert enough to mouth two words, 'Purse, Megan.' I opened her purse and found an envelope with your name written on it. I believe she wanted you to have this. It's the primary reason I called you."

Megan's eyes filled with tears, as she watched the nurse wheel the monitoring equipment from the room. Taking the envelope, she turned to Sam.

"Should I read this here?"

"I think you should sit in this chair and read it before Dora's body is removed," answered Sam.

Megan took a seat and reverently opened the envelope. It contained a personal letter, which Megan read aloud.

"Megan,
I wish for you and Sam to have a long and enjoyable time together. However, never forget that this world isn't heaven. There are few guarantees in life. If the world appears to be turned upside down, know that God's hand will still guide you. There may come a time when the world proclaims that that faith is finished. But remember, in the end God wins. He sees all, and His unseen plan will not be denied. Don't let

anything or anyone rob you of your personal faith.

Charles Worthington was your father's closest friend. However, you don't really know him. I advise that you not put your trust in Charles – even in financial matters. Don't be bound to him. He may believe that his intentions are for good, but he is an extremely arrogant person. Arrogance always blinds – even while active in what we believe to be a noble endeavor. It strangles perspective, and it's deaf to the wisdom of others. Arrogance is the sister of vanity, born from self-absorption. It impairs a person's ability to recognize value in people, ethical boundaries, dangers, and sometimes even the truth itself. There have been several occasions throughout history where arrogant individuals in power have oppressed people and brought those around them to ruin. The Bible warns us that pride comes before destruction, and a haughty spirit before a fall.

Lastly, Sam may not be as close to God as you would like, but he knows people. If he senses something about someone, listen to him.

Love, Dora"

"I feel privileged that she wrote a personal letter to me before she passed away," said Megan.

"She was special," added Sam. "It's sad that she died without the comfort of family."

"I'll handle the arrangements," assured the pastor. "You two can go."

In silence, Sam and Megan walked hand in hand from the hospital room. When they stepped into the cool evening air, Sam pulled Megan close.

"Dora was something else, wasn't she?" he said.

"She was a very unique woman," Megan answered. "What's with the warning regarding Charles Worthington? People don't usually leave a letter to be read after their death unless it contains something of personal importance. Why would she specifically warn me not to trust him?"

"He was part of that weird group."

"So was my father."

"I know, but your father advised you to not become involved in a group like that one. It's possible that he may have been warning you to stay clear of its members."

"She told me not to trust my father's best friend. I don't understand."

"Maybe she knew things about him."

"If that's the case, why didn't she just explain it – instead of simply telling me that he is arrogant? He's extremely intelligent, so I'm sure he has a valid basis for thinking highly of himself. He was my father's financial advisor, and my father was a brilliant man."

"Who did you better know, Dora or Charles Worthington?"

"Dora and I have talked for hours over the years. I saw Charles several times a year, but our conversations were brief. I would have to say that I knew her best."

"Did you trust Dora?"

"Yes."

"Then, maybe you should reconsider your trust in Charles Worthington."

"You're serious."

"He was your father's friend, so initially I didn't have a reason to question his advice. I trusted your judgment in the matter. Dora was a straight shooter, and she's seen life from a variety of perspectives. For her to go to the trouble to issue you a personal warning about Worthington, she must have known something."

"I've known Charles Worthington since I was a child," replied Megan.

"You've been associated with both the Worthingtons and the Galluccis. That does not mean that you actually knew them. Do you remember your shock when we witnessed those rituals in the cave?"

"You're right. I would have never guessed that they were involved in something that weird. But, then again, my father was also involved in that. However, his behavior was very different after my mother left. I'm confused about all of it."

"These people are extremely respected by society, but you know that there is something deeply wrong. Your mother abruptly left the country without even speaking to you, and Tony Gallucci…I'm not sure where to begin with that guy."

"Maybe Dora was right," said Megan.

"I think you should play it safe and take control of your finances. Keep the diamonds in the safe deposit box. You currently have total control over that. But consider moving that fifteen million out from under Worthington and invest it in a long-standing reputable firm. Dora's last advice to you was to not trust the man."

"He's been extremely kind to me, but it doesn't mean that I have to give him control over the money my father left to me. OK, I'll talk with him in the morning. I'll tell him that I want to diversify the money – spread it out over three firms. I think he'll understand the wisdom of that."

MEGAN MET WITH Charles Worthington the following morning and notified him of her plan to diversify her inheritance.

"I've always suspected that you have a mind of your own," he stated. "You're Allen's daughter, and I imagine that he shared fiscal insight over the years with you. You're always welcome to bring the money back under my management."

Megan then met with three investment firms and completed the transactions. After leaving the last firm, she placed a call to Sam.

"I think you were right. I feel better about taking control over my inheritance. Charles Worthington was right about something."

"What about?" questioned Sam.

"My father gave me advice all my life, and I believe he prepared me to handle my own finances. It's time I charted my own course, with you at my side. The investment with Charles is finished."

TUESDAY EVENING CHARLES met with the other five Princes in London. They sat around a circular ancient oak table. Standing beside his assigned seat, he removed his ring and laid it upon the table. In front of his empty chair, was a small bronze box. He opened it, removed the new ring and placed it on his finger. He was invited to sit. Each of the Six Princes wore gold rings with an image of six connected sixes, the stems of the numbers joined and laid out circularly in sixty-degree increments. A small red ruby was fitted in the looped bottom of each number, so that the design resembled a flower. However, this new ring contained a larger ruby in the center. After a few moments of talk about situations in various regions of the world, Charles began his planned address.

"For many years in secret, the Princes have determined which nations prosper and which do not, all according to a master design. They've operated above warring factions, political structures, ideologies, and religious frameworks across the globe. In truth, there exists a one world government -not recognized as such, but empowered as such. With each passing century, our power has increased. We've positioned the world to be ready for what we offer. This is understood by everyone in this room.

The world is in chaos, and this has been so for a long time. Advances in the speed and content of international communication have brought awareness of the chaos to ordinary citizens of this planet. People are now frightened by the scale of it, and soon they will demand that something be done about it on a global scale. With the current intertwined technologies, we have the world at our fingertips. Almost every week, satellites are launched into space. Cameras from on high capture actions taken on our world in incredible detail. Other satellites form a global network of communication. Because of our greater awareness of violent crime, we've populated cities with cameras which record the actions of people constantly. The world is quickly becoming comfortable with the idea of being continually monitored.

None of the monitoring, awareness, and massive

strides in communication has helped reduce the chaos. The world is ready for someone to step in and bring order. We will soon come out from the shadows to be embraced by those who understand their need for us. The preparation made by gatherings will be fulfilled. The order will evolve swiftly, giving birth to the One. We will eliminate war, poverty and hunger. How shall we bring this about? This is why I've called us to meet."

One of the Six sat in a chair with a high back with engraved Latin words, *Coitio Princeps*. He had served the order longer than anyone in the room.

"For many years, we've debated this point, and I'm interested in hearing your proposal," stated the man.

"The sheep of the world are ready for shepherds," began Charles. "From the beginning of time, people have yearned for self-determination and self-rule. But the vast majority of them are sheep and are in need of being shepherded. Nature dictates that common people be led by the elite. For hundreds of years, a degree of order was maintained by kings, emperors and other elite leaders. None of them had the advantage of global communications and a world organization. They were far too occupied with conflicts against other kings. But now the world is ready. I believe mankind is ready to welcome our guidance and knowledge. Our species is ready to be ruled by the elite, by shepherds that nature itself has raised up. There is no need for common people to continue in their worship of gods because they will soon recognize that we can provide what they deeply desire. We are ready to be the saviors of the world."

"Yes, but let's get to the subject of how to bring

this about," the man in the engraved chair stated, becoming somewhat impatient. "Stop stating the obvious. Please get to the point."

"I propose that we begin with the European Union," suggested Charles. "The populations aren't as independently minded as people in the United States. When many Europeans left lives ruled by kings and lords for what is now the United States, these are the descendants of those who remained behind. Their ancestors saw no need for self-determination, and to this day Europeans are more compliant. The people in those nations are already accustomed to working as a group, but they also recognize the failures of the current union. Plus, those nations have the technology needed to establish our system throughout Europe. We have the financial ability to prop it up until it becomes functional. We should then target South America because it is the most volatile. We can easily cause a degree of economic collapse in most of those nations. As each adopt our system and begins to prosper, others will wish to join."

"South America isn't the most tech savvy in the world," interrupted the man in the engraved chair.

"True, but the people are some of the most manageable," replied Charles. "They are accustomed to being ruled by strong leadership. We will reach out to the leadership of those nations and ensure them of the stability that they need to remain in power for a time. Once the world sees our success in those two continents, we will have the attention of everyone.

We will then target Asia, beginning with putting economic pressure on India. That nation has already nationalized many resources that were once owned by individuals. The poverty in many areas of the country is enormous. Russia is another nation that has a history of the common people being tightly controlled by a powerful leader. We can offer them what we've already done for those in the European Union. Once we are invited to bring order to India and Russia, we'll build the economies of those two nations while putting pressure on China. China is the real key. Once we are established there, the rest of Asia will fear being left out."

"The common people are one thing, but dealing with very accomplished individuals is different," a woman at the table interjected. "I see the most serious problem coming from those who have risen to power in politics and in business."

"True," replied Charles. "We simply need to convince them that they are key elements in what we are bringing about. Most have huge egos. Once prosperity comes to the first nations placed under our system, many of the accomplished will want 'a piece of the action' - so to speak. Systematically, more pressure will be placed on troubled nations. People will rise up, and some of those leaders will come to us. Initially, we can grant them assurance that they will remain in power. But they will become somewhat impotent figureheads – much like the current monarchs in Britain. All they have to do is give themselves over to our care, and they will have peace and prosperity."

"We can't afford to prop up nations forever," added the man in the engraved chair. "Our global system will need to be put in place quickly."

"Agreed," said Charles. "For those who resist at the end, we will be forced to take control. We can't allow exceptions. It may seem a bit harsh to some, but everyone must adhere to this system in order for us to effectively establish what is needed. No one will be able to buy or sell without being a subject in this system. Unlike past efforts to bring about a world empire, we will not need to fund massive military assets. Our control will be economic, and global technology will facilitate this effort."

"The US has the most wealth," stated another of the Princes.

"I believe the most difficult areas of the world will be the United States and the Middle East," replied Charles. "However, wealthy Americans will begin to feel isolated once their economy slips in the world market. They will not want to hold out. Those of lower incomes will demand the stability our system exercises, and we will use the democratic nature of the US to our advantage. The predominantly Muslim nations will be last to relinquish control. Elements in those nations are less predictable."

"I agree that nations of fervent religious practices will be difficult," stated the man in the engraved chair.

"Even the most devout Christians in the United States should understand that what we are bringing is the fulfillment of what Jesus spoke of," said Charles. "Jesus preached peace, and we will bring peace. He preached healing, and we will establish health care. We will begin to unify the world as it has never been. All the sheep of the world need to do is to relinquish their fantasy of self-determination and the strife of personally handling things themselves. Most now understand that they are incapable of accomplishing peace, and they see a world that is spinning out of control. Mankind has hoped for an unseen savior, but true salvation is at hand. Unlike exercises of faith in the unseen, we will be highly visible. We are flesh and blood. There will no longer be any need for beliefs in the supernatural because we will handle the aspects of life that cause them to fear. You are correct. The most fervent of the religious will be the most difficult to deal with, but religion must go."

"You believe that we can't work with the religious?" asked another woman. "Can't we allow the religious leaders to function just as the political figureheads?"

"At first, maybe," answered Charles. "But history has shown religion to cause unpredictable and disruptive situations. Religion carries a power of its own, and a competing power can't be allowed. The entire concept of supernatural powers must cease. The true salvation of the world is coming. People will be educated in the fact that unseen myths and fantasies cannot be allowed to hold the world back from prosperity and peace. Humanity will need to understand the power and purity of nature itself. Nature has raised the elite up to save mankind, and nature will not be denied. Unity is needed for world chaos to be removed, and we will bring about this unity.

In the natural world, no fit shepherd would allow individualism for common sheep. Human sheep may wish for individual freedom of self-determination and personal religious liberties. But those two aspects will endanger stability for the entire flock. They threaten world unity, which is required for world peace. This cannot be allowed. People will adapt, just as the actual sheep became dependent on others to shepherd them.

The age of faith in the unseen is over. The era of self-determination for common people is coming to a close. The age of our unifying world system will be established. To borrow famous words attributed to someone who for many centuries was thought to be a savior; we will soon be able to say, "It is finished."

Read another of Rob's books, Cabin by the Stream. Enjoy the first chapter here.

Chapter 1
The Woman

Glancing upward, John Walker's eyes met an unfamiliar shade of sky.

It has a pink hue. Red sky at morning, sailor take warning. I wonder if the weather is about to turn.

An unexpected eerie chill ran down his spine as he cast his fishing line into the slow running stream. The bobber on the line rose and fell with the moving water, but it was obvious to him that no fish toyed with the bait. As he reeled the line in, he heard a female voice.

"What do you think you're doing, sir?"

He turned to find a woman in a flowered pale peach dress moving in his direction from the trees. Suddenly, she stopped beside the stream bank and issued a warning.

"If you don't leave this instant, I'll call for my husband. You have no right to fish on this property."

"Seeing that I own this property, I believe that I do," he replied.

John pointed to the cabin on the edge of the woods. The woman starred at the structure momentarily, before her eyes moved back to him. She watched John pull the night crawler off the hook and toss it into the water.

"If the weather is about to change, I should probably continue the fishing later," he stated, his eyes turning upward.

He was somewhat surprised to see that the sky had become clear blue. John fastened the hook to a guide on the fishing rod, before turning his attention back to the woman.

"I….. when did you build that cabin?" she stammered.

"About three years ago," John replied. "I love it here."

The color of her face drained; her eyes widened. She turned and quickly made her way back into the forest.

Talking about weird! She wasn't close enough for me to smell liquor, but ...what was her problem?

———•●•———

Just before dusk, John stepped out of the cabin to check the coals on his grill. From the porch, he spotted the woman standing near the water's edge. Her eyes met his. He raised his right hand and gave her a quick wave, but the gesture wasn't returned. Noting that the coals needed to heat for a few more minutes, he focused his thoughts on the woman.

I've never seen her before today. I have no clue why she's here. She couldn't have been hiking in that dress, so she must have a car parked on the road.

He slowly moved in her direction, studying the woman as he neared.

"Can I help you with something?" he called out.

Her wild eyes locked on his. John stopped within five feet of the woman.

"Is there a problem?" he questioned.

She turned away; her hands trembled.

"What can I do to help?" John again asked.

She took a step towards him, but no reply was given. He slowly moved closer and held out his hand. She took a step back, but then reached out. Taking her hand in his, he quietly spoke.

"Tell me what I can do to help."

Her small hands griped his. Her eyes again fixed on his, her head slightly moved back and forth.

"You seem to be somewhat distressed," observed John. "You're welcome to rest in a chair on the porch while I prepare supper. I'm about to cook something on the grill."

He released one of her hands, and gently escorted her toward the porch. Her eyes scanned the building and looked back at him. The two moved up the steps, and he led her to a Klondike chair.

"Have a seat right here," he said, releasing her hand. "I'm going inside to get the meat for the grill. I'll be right back."

"Who are you?" she finally asked, reaching for his hand again.

"I'm John Walker. What's your name?"

"Rebecca Johnson… Mrs. Rebecca Johnson."

"Can I get you a cup of coffee?"

"Thank you."

John released her hand a second time and moved into the cabin through a screened door. He returned momentarily carrying a cup of coffee, sugar, and cream on a small wooden serving tray with legs. He placed the tray beside the chair to her right.

"I have sweetener in the cabin, it you like," he offered.

"No, you're more than hospitable."

"The coals are ready. I'm going back inside for the meat. Just relax with your coffee."

Within a couple of minutes, he returned with a plate holding two thick red steaks.

"Hungry? It's getting late, and you might feel better after a meal. You're welcome to share these with me. I plan to cook them both."

"The coffee is fine for now," she replied. "Thank you."

John dropped the two steaks on the grill and moved back up the steps.

"I need to get a few things," he said, stepping back inside the cabin.

He soon returned with a matching tray holding garlic salt, black pepper, a sauce, and metal tongs for turning the meat. Satisfied that the steaks were properly seared on one side, he turned them. He added sauce, and then the garlic salt and pepper. Turning his eyes to the woman, he saw her lips gently sipping the cup of coffee.

"It's not a special blend, just Colombian," he told her.

She gave him a polite smile.

"I guess you've noticed there's spotty cell reception out here," John stated. "It took me a while to find a carrier that gave me fair reception at the cabin. I have a land line inside, if you need to make a call."

Her hands shook as she placed the cup on the tray.

Her eyes were deeply troubled, but John focused his attention back on the grill. He turned the steaks for a second time, adding the pepper and salt to the sizzling meat. When he turned back, he was started to see that she now stood beside him. A strange, unsettling sensation came over him.

Maybe she has mental or emotional problems, and off her medication. Earlier, she was on my case about fishing the stream, and now she is hanging around like an old friend. This young woman could be totally nuts.

"What's the matter?" he asked,

She silently stared at him.

"Is there someone we should call?" he asked. "You have no bag or purse. Maybe you left something in your car."

Her eyes narrowed. John's uneasy mind raced.

She says that her name is Rebecca Johnson, but she could be anybody. I'd like to see some ID on this woman. If mentally stable, she could be setting me up. There could be some guy of hers waiting at the car, waiting for dark to settle with plans to rob me. Or, maybe the two are on the run and are looking to use this cabin as a hideout.

Fear gripped his mind and soul. He thought about the pistol he kept in a drawer in the kitchen.

"As soon as the steaks are done, I'll be glad to walk you to your car," he offered. "We should at least get your purse before it turns dark. I'll get a couple of flashlights, in case they're needed on the way back. We should go before dark."

"Go?" she asked.

"Yeah. Most women hate to be without their

purse."

Her hands began to shake again.

"What's going on?" he asked. "Earlier, you complained about my fishing and then walked into the woods. Why did you come back?"

"I don't know."

Her body began to shiver.

"Are you cold?"

She nodded.

"The steaks are about ready," John said. "I'll go back into the cabin for a plate, and I'll get you a coat. Would that be all right?"

She nodded.

He raced back into the cabin. He grabbed two jackets, putting on the one that held his SUV keys in a pocket. He took the loaded pistol from the kitchen drawer and placed it in the other pocket. Taking a plate for the steaks from a cabinet, he quickly made his way back to her.

"It's a little large for you, but it should warm you up," he said, handing her the jacket.

She slipped it on, as he put the steaks on the plate.

"I forgot the flashlights. I'm going to put the steaks in the microwave to keep them warm, and I'll be right back with the flashlights."

Returning with the flashlights, he turned them on and handed her one. He opened the screen door of the cabin, inviting her inside.

"No!" she said emphatically.

"I thought we could cut through and leave out the front door," John explained.

"I don't want to go inside; I don't know you," she replied.

"Fair enough, we'll walk around from the back."

He took her hand and led her down the stone steps of the cabin. She abruptly halted, as they neared the grill.

"The road is only about fifty yards from the cabin, so your car can't be far," he said, releasing her hand.

"I don't know…" she mumbled.

"You don't know what?"

"I don't know what you are doing."

"Going to find your car, and your purse. It's almost dark, so we should be going."

Her eyes were wild with fear.

"Don't you want your purse?" John asked.

"I don't know…" she replied.

"You don't know?"

"I don't know anything."

Her eyes wide and wild, she seemed almost frantic. Suddenly, the motion detecting floodlights of the cabin flooded the yard with light. The startled woman stepped back, tripping over a small wooden bench he had earlier placed near the grill. Losing her balance, she fell and hit her head on the stone steps. The flashlight dropped from her hand.

"Are you OK?" John frantically asked.

She was motionless. John stepped closer and stood over her. He heard leaves rustle in the woods. Turning his flashlight in the direction of the sound, he saw nothing.

"Who's out there?" he bellowed.

Placing his hand on the gun in his jacket pocket, he nervously scanned the forest with the flashlight. Seeing nothing out of the ordinary, he turned his attention back to the woman. He knelt beside her and touched her face.

"Are you all right?"

There was no movement or response. He lifted her head and saw quickly that her body was totally limp. John checked her neck for a pulse and found her heart to be slowly beating. She appeared to be unconscious.

John's emotions ran in all directions. He couldn't leave an unconscious woman on the steps of his cabin, but he wanted desperately to find her car and see if a man was waiting.

She objected to coming inside the cabin, but I can't just leave her here. I doubt she's alone; she earlier mentioned a husband. If I bring her inside, she could come to and open the door for a guy to enter and shoot me dead. If she's truly alone, she could be crazy. She might put a kitchen knife in my back!

He tried to help her sit up, but her body was limp. Her head fell to one side.

Something could be seriously wrong. A lack of medication could have cause her to become dizzy and fall. She hit the steps hard. She could need medical attention. I should call someone to check her out.

Under the floodlights, John turned off both flashlights and placed them in his jacket pocket containing his keys. He lifted her limp body in his arms and carried her up the steps and into his cabin. John laid her on a couch and turned on a table lamp.

Fearful of an accomplice, he quickly turned the lock on the door and fastened the dead bolt. John knelt beside her and felt the back of her head. A large lump had formed. Bringing his hand back, there was blood. Checking her neck for a pulse again, her eyes blinked. She seemed disoriented.

"You're inside my cabin," informed John. "You fell onto the steps. I believe you became dizzy."

Suddenly, her body tensed. Her desperate green eyes fixed on his, she grabbed his jacket with both hands. Her lips trembled.

"Please, help me!"

About the Author

Rob Williams, currently residing in Nacogdoches Texas, has served in multiple roles supporting the Christian community. Included in this long list of mentorships was his service as youth director of an inner-city church in Atlanta and working with children in some of the toughest housing projects in that city. Rob worked at a rehabilitation center for five years, where he became acquainted with the homeless. The center helped those on work release from jail and those who were physically and mentally handicapped. He has taught adult Sunday school classes for more than thirty years and led youth in Boy Scouts and Cub Scouts for twenty years. Retired from the high tech industry in Huntsville Alabama, he writes Christian fiction and science fiction in his free time. Rob is a husband, the father of four, and a grandfather. He is the author of the three novel Brandon Springs Christian fiction series, the dystopian science fiction novel *Sins of Variance*, the Christian fictional crime novel *Gathering of Six*, and Christian mystery *Cabin by the Stream*.